DEATH BY MISADVENTURE

Anna Legat

Headspace Books

Headspace Books
Cover design by: ABE
Printed in the United Kingdom

CONTENTS

Maggie Kaye and Samuel Dee

in

The Shires Mysteries

Book 5

DEATH BY MISADVENTURE

Anna Legat

CHAPTER 1

There is nothing like a party to dispel winter blues. What could be better than the company of friends, a glass of mulled wine with a hearty beef stew, and a woman you love by your side? Sam Dee couldn't think of anything.

When he had proposed to Maggie a couple of weeks ago, he couldn't be sure whether she would say yes. In fact, she hadn't. She'd fixed him with a probing gaze and mumbled, 'Hm, that was sudden. I didn't expect this. Let me have a think.'

'You need to think about it?' Sam was deflated.

'Yes, sort of. Leave it with me.' At that she had fled to her house.

Sam was left behind with his mouth gaping and a black despair crawling up his spine.

It was quite some emotional height for Sam to climb down from after Maggie's abrupt departure. He had whipped himself into a state of frantic anticipation only to be shot down to earth with her non-committal response. What was there to think about? Sam pondered. Insecurities crept in. The most plausible explanation was that she, plain and simple, didn't love him. What had made him think that she did? He was a friend, a business partner and a neighbour, she always said that. She had never given him any encouragement, nothing more than her effusive but rather glib *knight-in-shining-armour* compliment. But that was gratitude, not affection. And then there was his rotten timing. Maggie had only just discovered that her one-time fiancé had tried to kill her, twice. Only a fool would jump into another romantic entanglement on the back of that life experience. Sam kicked himself for being a presumptuous old fool and sulked.

His mother, Deirdre, glided from the kitchen carrying a bowl of stewed pears to find him alone and morose. The little box housing the engagement ring sat on the table, unopened. That box was well travelled – all the way to Russia, and back – but it was still *virgo intacta*.

'So?' she prompted him. 'Did you ask?' Deirdre was a frisky octogenarian with quick, beady eyes and an even quicker, and sharper, mind. Her tongue usually kept pace with her mind.

Sam nodded.

'And?'

'And she said she'd think about it.'

'What sort of answer is that?'

Sam dropped his shoulders. 'I want to be alone.'

'What about the pudding? It's a perfectly lovely pear. With cinnamon and sultanas – just how you like it. Give it a try.' His mother would not allow good food to go to waste and in her considered opinion food is exactly what Sam wanted.

'Please, mother,' he implored her without lifting his eyes.

Defeated, she sighed and left the room.

Sam stared vacuously out of the window at the grey, wintry world outside. It was February. The hedgerow was latticed with contorted dead leaves and dry twigs. There was no sign of spring. A vituperative robin had chased a couple of sparrows away from the bird feeder and tucked into a fat ball. The robin, in its turn, was disturbed by the slamming of a door and hurried steps crunching the gravel on the path. It was Maggie. She was on her way back. It couldn't have been more than a quarter of an hour since she had left.

A knock on the door confirmed that Sam wasn't dreaming. He raced to answer it, then paused for thought before pulling down the handle. He inhaled deeply, preparing himself for whatever disappointment was coming next. Like a dumbstruck teenager, he beheld Maggie, taking in her lipstick-enhanced features, her freshly brushed locks and her figure-hugging, soft-wool dress that screamed to be touched and stroked, especially over the well-rounded curves of her hips. Sam composed himself.

'Did you forget something?' he asked with the poise and dignity that any other rejected admirer could only wish to possess.

'Forget?' Maggie scowled, giving his question some intense consideration. 'No, I don't think so. Yes. I mean, no.'

So that was it, Sam thought dolefully, the answer was *no.*

'I didn't forget anything. What makes you think I did?' Maggie quizzed him. When he couldn't come up with a reason, she said, 'I have an answer for you. I couldn't give it to you wearing my everyday jumper and those dreadful leggings. It just didn't seem right. It's not every day that someone asks me to marry them. I wasn't ready, you see.'

'I understand. My timing was off,' Sam conceded.

'Well, only by five minutes.' She blinked at him, dots of mascara falling from her eyelashes onto her cheeks. 'Five minutes was all I needed to change into something more appropriate before saying - *yes.*'

'Yes? Sorry, say again – did you say *yes*?' He stammered.

'Yes, of course I'd love to marry you, Samuel Dee! I didn't think you'd ask, but yes, I'd like nothing better than to be your wife. Even if it's only your second wife...' It was a tenuous, but affectionate, nod to Alice, Sam's first wife. Maggie's voice wobbled a little at that moment. Sam detected tears of emotion swelling in her eyes. His throat constricted. He pulled her into his arms.

'Oh Maggie, you're impossible!' he laughed. 'If I cared about your dress sense, I would nev —' Sam stopped himself just in time. Maggie's fashion statements would often be the talk of the town. Her foray into Sexton's Canning wearing her Christmas jumper in the middle of July three years ago would stick in Sam's mind for eternity. From that point on nothing surprised him: not the frayed straw hat at best fit for a scarecrow, nor her school-girl dungarees with the checked patch on her left buttock, or her pink, crushed-velvet tracksuit. Maggie wouldn't be Maggie without her peculiar dress code. Sam cooed over Maggie's head as he held her in his arms, 'You really didn't have to change just to say *yes.* It'd be just as good if you wore a brown paper bag.'

Deirdre found them frozen in an embrace on the doorstep when she came to investigate where all the cold air was coming from. She quickly realised things had moved in the right direction.

'Shut that door and come inside, you lovebirds,' she chimed. 'Let's have that stewed pear. Best to have it when it's piping hot.' There was a slight tremor to Deirdre's voice.

Two weeks later Maggie and Sam were holding an engagement party at Badger's Hall, their joint B&B enterprise. Everyone and anyone were invited, and most of them made it to the party. Sam gracefully received seven bottles of wine and one of champagne, and Maggie squealed with joy at the sight of a box of Rum & Raisin Fudge Extravaganza presented by Kev and Jane Wilcox, Bishops' master chocolatiers and fudge makers. They were the last to arrive but were well worth the wait, according to Maggie.

The first to arrive were Vera and Rumpole (he being her dog, not her husband).

'Henry's back in Westminster, I'm afraid,' Vera apologised on her husband's behalf. Nobody was particularly concerned about that given that the Right Honourable Henry Hopps-Wood MP was a pompous clown. Rumpole on the other hand was cuddly and sociable. He wagged his tail enthusiastically when Maggie patted his shaggy hind, a reaction that could never be evoked from Henry.

Hot on Vera's heels, her cousin Sabine bundled in, rattling her many charms on her many bracelets and emitting fumes of fragrant incense. Sabine was a hippie throwback, but she was also an activist and astute businesswoman.

She ran a shelter for recovering addicts and victims of domestic violence.

'The car stinks of wet dog,' she remarked, giving Rumpole an evil eye. She had given a lift to him and his mistress, and seemed to be regretting it.

'I told you we were happy to walk,' Vera snorted.

'In this downpour?' Sabine rolled her eyes. 'I couldn't let you. I do have a heart, I'll have you know,' and to prove her point, she presented Sam with a bottle wrapped in pink-tinted foil, 'Something very special for the two of you – an alcohol-free elderflower wine, homemade.'

Maggie wrinkled her nose, but Sam expressed his delight.

James Weston-Jones, the son of the local land gentry, arrived without his wife and children (they lived in France more or less permanently), but he delivered Cherie and her partner Lisa to the party. To Maggie's delight they came armed with alcoholic beverages. James's French Bordeaux was welcomed with open arms.

The reception room of Badger's Hall was quickly filling with guests: Mary and Dan (finally married after eloping to Gretna Green last summer – an opportunity for a booze-up inadvertently lost), Edgar (doctor of psychiatry and a confirmed bachelor), his mum Hermione accompanied by her latest knitting project, Kev and Jane Wilcox with their fudge as aforementioned, and sweet Vanessa with the chunky accessory of her police superintendent husband, Alec Scarfe. When the forensic pathologist, Michael Almond, turned up with his snotty detective girlfriend Gillian, the dynamics at the party became destabilised – a whiff of crime, policing and dead bodies sneaked into the room. After exchanging a couple of snipy work-related remarks, Gillian Marsh and Alec Scarfe were forced to call a truce.

'I thought we left murder at home, Alec,' the usually amiable Vanessa sounded stern. Alec relented and told DI Marsh to forget work and enjoy herself.

'I fully intend to, sir,' she replied.

'Good,' said he.

'Good.' She insisted on having the last word.

Vanessa pulled her husband by his sleeve and led him away before he attempted another riposte.

Maggie trotted to the kitchen on the pretext of helping Deirdre with the dinner, but mainly to sample the French Bordeaux and to see how well it went with rum and raisin fudge. Sam followed her to also offer a helping hand to his mother, but mainly to keep an eye on Maggie.

'What are you two doing here? Don't you have guests to entertain?' Deirdre groaned.

'Came to see if you need help, Mum.'

'Help? You? Stop getting under my feet,' Deirdre warned them. 'I've got it under control.'

Indeed, the stew was bubbling in a large pot on the hob and Deirdre was working her magic on turning boiled spuds into a creamy mash. With her sleeves rolled up and her wrist as fast as an electric whisk, it was hard to believe that the woman was going on eighty-five. Sam thanked his lucky stars for blessing him with an indomitable mother. She was his mainstay, and that enabled him in turn to be Maggie's. With both her parents dead, her brother undergoing an identity crisis in London and her sister living in far-away New Zealand, Maggie had no one. But now that she had Sam, his family would become hers. She would acquire a loving, if slightly rough around the edges, mother-in-law, and two grown-up stepchildren: Campbell and Abigail. He intended to take good care of Maggie, and on that note, intercepted a second piece of fudge that was on its way into her mouth. Before she snatched it back, he gobbled it up.

'Don't spoil your appetite before dinner, Maggie.'

'And you can?'

'It didn't touch the sides. I swallowed it whole.'

'What a waste!' She licked her fingers and knocked back a glass of wine, glaring at him but only after a fashion.

'Dinner's ready,' Deirdre pronounced. 'Sam, get them all to the table. Maggie?'

'Yes, Deirdre?'

'Are you steady on your feet, or shall I do the honours?'

With an indignant sparkle flashing in her eye, Maggie declared herself fit and stable to set the table, serve the stew and even to crack open a bottle of bubbly.

'To Maggie, my beautiful wife-to-be!' Sam raised a toast and everyone joined him in saluting Maggie, including his mother. Deirdre wasn't a drinker, but this occasion called for an exception. She drained her glass. Her cheeks filled with colour and her eyes twinkled. It wasn't her first glass, either. Sam couldn't remember his mother this happy – and this tipsy – in ages.

She leaned across the table towards Maggie and slurred, 'I thought he'd never get over Alice. If it wasn't for you he wouldn't have. I know my son – obtuse and set in his ways.'

'He isn't that bad, though you may have a point there,' Maggie concurred to Sam's astonishment.

'Oh, I do. He's on his best behaviour now, but give him a chance and—'

'Mother, what exactly are you saying?' Sam interjected before she put Maggie off him for life.

'Nothing that isn't true. All I'm saying is this: keep him on a short leash, dear. He can take it.'

Maggie swore to do her best.

'Good,' Deirdre muttered. 'All men are the same – they need taking in hand and to be given clear boundaries, like small children.'

'So, have you set the date yet?' The inevitable question came from Vera.

'The sooner the better,' Sam said.

Maggie peered at him sweetly. 'You really think that?'

'I do.' Sam kissed her hand, making her blush.

'Well, in that case, how about this summer? August?'

'A perfect time for a wedding,' Vanessa gushed.

'We'd better book a date with the vicar.'

'A church wedding? How unimaginative!' Sabine exclaimed. 'Why don't you do the real thing?'

'I thought a church wedding was the real thing,' Sam argued.

'Not in Bishops Well, it isn't,' Sabine countered. 'We have a longstanding tradition of pagan betrothals – in the Stone Circle in Harry Wotton's field, the way it's been done it since time immemorial. The right way.'

'Oh, Sabine, get off your high horse,' Vera tried to bring her wayward cousin to order. 'Let them do it their way. Not everyone still lives in the Neolithic age. Some of us have moved on.'

'It's how it's always been done in Bishops. Full stop.' Sabine persisted.

A staring standoff followed and an awkward silence fell on the gathering. Sam gazed towards

Maggie, desperate for her intervention. As a native Bishopian she was entitled to voice an opinion. Sam, a newcomer, had no say in the matter.

Maggie tilted her head and pursed her lips pensively, thinking. Everyone sat still, awaiting her verdict.

'We'll do both,' she said at last. 'We can't break with tradition, so we will have the Stone Circle ceremony.'

Sabine beamed.

'But my dear grandad Bernie would turn in his grave if I didn't go for a proper church wedding, so we'll do that too.'

Sam recalled that Grandad Bernie used to be the vicar at St John's.

'Quite right, a decent Christian rite,' Deirdre agreed. 'I wouldn't like you living in sin.'

'So, that's settled,' Sam exhaled his relief. 'We will book a date with Vicar Quentin.'

'And with Harry Wotton,' Maggie added. 'He needs a longer notice period – it'll be harvest time in August.'

Festivities resumed around the table. Wine was poured by the barrel, jokes were being cracked like eggs, the cook was praised for her delicious cooking and at last, after nearly five years of mourning, Sam Dee stood on the doorstep of Seventh Heaven. Until it all went belly up.

CHAPTER 2

Maggie's Journal

Sometimes I wonder if I've been cursed for something awful I did in a previous life.

My engagement to Samuel (the most wonderful man on earth and widely acknowledged as my knight-in-shining armour) was supposed to be a joyous occasion, but it turned out the first in a sequence of catastrophic events which, at first glance, appeared to have been orchestrated by dark forces hellbent on throwing our best laid plans into disarray. And I don't mean the fast-approaching pandemic that was about to grip the country and put our wedding plans on ice. I mean events much, much closer to home.

The party was over by midnight. Most of our guests had gone home. Edgar's mother,

Hermione, had fallen asleep with her knitting needles in her lap. She was a sound sleeper, or possibly a deaf one for Edgar's attempts to wake her fell on deaf ears. Reclined in an armchair, her arm dangling by her side, she was snoring merrily and ignoring him.

The other octogenarian, Deirdre, on the other hand, was still on her feet, insisting on tidying the kitchen before we went home to Priest's Hole. Our protestations that the cleaning could be done tomorrow were dismissed as sheer idleness, so Samuel and I joined in the clean-up effort. I was shuttling between the dining room and the kitchen, collecting plates and glasses while Samuel was loading them into an industrial dishwasher. Deirdre was busy pouring the leftover stew into a Tupperware container, ready for tomorrow's supper.

'There's nothing like a stew re-heated on the second day. And it's enough for the three of us. You would've chucked it in the bin if you had it your way,' she tut-tutted while scraping the bottom of the pot.

Suddenly, her face became contorted in pain and her hands lost grip on the pot which tumbled to the floor with a clank, spitting remnants of the stew all over the walls and kitchen cupboards. Deirdre hit the floor too.

Samuel and I dashed to her side. He called out to her. She was conscious, but her face was twisted and she was gripping her arm.

'It's sore,' she managed to wheeze, 'I think I broke it.'

She was gasping for air. Droplets of sweat shone on her forehead. Samuel was frantic. He was trying to talk to her and make her more comfortable, using kitchen towels to make a sling for her arm. I dialled 999.

'It looks like she broke her arm,' I was telling the NHS operator. 'She's in pain, grasping it – won't let us touch it.'

'Which arm?'

'I don't know!' It took me a few seconds to work it out. 'I think it's her left one.'

'Is she breathing normally?'

'No. It's, um… shallow gasps. She's eighty-four! Hurry!'

'An ambulance is on its way.'

Alarmed by the commotion, Edgar ran in and stared. 'What happened?'

'She broke her arm,' I told him.

The pain must have worsened and Deirdre appeared to be experiencing a panic attack – she was panting and sweating profusely, trying to dig her fingers into her chest. Then she went still and limp. Samuel screamed her name but she didn't respond.

'She's gone into cardiac arrest!' Edgar knelt by her side and pushed Samuel away. He began chest compressions. My teacher's First Aid training kicked in. I remembered something about mouth-to-mouth (I really should've paid more attention to what the handsome instructor was saying). Rightly or wrongly, I started blowing air into Deirdre's mouth at intervals of thirty chest thrusts. When I noticed that Edgar was slowing down, I suggested we swap. He let me take over, and we carried on.

We were still at it when the ambulance arrived. I would never be able to say how long our resuscitation operation lasted, but by then I was exhausted. The paramedics' verdict was unequivocal – a heart attack with the additional complication of a cardiac arrest. We watched them as they used a defibrillator to kickstart Deirdre's heart into action. After that, they put her on oxygen. We followed them as they wheeled her to the ambulance.

'Where are you taking her?' Samuel asked.

'RUH Bath, Emergency.'

The ambulance departed with blue lights flashing and sirens blazing. We stood on the road until it disappeared round the bend of the High Street.

'She can't be on her own,' Samuel said. 'I should've gone with her.'

'They wouldn't have let you,' Edgar informed him.

'We ought to follow,' I said, but I knew we'd had too much to drink. 'I'll call a taxi.'

'I'll take you,' Edgar offered. 'It's on our way home, anyway.'

We went inside to fetch Hermione. She was

awake and rather bothered, demanding to know why we'd called an ambulance for her. 'I only had a nap,' she protested. 'I wasn't dying!'

'It was for Deirdre. She had a heart attack,' Edgar explained calmly and ushered his mother to his car. I carried her knitting bag. Samuel locked up, and soon we hit the road.

A stocky nurse with short, mousy hair and an air of frenzied busyness popped out from behind the curtain. Her movements were quick and her eyes alert. She reminded me of a field mouse stranded indoors and frantically searching for a way out. Her gaze fell on me.

'Maggie Kaye! Well, I never!' She rejoiced and pounced towards me.

I gawked at her, scouring my memory for my last medical appointment and whether it may have been with a nurse.

Seeing my consternation, she explained, 'It's Kylie! Bishops Well Primary! Come on, we were in the same class.'

'Kylie Cunningham!' I cried. I remembered Kylie as a skinny little thing with waist-long hair contained by a gem-studded Alice band and multiple hairpins featuring colourful butterflies. I had been so spellbound by Kylie's hair accessories that I rarely glanced at her face.

'Fancy bumping into you here. You're a nurse!' I stated the glaringly obvious.

'I am,' Kylie spoke with pride. 'I had a slow start – drifted for a while, but I went back to college ten years ago. And here I am, Senior Nurse, as it happens. What about you, Maggie?'

'Well… I teach. Sometimes.'

'Sometimes?'

'I'm a supply teacher. And I write for *Sexton's Herald* – small pieces on local history, travelogues, that sort of stuff.'

'You're back in Bishops, then?'

'Never really left, bar a few years at uni. You?'

'Same here. I married Jack – Jack Pearce. I'm Kylie Pearce now.'

'No! Giant Jack?'

'Him, alright.' Kylie chuckled. 'I haven't heard anyone call him that in years. He's lost all that weight. Listen, we've got to get together for coffee and a natter.'

Before I answered, Samuel cleared his throat ostentatiously, 'Sorry to interrupt. About my mother – Deirdre Dee… Have you any news? We've been told to come here and wait.'

Kylie clapped her forehead with the flat of her palm. 'Mrs Dee, yes! Are you family?'

'We are,' Samuel replied and that small word "*we*" forced my heart to skip a beat. I was *family*, wasn't I?

'Right, so it's good news, really. She is stable.'

'Can we see her?'

'No, not yet, I'm sorry. She's been moved to the Cardiac Ward for an angiogram.'

'What is it? Is it serious?'

'It's to check the extent of damage to her heart and the state of her arteries. It's a routine diagnostic procedure. Nothing to fear,' Kylie assured us. 'She's in good hands, the lovely Mrs Dee. Dr Edmunds is a miracle maker. He's the best.' Kylie leant towards us to continue conspiratorially, 'His wife, Indira, was given only a few months to live. Congenital heart disease, you see. Anyway, that was two years ago, and she is still with us. Jonas – that's Dr Edmunds – keeps her heart ticking, defying all the experts. He'll do the same for your mother. You can trust him. I, for one, would trust him with my life.'

After some confused meandering, we located the Cardiac Ward and, within it, a small waiting room where we camped, determined not to leave until we knew more about Deirdre's prospects of recovery. There was a water cooler in the room so we could rehydrate and keep our hangover-induced migraines at bay. Despite my earlier alcohol intake, I was as sober as a judge. Samuel couldn't sit still. He was pacing the length and width of the room, biting his lip and repeatedly telling me that he had let his mother down.

'She's a feisty lady, Samuel,' I continued to remind him. 'She'd have done as she pleased with or without your permission.'

'Still, I should've—'

'Should've what?'

'Stopped her.'

'From what? From buzzing with excitement? From taking charge? From being Deirdre?' I did my best to talk sense into him. He had nothing to blame himself for. I forbade him. His mother may have overestimated her strength – gone too far, worked too hard, had one drink too many...

'That's the thing, Maggie! She doesn't drink. She shouldn't have been drinking!' He cried and punched the air to punctuate every point.

'Do you really think you could've stopped her? She was celebrating. She drank a toast to us. Perhaps she had a glass too many, true. Her body gave her a timely warning, but that's all it was: an alarm bell. But she will be fine. She just wouldn't do it to you. She will yet dance at our wedding, mark my words.'

He smiled – weakly, but he smiled.

'That's better,' I said. I believed in Deirdre. She was a fighter. She was alive. This particular fact I could state with certainty. The hospital corridors were chock-a-block with the stranded souls of those who had given up the ghost, but Deirdre wasn't one of them. I kept checking, just in case.

Dr Jonas Edmunds was a man in his prime, six-foot tall and athletic. He approached us bristling with healthy energy despite having just come from a long and frantic night shift. He had calm, grey eyes and large hands. You could trust those eyes and especially those hands, I concluded. Kylie was right: this man could well be a miracle maker.

He showed us to his office and sat us down before proceeding to explain that Deirdre had been stabilised and was out of danger. 'She's a strong lady for her age.'

'Didn't I say?' I peered at Samuel, exuding positivity. He took my hand and gave it a firm squeeze. My compressed knuckles cracked. A thought occurred to me to get him one of those stress-relief balls at the first opportunity.

'When will she be able to come home?' I asked the wizard-doctor.

'Not so fast – we've only just started,' he chuckled. He had a charming smile that radiated from his lips to his eyes. 'She'll have to undergo a coronary artery bypass graft. There's some clogging in her arteries. This procedure will divert blood around those obstructions and improve her circulation and oxygen supply.' He showed us a diagram and took us through the whole process.

'When?' Samuel asked.

'As soon as possible. I'll have her booked in by the end of this week. We'll keep your mother in until the surgery. After the procedure, provided all is well, she will stay with us for about a week to recuperate. Then you can take her home.'

CHAPTER 3

Maggie's Journal

I spent the rest of the night at Samuel's to make sure he got some sleep. I had given him an invigorating pep talk about the importance of rest and staying strong for his mother. After that, he'd slept like a baby. We rose at ten. I ran home to shower and change from my party dress into my everyday jumper. It was the one with holly leaves and snowflakes. I had worn it for three weeks on the trot and it was beginning to smell a little musky. It was too warm for this time of year. We had come to the end of February and the weather was taking a decisive turn towards spring. Still, I didn't have the presence of mind to search for something suitable, such as my dungarees. I went back to Samuel's.

He was having his habitual mug of black coffee, and had another one steaming on the kitchen table, witing for me. He remembered to put milk into mine. He is such a darling, and I am the luckiest girl in the world (I use the term "girl" loosely). I gave him a hearty hug.

We established that the visiting hours at the hospital were between two and three-thirty in the afternoon, and then again at 6pm. Samuel called the hospital to confirm that Deirdre would be able to see us. He was told that she was awake, in good spirits and looking forward to seeing us. I could literally see the weight lifting from his chest.

As we had time to kill, and our stomachs were turning on themselves and beginning to chew on their own walls, I decided to re-heat what was left of Deirdre's beef stew. We had it with bread rolls.

'Mum was right,' Sam observed. 'It's even better than yesterday.'

I concurred and swiped my plate with bread to soak up all the juices. For dessert, I generously offered Samuel my rum & raisin fudge and he, even more magnanimously, declined. I ate two pieces: his and mine. Rested and restocked, we were feeling much more optimistic.

At half-past-one we jumped into Samuel's Jag. And that was when the second calamity occurred.

Had we emerged into the road a few seconds

later, Samuel's car with us in it would have been squashed against the wall like a swotted fly, and we would be dead.

Things happened very quickly and right before our shocked eyes. Firstly, we heard the roar of an engine and smelled diesel and the burning of tyres. Then, as Samuel slammed on the brakes, we watched a quadbike plough through the air right in front of us and crash into our wall. Dry stones crumbled away and flew in all directions, one hitting the bonnet of Samuel's Jag. The wheels of the quadbike, even though enormous, became airborne but in the end came to an abrupt halt on top of the rubble of our wall. And as they did, the rider was catapulted out of the vehicle and landed awkwardly in my dormant flower bed. His foot seemed to be pointing in the opposite direction to his bent knee. He screamed in pain.

His cries for help stirred us from our shock. We hurried towards him. I glanced under his hood and, despite his face being twisted in agony, I recognised Isaac Wotton. I wasn't surprised to see him, to be perfectly honest. Young Isaac had a reputation for disorderly behaviour. His youth notwithstanding, he had already built up an impressive portfolio of ASBOs, injunctions and a suspended sentence for breaking into the off-licence to steal liquor after the shop assistant had refused to serve him due to Isaac being under eighteen. Isaac Wotton was a menace.

'Help me! It hurts!' He was curled up in pain and trying to reach for his knee. It didn't look good. Apart from his knee being unnaturally twisted, his bone had been snapped and its sharp edge was peeking through a hole in his joggers.

'You've broken your leg,' I told him calmly. 'Stop twisting and turning. You'll only make it worse.'

'Call my dad!' He screamed.

'And what is your dad going to do other than tell you off for joy-riding his quadbike and demolishing our wall?' I asked him. I didn't expect an answer, so I went on, 'No. As it happens we're going to the hospital to visit Samuel's mother. We'll take you. It'll be quicker than waiting for an ambulance. And it's only a broken bone. Sit still. Don't go anywhere.'

'As if I would!' He snorted. There was always room for defiance in Isaac's attitude.

I went to fetch two pokers from my fireplace, plus a couple of scarves. Again, my First Aid training was paying off big time. I returned to the groaning Wotton Junior and went about immobilising his leg with the aid of said pokers which I tied around his lower leg with said scarves. After the procedure, Samuel and I lifted the youngster from the ground. Samuel placed him over his shoulders in a fireman's lift and carried him to the car, while I supported his twisted knee from moving too much. His arms wrapped over Samuel's neck and totally at our mercy, Isaac still had the audacity to scream at us for *dragging* him and making it *worse*. I was close to giving him a therapeutic slap. I held my nerve. We helped him into the back seat.

'Try not to bleed on Samuel's seats,' I had the pleasure of instructing him. One glance at my blood-soaked scarves and I knew they were a write-off.

Leaving our wall in ruin and Mr Wotton's quad bike draped over it, we drove to Bath.

In the Emergencies forecourt, we joined a line of three ambulances which were waiting to unload their human cargo. Our cargo was expelling not entirely human shrieks and increasingly colourful curses. He was clearly in agonising pain, and bleeding profusely. My scarves were saturated and so was the seat. I did my best to keep Samuel's attention on other matters.

'Why don't you run in and get someone to collect him,' I suggested. 'I'll stay here and keep him entertained.'

Isaac groaned. Samuel left.

'Please don't tell my dad,' a small voice squeaked from the back seat.

I twisted my body to look Isaac squarely in the eye. 'First you ask me to call him, now you're begging me not to tell him. Which one is it?'

He winced, probably because of the pain rather than the moderate harshness of my words. 'He'll bust my balls, Miss Kaye, if he finds out.'

'As he should.' I was merciless. 'Never mind your leg, but our wall and Samuel's car will need mending, I'm afraid.'

The back door was flung open.

'What do we have here?' A pair of large brown eyes peered in and scrutinised Isaac's slumped frame from head to toe, pausing briefly on my poker-and-scarf handiwork. 'I see...' The paramedic provided his vague diagnosis. 'My name is Rahim. Me and my colleague, Martha, will help you into a wheelchair. I want you to put your hands around my neck, okay?'

Isaac whimpered but did as he was instructed. Martha dexterously repositioned the wheelchair in such a way that it slid smoothly under Isaac's bottom as Rahim lowered him gently into the seat. Off he went without a second glance at the bloody mess he left behind. Samuel stood gawking at it in horror. There was blood everywhere and it appeared that one of my pokers, when transported in or out of the car, had caught on the seat and ripped the leather upholstery.

'Oh dear,' I bleated sheepishly. I felt partially responsible for the damage. 'On second thoughts, it might have been wiser to call an ambulance.'

'Yes...' Samuel showed great restraint. 'I'll have a word with Harry Wotton about this.'

'And about our wall,' I chipped in.

'That too.'

By the time we made it to the Cardiac Ward and found Deirdre it was a quarter to three.

'You're late. They told me you'd be here at two,' Deirdre greeted us. She grimaced humourlessly from her bed. She was slightly elevated and it seemed like she was looking at us down her nose which, in a metaphorical sense, she probably was. All the tubes, drips and electronic machinery aside, she looked better than I had expected.

Samuel apologised for our lateness *due to unforeseen developments,* and I gave her the long version. Deirdre, and all the other patients on the ward, were riveted by my account of Isaac Wotton's antics and his ultimate demise in my flower bed.

'That young man needs reining in. He's out of control,' Deirdre remarked. 'He's lucky I wasn't there. God help me, he wouldn't know what hit him!'

'As things stand, he just hit our wall and made a mess of Samuel's car,' I said. 'But he knows we won't let it slide. I told him as much.'

Deirdre squinted towards her neighbour occupying the corner bed by the window. 'Did you hear that, Indira? I leave them on their own for one day and this is what happens – Sodom and Gomorrah!'

Indira smiled weakly and said, 'The sooner you get well the sooner you can sort things out at home.' Uttering just that one sentence took some toll on her for she inhaled laboriously through her nose and exhaled with a deep wheeze through her mouth. Her eyelids flickered as she tried to keep them open.

'That's exactly what I intend to do. As should you, dear.' Deirdre gave her an affectionate wink.

'I'm just glad to be alive.'

I gazed at Indira, intrigued. Despite being bedridden and emaciated, she was a woman of striking beauty. Her eyes were enormous and virtually black and her thick raven hair lay arranged in coils over her shoulders. Someone was taking real good care of this patient. I remembered Kylie telling us that Dr Edmund's wife's name was Indira and that she had a terminal heart condition. *Indira* was a rare name. What were the chances that this was Mrs Edmunds?

'I hope I don't sound presumptuous, but is Dr Edmund's your husband by any chance?' I had to know.

She smiled warmly at the mention of his name. 'Yes, he is.'

'A very loving husband, I should add,' Deirdre interjected. 'Since I woke up this morning, and that must've been around seven, he's been here six times. And counting. He cares about you a great deal, dear.'

'He does. I wish I could—' Indira's voice trailed off, perhaps from exertion but more likely from emotion. A small tear rolled across the side of her cheek. 'I can't give him anything back. All I'm doing is dying.'

Samuel and I exchanged shocked looks.

'Come now, Indira, don't give up,' Deirdre shook her head. 'Don't ever give up. There's a lot to be said for positive thinking. Take it from an old woman who's seen a few miracles in her time.'

'That's my only hope – a miracle. A new heart from a donor with an AB-negative blood type. I can't say I'm holding my breath.'

'Patience, my love, we'll get there. Have faith.' It was Dr Edmunds. He must have heard us talking before we heard him arrive. He approached his wife's bed and without any awkwardness leant over and kissed her. It was a long and passionate kiss. He then gazed into her eyes and stroked her hair. He rearranged it lovingly around her face, pushing it behind her ear on one side and laying a thick strand over her shoulder on the other. It was an extremely tender and intimate scene to watch. My eyes welled up.

Dr Edmunds turned his attention to Deirdre. 'And how's my second favourite patient?'

Deirdre mumbled something, trying to compose herself.

'Looking good.' He checked her chart at the head of her bed. 'All's ready for the bypass. We have a date: this Friday.'

CHAPTER 4

Maggie's Journal

As soon as she awoke after her surgery, Deirdre peered at us with moist eyes and declared weakly but conclusively, 'I'll yet dance at your wedding. Just don't make me wait too long.'

Samuel leant over and gave her a tender peck on her forehead. 'Let's focus on your recovery first.'

'Dr Edmunds tell us that you'll have to take it easy,' I chipped in.

'I'll take it easy,' Deirdre conceded. 'But you don't have to. While I'm lying here, taking it easy, I want you to press ahead with the wedding arrangements.'

'The wedding can wait until—'

'But I can't!' Deirdre interrupted Samuel

forcibly. She even managed to lift her forefinger to him by way of warning. 'I had a timely reminder of my mortality, son, and I did some thinking. I want to have everything sorted out before I leave this mortal coil for good. That includes seeing you married and in the hands of a good woman, like our

Maggie here.' She flashed me an approving look.

Flattered, I pulled a silly face and felt blood rush to my cheeks. I mumbled, 'You may be overestimating me, Deirdre.'

'You'll be better than nothing, Maggie, trust me.'

That brought me down a peg, but precisely because of that, I felt more comfortable with the conversation. I don't like people having too high an expectation of me. I wouldn't want to disappoint anyone. I grinned happily. 'If you say so, Deirdre.'

'Well, I do. You give this idle boy purpose in life,' she gestured towards Samuel with a slight jerk of her head. 'And I want you to promise me that you'll make the bookings today. Don't waste time thinking about it. Promise me and make an old lady happy.'

I nodded. 'Cross my heart and hope to die.'

'Good. And don't leave it up to him,' she blinked towards Samuel. 'He's a procrastinator, like his father.'

Samuel rolled his eyes.

'Now be off with you. I need my beauty

sleep.' She closed her eyes. She did look tired. The conversation must have taken a lot out of her. We tiptoed out of the room and left her to rest.

Tasked with our urgent mission, we went to see Vicar Quentin. Everything else, including dinner and arrangements for repairs to our wall and Samuel's car would have to wait.

The vicarage was conveniently located behind St John the Baptist's church, just across the cemetery from Priest's Hole. By Bishops Well standards it was a relatively new building, dating back to the late nineteenth century. It was Victorian in every sense of the word: grey stone walls invaded by aggressive ivy, steep gables with ornate patterns and bay windows with latticed panels. Before becoming a vicarage, it used to be the village school.

We crossed the graveyard, torches in hand. It was a late hour – well past seven. The sky was overcast with rain clouds so heavy that they seemed to sag onto our shoulders. The thin drizzle wasn't enough to relieve them of that weight. The westerly wind was beginning to pick up. Perhaps it would blow the nasty clouds away to let them do their worst somewhere over Sexton's Canning. One could only hope. Here, in the valley of Bishops Well parish we'd had more than our share of the record-breaking February rainfall. The ground was saturated beyond capacity. The Avon had broken its banks in a couple of places and was burbling out into the surrounding fields. Parts of Holbrook Estate were under water. I felt sorry for the residents. The property developer who had built the estate twenty-odd years ago had been told that they were building on a flood plain, but did they care?

We rang the bell. Expecting to see the six-foot tall bulk of Quentin Magnebu and hear his sonorous baritone voice, we were confronted by his wife, Leanne. At a mere five-foot-one (in high heels), petite and with a pale complexion, she is a frail sapling to her husband's mighty baobab. Inside that tiny parcel dwells a busy personality charged with energy and purpose. The woman seems to have a finger in many pies. Since her arrival in Bishops a year ago, she has taken control of Bishops Women's Institute, started a few charities (which are flourishing to this day) and put the Folly Halfway House for Children Refugees on the map of political conscience in the highest echelons of society (she lobbied Westminster for extra funding, and got it!). She is a force to be reckoned with. I hope she has no interest in local history and never applies to join our Archaeological Association. It bears no imagining how Cherie would react to that.

'Yes?' Leanne Magnebu asked, peering at us through a gap in a narrowly open door.

'Good evening,' ever the gentleman, Samuel began and instantly apologised about the late hour. 'We should've waited until tomorrow morning, but my mother—'

'She's in hospital,' I interjected, 'and asked us to sort this out sooner rather than later.'

'You want to make funeral arrangements?' Leanne sought our clarification.

'No! Good Lord, definitely not!' I cried in horror.

'No, not that,' Samuel concurred, and added, 'We've come about our wedding.'

Leanne's face softened in a smile. 'My congratulations. How lovely! Come in. Let's talk about a date.'

We bundled in, glad to be in the warmth and out of the way of the raging elements.

'It's blowing gales out here,' I commented.

'It's fortunate you didn't have to travel far.'

She led us along a poorly lit hallway and into an equally poorly lit study. For a moment I feared we had entered the film set of *The Christmas Carol* and were inside Scrooge's office. The vicar's wife sat down at a dark mahogany desk and gestured towards two chairs. We took our seats and waited while her computer was coming on.

'Is the vicar out and about on church business?' I inquired just to strike a conversation.

'He's been called out to Mrs Cripps. She's taken ill.'

'Oh dear, I hope it isn't the final rites!'

She gazed at me with a faint spark in her eye. She probably thought I was joking. To some extent, I was. Mrs Cripps was infamous for her hypochondriac tendencies. She was hardly in her sixties, but as far as I could tell, she had been threatening her poor husband with dying for decades. One week it was her heart, the next a brain tumour. Nothing had ever materialised. She was actually blacklisted at Bishops Surgery and was only given last-minute-cancellation appointments. John Erwin, the postman, told me. His wife worked there as a receptionist.

'Mrs Cripps appears to have pneumonia.' Leanne Magnebu informed me, emphasising the word *appears* ever so subtly.

'Should we come back tomorrow morning when the vicar is back?' Samuel asked.

'No, no need. I expect him any moment, but even if he isn't here we can look at a date. I keep the church diary.' Mrs Magnebu sounded very efficient indeed.

At long last, her computer glowed at her face, illuminating her paleness. She was hitting the keyboard buttons with ferocious fingers. She may have been a typist in her previous life, before she married Quentin, because she used all her fingers to type, including her thumbs and pinkies. 'What date do you have in mind?' she asked, her eyes rivetted to the screen.

'This summer – some time in August, if you have spaces,' Samuel said.

'We're pretty full in August. Everyone wants August,' she frowned at the screen, 'but you're in luck – I can give you the twenty-second. That'd be Saturday. I've a slot in the morning, at ten,' she lifted her eyes and gave a questioning look, 'unless you prefer Sunday.'

'We'll take the Saturday, the twenty-second,' I said. 'But could we have a later slot, please? Early afternoon? We're planning to have the Stone Circle ceremony first. It's an old tradition here in Bishops—'

She puffed out her cheeks and shook her head as she warned us, 'Just don't mention that to Quentin. He doesn't approve of mixing pagan rites with Christian sacraments. He's quite particular about such things.'

'That's a bit...' I looked for an unoffensive word.

'Old-fashioned,' Samuel helped me.

'Yes, I suppose he had a pretty conservative upbringing in Mombasa,' Leanne smiled almost apologetically. Her eyes returned to the screen. She scowled, 'I'm afraid the afternoon of Saturday, twenty-second is full. Should we look at a date in September?'

'I was hoping to have our wedding at the height of summer.' I couldn't hold back my disappointment.

'Why don't we stick with the morning ceremony in church and do the Stone Circle in the afternoon,' Samuel suggested.

The front door slammed and we heard heavy footsteps in the hallway.

'I'm home!' It was Vicar Quentin's resonant

baritone. 'It turns out it was a false alarm. A touch of indigestion. In the end, Mrs Cripps was well enough to get out of bed and offer me a cup of tea.' His voice carried from the hallway and grew in volume as he approached the office. He entered and as soon as he saw us, his face broke into a wide smile.

'Miss Maggie! Samuel! What a surprise! What brings you to my humble—' His face dropped suddenly and he gave a sharp gasp. 'It isn't Deirdre! Tell me it isn't—'

'No, not at all. Mum is fine. We saw her this morning. She's on the mend – should be home by the weekend,' Samuel assured him. 'We are – Maggie and I are booking a wedding date.'

'Get out of here! Congratulations!' The vicar shook our hands. His were enormous, but soft and warm. 'When is the happy day?'

'August, the twenty-second,' Samuel replied. 'We've just been negotiating the time with your good wife, though it looks like that Saturday afternoon is full so we'll have to settle for the morning.'

'Saturday?' Vicar Quentin's face dropped in disappointment. 'Sundays are holy days, better placed for such ceremonies. Did you check availability for Sunday, the twenty-third, dear,' he addressed his wife, but before she looked it up herself, took the mouse out of her hand and leant over the computer.

'We are happy with the Saturday,' I said.

'And that's coming from a vicar's granddaughter,' Magnebu tut-tutted, giving me a hurtful look. 'Do you forget, Miss Maggie, that the seventh day is a sabbath to the Lord your God. Remember the sabbath day.'

'And we do – we will, I mean, but the wedding will be on Saturday,' I put my foot down. I don't take kindly to people hectoring me.

'Christians should marry on the Sunday, in my view, but I shan't deny you the sacrament of marriage even if I have to perform it on a different day,' he conceded, although the judgment in his tone was unmistakable. In Vicar Quentin's estimation we were heathens.

'Thank you, Vicar,' Samuel said dryly.

'Leanne will take you through the paperwork that needs soring prior to the date,' the vicar sounded equally business-like. 'I will open the church an hour in advance.'

'Isn't it always open?' I was surprised. Grandpa Bernie, who used to be the vicar at St John's forty years ago, used to say that the church door should never be closed.

Quentin looked saddened. 'I'm afraid we've had a spate of break-ins of late. Nothing serious – what I mean to say, no sacrilege was committed, but they stole the communion wine.'

'Twice,' Leanne quantified, and added, 'Don't forget what they did to the pew cushions!'

'Oh yes, that! They set fire to a few of them.'

'Arson?' I was shocked.

'Indeed,' the vicar hung his head. 'And if that wasn't bad enough, some unholy lunatic has been lurking in the graveyard at night, hanging weird amulets in the trees.'

'Amulets?'

'Bizarre trinkets: pentagonal stars with feathers and wind chimes,' Leanne explained.

'Do you understand what I'm saying to you?' the vicar's volume went up and his accent thickened, 'We Christians are under siege from those devil worshipers. They may call themselves pagans, but we all know what they really are—'

'A pagan and an arsonist isn't one and the same thing,' I pointed out. I was a little aggrieved by his wanton accusations, 'and without any proof—'

'What more proof do you need?' He glared at me with self-righteous indignation.

'I bet it was some bored teenagers looking for thrills. They wouldn't know a pagan if he bit them on their backside,' I speculated.

'That's how the greatest evil begins – with ignorance,' Quentin lectured.

'Yes, you're right there, Vicar,' Sam, the mediator, stepped in. He sounded conciliatory, reminding me that all we wanted was to book a wedding date, not earn ourselves an excommunication. 'Nobody approves of what those hooligans did. I'm sorry if it came across differently. Those rascals, whoever they are, deserve punishment. Did you report it to the police?'

'No, we didn't,' Leanne said. 'But we decided to lock the church. Like you said, Miss Kaye, it was probably some kids getting up to mischief. No need for the police to get involved.'

'They wouldn't bother to investigate,' Quentin added. 'I don't blame them. They have their hands full. And anyway, matters of faith have to be resolved on a different plane altogether. Truth will see the light of day sooner or later,' he concluded in his typical high-brow and confusing fashion.

We nodded, pretending we understood and agreed with him.

'Back to your wedding,' his big smile made a welcome return, 'what time would you like to exchange vows?'

We promptly agreed on ten o'clock in the morning. Leanne pencilled us in and told us she would be in touch about the arrangements. She saw us to the front door.

'Do you see now why I asked you not to mention the Stone Circle rites?' she whispered.

Trudging back home in the now howling wind, Samuel and I agreed to cut across the graveyard to my back gate. It would be quicker than taking the long way around the church and through the High Street. I don't use that gate often, but although it is overgrown with weeds, it isn't locked. Grandpa Bernie used it all the time.

As we approached it, the beams of light from our torches dancing unsteadily in the wind, a crouched figure rose abruptly and scuttled away. It could have been a crouched figure or a four-legged animal – a dog, or even a large tabby cat.

'Did you see that!' I shouted to Samuel.

'See what?'

'Someone took off from over there!' I pointed to the spot.

'A ghost?' Samuel grinned. 'Only you can see them, Maggie!'

It wasn't funny. I shrugged. 'Oh well, I'm sure there was someone—' That was the moment when I slipped on something.

My hands met with the soggy ground and sunk into the mud. 'Bloody hell!' I cursed.

'Maggie?' Samuel hooked his hands under my armpits and hauled me up. 'Are you okay?'

'Fine. I've lost my torch.'

He shone his on the ground. We discovered the offending item that tripped me up. It was a beer can, or rather one of many beer cans scattered all over the place. There was also a nest of cigarette ends and a few crumpled crisp bags wedged under the roots of a holly bush.

'I told you I saw someone!' I felt vindicated.

'We'd better keep an eye on this – see who it is,' Samuel said. 'But they aren't coming back in a hurry. Let's go inside and clean you up.'

CHAPTER 5

Harry Wotton was a stocky man with a ruddy complexion and a shock of electric-silver hair sprouting from under his crumpled hat. He rarely, if at all, visited the barber judging by his misshapen and windbeaten coiffure and the glaring discrepancy in the length of his sideburns. One reached halfway across his cheek, the other ended level with his cheekbone. Mr Wotton's attire complimented his hairstyle. His chinos were frayed and filthy where they came in contact with the ground, which they did because they were a couple of inches too long. His anorak pockets bulged with the various items of interest he kept in them. Underneath he wore a padded vest, whatever the weather. His hat with a drooping brim was adorned with colourful badges sown on by an unskilled hand. That hat was nearly as old as Mr Wotton, and he was in his late forties.

On Saturday morning, a week after his son

Isaac's collision with Sam and Maggie's wall, Mr Wotton was toddling along the High Street, carrying a large package. Two steps behind him, Isaac was hobbling on crutches. His right leg, which was encased in a cast and therefore not of much use to him, was bent at the knee; his left leg was doing all the work, assisted by the inexpertly handled crutches. Isaac had just been released from the hospital.

'Hurry up, boy!' Mr Wotton shouted over his shoulder as he turned into Sam and Maggie's driveway. Isaac quickened his pace.

Sam saw them through his study window. They were heading for Maggie's house. He stuck his nose to the window from where, at an angle, he could see that they were admitted inside. Five minutes later however, the Wottons accompanied by Maggie were knocking on Sam's door.

'Mr Wotton came to apologise,' Maggie began.

'Not me, as such. I brought him to do that.' Harry Wotton elucidated and clipped Isaac around the ear. Isaac flinched and yelped, but didn't protest. 'I came, more like, to compensate you for the damage, and that.'

'Come in,' Sam invited them in.

He took them to the sitting room and gestured to the couch. 'Make yourself comfortable.'

'He can stand,' Mr Wotton waved his hand at

Isaac dismissively while he lowered himself into the couch.

'Are you sure?' Maggie inquired. 'It's a bit awkward for him, being on crutches and—'

'Bloody sure.'

Mr Wotton nodded at Isaac. 'Go on, then! Speak up! Like you practised at home.'

Isaac grunted, 'I ... I'm ...' Apologies were not his forte.

Mr Wotton gave his son an evil eye and hollered, 'Did the cat get your tongue? Get on with it or I'll have to re-acquaint your sorry arse with me belt! And take that blinking hood off your face!'

The scrawny body of Isaac Wotton shuddered and the pimples on his chin darkened. This was evident the moment his hood fell, leaving the very contrite Isaac exposed to scrutiny. 'I'm sorry Miss Kaye and to Mr Dee for ... what I done. It won't happen again.'

'It won't happen again,' Harry emphasised, 'or I'll personally get the cops onto him if it does.'

Isaac shrivelled inside his coat.

'It's good to hear you're sorry, Isaac. Very kind of you,' Maggie said. Sam only nodded. He didn't quite recognise this faltering speech as an act of kindness though. And neither did Mr Wotton, it seemed.

'Kind? That's a first!' He guffawed. 'Never heard no one before call him that in his life. No, it's your good self, Miss Maggie, that is kind.'

Maggie glowed, looking rather pretty.

'God's honest truth!' Harry Wotton reiterated with conviction.

'Well, apologies accepted,' Maggie surrendered. 'Do you think young Isaac could take a seat now. He looks a little wobbly on his feet – well, on his one foot.'

'Nah, he don't need to be sitting. He'll be hopping off home now. Not good for anything as he is now, what with his leg in the cast, but soon as he's fit he be at your service – no job too big, Miss Maggie: gardening, washing your cars, you name it.'

'We couldn't possibly—'

'Oh yes, you could. Think of it as his community service. And that's getting away with it lightly in me books.' Mr Wotton jerked his head at his son. 'What you still doing here? Be off with you. I got matters to talk over with Miss Maggie and Mr Dee. Hop off!'

Isaac mumbled something fractionally defiant under his breath, but his father didn't hear it. He then hobbled out of the room, shutting the door behind a little too enthusiastically.

As soon as he was out of earshot, Harry Wotton removed his badge-enhanced hat, revealing a large bald patch on top of his head. With that patch and the frizz of silver hair sprouting around it, he looked deceptively like someone closely related to Albert Einstein.

'Now we can have a serious talk,' he said and slammed on the table the bag he had brought with him. 'A leg of lamb for your kind selves. From me and Mrs Wotton for all you done for that good-for-nothing son of ours.'

'You shouldn't have, really,' Maggie protested.

'I'm quite partial to lamb,' Sam pointed out.

'In that case,' Harry grinned, 'there's more where this came from. We are much obliged to you for rushing our Isaac to the hospital as quick as you did.' There was a quiver of tenderness in his voice, which for as long as his son was around hadn't made an appearance. ''Tis not about the broken leg per se as that he bled a lot, more than he should of. Turns out he's got a very rare blood group, our Isaac – they had to jump out of their skins to get him on a drip fast. It was touch and go. If it wasn't for you, it bears no thinking. They might of not saved him.'

'It was worth the bloodied seats after all,' Sam reflected.

'On that note, Mr Dee, I'm here to cover your expenses: the wall and them bloodied seats.'

'A stone came off the wall and dented my bonnet,' Sam added to the list.

'And all the dents in your car – the lot!'

'I'll pass the invoices to you, then.'

'Right you are!'

'All's well that ends well,' Maggie cheered.

Harry Wotton fidgeted a bit and wrung his

hands. 'One more thing that been bothering me and me wife, if I may ... You see, Isaac is on probation, so if you was to report the ... assault against your wall to your insurance company, or God forbid, to the coppers, he'd end up behind bars. He be only twenty in May. Half of the time he doesn't know what he's doing though he doesn't mean no harm as such.'

'We'll keep the insurers and the police out of it,' Sam said.

'Thank you. Thank you, both. Much obliged. You can count on a supply of Wotton lamb as long as you want it. And if there be anything else —'

'Actually, there is,' Maggie cocked her pretty little head and beamed her dimpled smile at the farmer. 'You see, Mr Wotton, we're getting married in August and as the tradition has it we'd like to have the proper Stone Circle ceremony.'

'Consider it done. When would that be?'

'August, the twenty-second. Shall we say at noon?'

'Noon it is.' Harry was very amiable. He would have agreed to a midnight session with fireworks at his expense if they had asked. He rubbed his hands. 'I'll have it all ready for you. I'll clear the access path and tidy up around the Circle. It's gone to seed of late, if you know what I mean.'

'Has it?' Maggie was surprised. 'I thought the

Parish Council was responsible for the upkeep.'

'Ooo, it was, it was. Until, that is, the new vicar started interfering: sticking his beak into what wasn't his business, telling folks how to run the place.' Harry halted and blinked nervously. 'I hope I'm not treading on no toes. You not friends with the vicar, are you – by the reason of your grandfather?'

'No, not at all. I haven't been to church in years. Go on, Mr Wotton, you can speak freely.' Maggie sounded as keen as a bean to find out the nature of Harry's grievance.

'Well, as you well know he be on the Parish Council – on account of being our vicar. As if we need one what interferes with our ways every step of the way! Supposed, he *nourishes our Christian faith,*' Harry Wotton twisted his lips with disdain. 'So he joined the Council as soon as he arrived, which is as it should be – Vicar Lawrence was no trouble in all his time here, God rest his soul ... But the new vicar! He be a different kettle of fish altogether right from the world *go*! It wasn't more than three month into his joining the Council that he started bossing the lot of them. The Chair, Mr Jacobsen rolls over. He sends us a letter – an official letter, by post and that, on the Parish stationery paper, to tell us that the funding for the Stone Circle maintenance been taken back, as in it's me Circle and me responsibility to look after it, if I care to.'

'Oh dear!'

'You can say that again, Miss Maggie. So I get up in arms and march to see Mr Jacobsen in person to have it out with him face to face. I tell him how many feet trample over me fields every summer, and the cost of keeping the footpath, but – I say to him – if they don't pay then I'll block the path – put a padlock on the gate. I'd given right of way out of the goodness of me heart, but without the funding I'm not having tourists leaving the gate open and me sheep getting into the road and being mowed down by cars. No funding, no access.

'And that's where Mr Jacobsen starts apologising, and says that's naught to do with him, but all due to Quentin Magnebu campaigning for the Christian values in the community, or some such nonsense. It was all his doing, Miss Maggie. But don't you worry your little head, I'll have that Stone Circle up and running for your wedding.'

Maggie sat through Mr Wotton's account with her mouth gaping. Sam could tell she was seriously rattled. Her face transformed from shocked to furious in a matter of minutes. At last, she squared her shoulders and declared, 'That's all very kind of you, Mr Wotton, but we can't have Mr Magnebu dictating to us. It's our way or the highway, I say, and I will say that to his face. Watch this space, Mr Wotton!'

He gazed at her admiringly. 'Well, if you can put a good word out for me with the Council, I'll be obliged. Still, be careful with that man. Big and mighty like a brick house – I couldn't handle the bugger on me own, and I ain't no ninny.'

CHAPTER 6

Maggie's Journal

Both Deirdre and our hot tub were due to arrive on the same day. It was the first Monday of March. After weeks of incessant rain and howling winds, the weather was beginning to lean towards spring, although still erring on the side of caution. The sky was grey and heavy but at least it wasn't raining, and the temperature hovered comfortably in the mid-teens. We were working on a tight schedule conceived with military precision: collect Deirdre from the hospital at eleven-hundred hours sharp, install her in her new bedroom downstairs (converted from Samuel's study) by fourteen-hundred hours at which time we would be shooting off to Badger's Hall to take delivery of the hot tub.

At the hospital we again bumped into Kylie Cunningham (nee Mrs Giant Jack Pearce) and she and I agreed to meet at The Old Stables for coffee and cake on Thursday. We couldn't chat for long – she was run off her feet and I was on a tight schedule. We thanked Dr Edmunds for taking such good care of Deirdre. He appeared a little less jovial and a little more distracted than usual. The heavy bags under his eyes looked like bruises. He patted Deirdre's shoulder and said, 'I'll see you Wednesday week.' He gave Samuel a comforting nod, 'Just a routine follow-up appointment. Nothing to worry about.'

We wheeled Deirdre to the car and drove off.

As we approached Priest's Hole, we were delighted to discover that the stonemasons organised by the ever-efficient Harry Wotton had commenced remedial works on our wall. He had telephoned on Saturday to inform us that they would be starting on Monday. 'If you can take their word for it, that is. Tradesmen nowadays aren't what they used to be, if you get me drift. They say one thing and do another.'

It transpired that these workmen were the reliable sort.

We abandoned the wheelchair in the boot of the car as Deirdre insisted *she still had the use of her legs, thank you very much!* She hooked her arm over Samuel's and let him escort her. Slowly, one small step after another, they made it to the house.

'You're not seriously thinking of *storing* me in your office!' She exclaimed upon discovering the new location of her bed. She was fuming. 'Whatever next? The garden shed?'

'It's only temporary, Mother, to spare you the stairs.'

'I want to negotiate the stairs! I'll not be treated like an invalid!'

Poor Samuel pressed his hands to his mouth to stifle a groan. 'It's for your own good—'

'No,' she was resolute, 'I'll wait in the lounge while you two carry my bed back to my bedroom. Then I'll have a nap.'

We were in the middle of dismantling the bed when someone knocked on the front door. It was just twenty past one and we were yet to put the bed together in Deirdre's bedroom and tuck her in.

'It can't be the hot tub?' I asked Samuel.

'They aren't due until two.'

'Maybe they're early?'

'They would've gone to Badger's Hall anyway, not here.'

'True. So who can it be?'

The knocking was resumed with redoubled force. Samuel expelled a resigned sigh, 'Let's see who it is and blow them off.'

'Politely,' I added. Being in a hurry gave us no excuse to abandon our good manners.

We propped the headboard against the wall and tread gingerly over the many loose parts, slats and screws.

'Good afternoon!' Vicar Quentin boomed. He and Leanne were standing on the porch. They made a handsome if eccentric couple: he large and as black as the iris of your eye, she a tiny porcelain doll with strawberry-blonde hair and rosy heart-shaped lips. In broad daylight, she looked healthier and younger than in the shadows of the dimly lit vicarage.

'A little birdie told us Deirdre was back from the hospital,' Vicar Quentin tolled in his sonorous voice. 'I said to Leanne, "My dear wife, we must go and visit my favourite parishioner to wish her a speedy recovery." And she said ... Well, what did you say, my love?' He peered at Leanne expectantly.

'I said I'd make a nice lemon drizzle,' Leanne offered a modest smile and presented the cake which looked and smelled delicious.

'And I said, "What a splendid idea!" So here we are. I hope you don't mind our dropping in without calling first?'

'Who's that at the door?' Deirdre's voice carried from the sitting room.

'And there she is!' Vicar Quentin rejoiced and pushed past Maggie and Samuel. Leanne followed.

'Aw, Mrs Dee, my dear, dear Mrs Dee! How we missed you!' the vicar stomped towards Deirdre and enveloped her in his octopus-like arms. 'I prayed for you day and night.'

'Well, Vicar, good to see you. There was no cause for alarm – and no need to get God involved,' Deirdre said dryly, 'I had it all in hand.'

I always wonder about Deirdre's relationship with God. She strikes me as a rational woman, but nonetheless she never misses the Sunday service. Apparently, she does the readings. Her posh clipped enunciation is much appreciated by the half-deaf elderly congregation of St John the Baptist. I think she enjoys being indispensable.

Vicar Quentin rattled with laughter. 'Always the joker, Mrs Dee! I'm glad you didn't lose your sense of humour.'

'Shall I cut the lovely cake and get some tea?' I offered and reached for the cake that rested forgotten in Mrs Magnebu's lap.

'Ah, the cake! A lemon drizzle especially for you, Mrs Dee,' the vicar exulted.

'I don't mind if I have a piece. You spoil me rotten, Vicar,' Deirdre beamed and gave a little chuckle. She may have even winked at him, but it could have been a reflection of light in her twinkling eye. She certainly seemed invigorated by his visit. Perhaps she fancied him on some transcendental level?

Leanne surrendered the cake to me a little reluctantly as if she feared I may run away with it.

'Tea will go nicely with it,' I said and promised to be back.

Samuel followed me to the kitchen to help. I

cut the cake and he prepared a pot of tea.

'You do realise, Maggie, that we won't be able to partake in refreshments. It's ten to two – we ought to be going to Badger's Hall to take delivery of the hot tub.'

'Damn it!' I cursed and hurriedly shoved a whole slice into my mouth. It was delicious. It dissolved on my tongue, bursting with the fresh flavours of citrus. 'You're right, Samuel,' I agreed as soon as I swallowed the last crumb, 'We'll have to leave your mum with her guests and get going.'

We brought the refreshments to the sitting room and offered our apologies.

'It's such a pity,' the vicar's face darkened, 'as I was hoping to revisit the question of your Saturday wedding.'

'Wouldn't Sunday be a better day for a wedding?' Deirdre inquired.

'You took the words out of my mouth, my dear lady! I tried to explain that to your son and Miss Kaye.' Although he was addressing Deirdre, he shot us a supercilious look. 'With your gracious backup, Deirdre, they may yet reconsider.'

'We really have to be going,' Samuel pushed me towards the exit.

We arrived at Badger's Hall just seconds before the lorry carrying our hot tub turned into the driveway. Badger's Hall used to be my childhood home and a cradle of many happy memories. It sat on the western-most edge of Bishops Well, next door to Mr Wotton's farm. Despite a recent fire, its thatched roof remained intact and its southern Tudor façade with the crisscross of age-blackened beams was still in one piece. When my parents had passed away, I had found myself on the brink of losing it until Samuel rode to the rescue and bought out my siblings. We had become business partners and converted it into a B&B. We had carried out refurbishment works with the help of our friends and after a short sojourn on the high northern seas we were ready to open for business.

The lorry with our hot tub backed into the garden, supervised by a man in his thirties with a tattoo of a snake wrapped around his neck. It was so realistic that it gave me the creeps. I kept well away from him in case a real snake slithered out of his sleeve. Samuel and I watched as our hot tub was being slowly lowered from the back of the lorry.

'Where do you want it?' The snake-man inquired.

'Over there please, on the patio by the rowan tree,' I pointed him to the very spot we had earlier identified as ideal.

'Right you are!' He gesticulated to the other crew members – the pot-bellied driver and a pimply lad of Isaac Wotton's age. 'You heard the lady, boys. Let's go!'

The ringing of the phone gave me a start. I had forgotten that last week we'd had a landline installed for the business. It was ringing! My heart burst into a frantic drumming.

'It's our phone!' I shouted to Samuel in case it was beyond him to understand this perplexing phenomenon. 'I'll take it.'

I raced inside and grabbed the receiver mid-ring. 'Badger's Hall, good afternoon. Maggie speaking. How may I help you?' I breathed into the phone in my best impersonation of Joanna Lumley.

'Oh, at last, I've been calling and calling, I was just about to give up,' said a foreign-sounding lady on the other side, 'I'd like to book a room for Friday week. I will probably stay the weekend – two nights.'

'Let me check the availability,' said I self-importantly. I don't know what possessed me. I knew we had no bookings whatsoever. 'So, that'd be Friday, the thirteenth? Let's see ...' I milked the moment.

'Yes – two nights if you can squeeze me in on this short notice.'

'I'll see what I can do,' I paused, then continued. 'Yes, no problem at all. I can offer you our deluxe suite with prime views of Bishops White Horse.'

'Would you have anything cheaper than deluxe?'

'Certainly!' I was still excited. I would be,

naturally, even if she requested a straw bed in the cellar. 'A small room with an ensuite on the first floor.'

'Perfect.'

'May I have your name and your credit card details, madam?' I was bristling with efficiency.

'The name is Daisy Rotich,' she said and proceeded to give me her card details.

As soon as I put the phone down, I ran out into the garden screaming at the top of my voice, 'Samuel! Samuel! We have our first booking!'

CHAPTER 7

Maggie's Journal

On Wednesday, ten days into Deirdre's home convalescence, Samuel drove her to the Royal United Hospital in Bath for her follow-up appointment with Dr Edmunds. Deirdre was lucky to have that appointment when she did. All over the town there was talk of the looming lockdown with the implication that all non-essential medical appointments would be cancelled. I stayed at home, fretting over the future of our budding B&B business. I would not speak of it however. Samuel had enough on his plate.

To keep myself occupied, I went through Badger's Hall, room by room, cleaning, dusting, polishing and making everything ready for our first guest. I banished the threat of coronavirus from my thoughts. I was finding it difficult to imagine that some microbe would really go to the trouble of travelling around the globe to settle in our humble Shires. Little did I know how virulent and well-travelled viruses can be.

After four hours of hard labour, though it was a labour of love, I returned home and waited for Samuel and Deirdre. I availed myself of a mug of coffee accompanied by a small pack of Jaffa cakes. The original plan was to have one or two, but the wait extended into infinity and to fill it I resorted to half a pack, or perhaps it was three quarters. Whatever the fraction, I remembered to leave two Jaffas intact: one for Samuel and one for Deirdre.

They finally returned at three in the afternoon, tired and famished. Over the late lunch, Samuel relayed to me the doctor's verdict, 'Everything is as it should be. Mum is on track to a full recovery, as long as she continues to take things easy.' He fixed her with an admonishing eye. 'No more running up and down the stairs, no more kitchen antics or any house chores. I'll be employing a cleaner.'

'Waste of money, if you ask me,' Deirdre muttered, but she looked resigned to the idea.

'I'm happy to help with house chores,' I offered.

'I wouldn't dream of accepting,' Samuel was firm. 'I can afford a cleaning lady, thank you all the same.'

I recommended Cathy Hicks. 'She's reliable and very discreet, not to mention that she needs the money. Her daughter, Amanda, has MS. Cathy is her sole carer and on top of that she looks after her two young grandchildren. I think the younger one has only just started school.'

'Cathy Hicks it is then.'

I gazed at Deirdre affectionately, 'You gave us such a fright! I'm so glad it's all behind us.'

'I'm made of stronger stuff than you give me credit for. I survived the Blitz. What's a heart attack compared to that?'

'A piece of cake, no doubt.' Samuel sounded marginally sarcastic.

'We can now look forward to the wedding.' A thought occurred to me: 'Perhaps we should invite Dr Edmunds? What do you think?'

'It's your wedding, not mine,' Deirdre pointed out, 'and anyway he may not come. He's a busy man, as you know. He couldn't even see me today. It was a Dr Wheeler. Nice enough chap, but he doesn't have Dr Edmunds's gravitas. He kept reading my medical notes out loud – wouldn't lift his eyes to as much as look at me. How can you call that an examination?'

'Oh, mother, don't read anything into it. He isn't familiar with your case.'

'I thought Dr Edmunds was to see you,' I distinctly remembered him saying so. 'What happened to him?'

'I don't know, do I?' Deirdre looked

disappointed. 'They don't tell you anything. You get pushed from one doctor to another – it's like speed dating.'

'What do you know about speed dating?' Samuel raised an amused eyebrow.

'More than you do, would be my educated guess. I read about it in *Sexton's Herald*.' Deirdre scowled. 'Everything is so impersonal nowadays. In the past, you'd have the same GP for every appointment. He knew everything there was to know about you. Health-wise, of course.'

'They still do. That's why they keep notes. It's all computerised, Mum. That's the way the world goes. It certainly doesn't stand still.'

'I wouldn't expect it to, but I would've liked to be seen by Dr Edmunds,' Deirdre declared mulishly.

In the evening I had an AA meeting to attend. Our AA stands for Archaeological Association, in case you wondered. Samuel declined to tag along, claiming that he had to look after Deirdre. I wasn't sure what that meant – reading her a bedtime story? Whatever it was, I didn't push him. He looked tired, poor thing. Driving to the hospital and back, being stuck in the notorious Bath queues and waiting for two hours for an appointment that had been scheduled for eleven o'clock would have wiped me out too. I headed for the Village Hall on my own. I had to be there tonight. There was the matter of the Stone

Circle upkeep to discuss and we, the guardians of Bishops' lore, were responsible for it.

Except for Samuel, everyone was present. Cherie, our chair person, had brought her partner Lisa who was to be initiated into the Association. That didn't involve blood-letting or any such savage rituals but simply parting with one's bank account details to set up a standing order for the membership fee, payable quarterly. As our treasurer, Vanessa handled these matters with her usual charm.

The agenda was full and it was my turn to take the minutes, but I asked Edgar Flynn to do the honours. 'I'm sorry to jump the gun, but can we go straight to Any Other Business?'

'We'll get there in due course,' Cherie informed me in a tone bearing no dissent.

'But this cannot wait, I'm afraid. I need to get it off my chest before I explode,' I insisted.

Cherie slid her thick-rimmed glasses down her nose and peered at me, 'Then explode you must. Go on.'

'It's about the Stone Circle in Harry Wotton's field. It's become endangered,' I began. That got everyone's attention.

James inquired with a puzzled expression, 'Do you mean *endangered* like a rare species of bird?' He was an avid bird-watcher and frequently resorted to feathered analogies.

'In a way, yes,' I confirmed.

The Stone Circle dated back to the early Bronze Age. It was constructed at about the same time as Stonehenge, give or take a thousand years. It consisted of five upright Sarsen standing stones, ranging in height from five to seven feet. The two tallest stones were topped with a horizontal lintel. The circle was twenty feet in diameter. In its centre was a spring. What an uninformed stranger would refer to as rubble was to us, Bishopians, a sanctuary.

'What precisely is wrong with it? Is it about to fall down?' asked James, alarm ringing in his tone.

'It has been abandoned by the Parish Council – abandoned and denounced. Poor Mr Wotton received a letter advising him that they were withdrawing funding for the maintenance of the Circle and the access road.'

'On what grounds, may I ask?' Vera's face coloured with indignation. She considered herself a patron of the Stone Circle. She walked Rumpole there every day. She referred to that as *communing with our ancient history*.

'Apparently the Circle doesn't align with the Christian ethos of the parish,' I explained.

'What sort of gobbledygook is that!'

'It's the vicar's gobbledygook. Quentin Magnebu sits on the Parish Council *ex officio*. He's of those religious nutters the world is full of, and soon after he arrived to take on the parish he took issue with the Circle being used for *unholy* pagan rituals—'

The room expelled a collective gasp of disbelief.

'It's true. I'm only repeating what Harry Wotton told me. The Council withdrew the funding at Vicar Magnebu's instigation. Harry Wotton is planning to lock the gates and no one will get through to the monument.'

'He's within his right to do so,' James commented. 'It's his land.'

'But it's our Circle …' Cherie hung her head, deep in reflection. 'Surely, he can't do that. It's his moral duty to—'

'It's all of our duty, not just Harry Wotton's,' I argued.

'No one should blame Harry,' Michael Almond backed me up. 'He is the keeper of the Circle as his father was before him, but he needs support. Could we apply for funding from English Heritage perhaps?'

'We shouldn't have to. It is *our* Circle. It belongs to Bishops Well and we, Bishopians, owe it to our children to care for it. We ought to fund it so that we can claim it as ours. We can't let English Heritage pull it from under us,' Vera struck a high note of local patriotism. She sounded like a seasoned politician on an election tour. Her husband's demagogic penchant must have rubbed off on her over the years.

'And how do we do that?' Edgar Flynn, who had so far been as quiet as a mouse, inquired. I think he was concerned that Vera would ask us for donations.

'We'll ensure that the Parish Council reverses its decision. I happen to know that there is a vacancy on the Council. Michelle Pyke resigned before Christmas. Her mother is on her deathbed, somewhere in Devon, if I'm not mistaken.'

'Her mother lives in Cornwall,' Lisa chipped in. 'Angela Cornish told me.'

'Wherever Michelle Pyke's mother lives is of no consequence,' Edgar Flynn pointed out, bringing the derailed debate back on track. 'Let's get back to that vacancy on the Parish Council. I can't apply for it. I'm not a local man. Anyone?'

We all looked at each other hoping for a show of many hands, but not a single one went up in the air.

'Someone has to volunteer,' Edgar pressed on. 'We must have an insider.'

'How about we draw straws?' James suggested.

The motion was carried out. Short on straws, we found a box of matches. One of them was beheaded by Edgar who then dropped them all into his tweed flat cap. We took turns to draw. Naturally, I got the short match.

I half expected that to happen. It's my rotten luck. I never gamble because I always lose. I put on a brave face. 'That's okay. I'll do it. I'll call George Easterbrook tomorrow to put forward my candidacy.'

'We'll all vote for you,' Vanessa cheered. 'I'll spread the word about town.'

'It goes without saying,' Vera seconded that.

'It's not George Easterbrook you need to call,' Cherie said. 'He's gone on a retreat. With some Buddhist monks in Tibet. He won't be back before Christmas.'

'Did he now?' Edgar looked intrigued. 'I considered doing that myself a while back. Couldn't do it now. Mum needs me at home.'

'So who has replaced George as the Parish Clerk?' was what I wanted to know.

'Claire Thackery. She's the clerk for Norton Parish. Lives in Upper Norton. I will text you her number.' Cherie was the font of all local knowledge, historical and contemporary.

CHAPTER 8

Although Sam had succeeded at extricating himself from last night's AA meeting, he stood no chance on Thursday. His services had become indispensable.

'This may be the last market for a long time if the rumours about lockdown are true,' Maggie elucidated. 'We need to stock up. And do I need to remind you that we're expecting our first paying guest tomorrow? There're tons of supplies to get for Badger's Hall. I don't have enough hands to carry it all by myself.'

Meekly, Sam armed himself with shopping bags and his wallet. He'd have to pay for the goods. The business account was empty, awaiting its first deposit. He was gearing himself up to educate Maggie about the ins and outs of proper account-keeping.

Maggie shot ahead of him. Her pleasingly voluptuous figure encased in her crushed-velvet tracksuit disappeared round the bend of the road. Sam had to pick up pace to keep up with her. Their first stop was at Vernon Leitch, the cheesemaker. Maggie acquired half a pound of five different types of cheese.

'Since we can't tell which one is Mrs Rotich's favourite,' she explained when Sam fixed her with a quizzical gaze. He had to think on his feet to remember who on earth Mrs Rotich was and why her taste in cheese was of such relevance. He remembered at last: Mrs Rotich, their first paying guest, of course.

'What if she doesn't like cheese?'

'Then we'll take it home and eat it ourselves. Simple.'

'There should be a clear distinction between our business and personal expenses, Maggie,' Sam began, and stopped. Maggie had tilted her head and knitted her brows to demonstrate she was mystified. This wasn't the time or the place to embark on lessons in book-keeping.

'I hear that Mrs Dee hasn't been well. A heart attack, I'm told. Not a trifling thing – the ticker – when it decides to pack up. My cousin, Stan – he was only sixty last year when it killed him. One minute he was mowing the lawn, the next he was dead. Please pass on to her my best wishes, Mr Dee,' Mr Leitch was saying as he weighed each of the five blocks of cheese and wrapped them in paper.

'Thank you, Mr Leitch,' Sam smiled.

'It's Vernon, Mr Dee. Just Vernon.'

'In that case, I'm Sam.' This wasn't the first time that they had decided to drop the formalities and move to a first name basis. The chumminess would only last until the next time when *Mr Dee* and *Mr Leitch* would re-surface again. Sam had learned that in Bishops Well familiarity took a long time to establish itself – several generations at the very least.

The bakery was next door to the cheese shop, so Maggie and Sam made a stop there on their way to the butcher's. Angela Cornish, Bishops' chief gossip, sold them three varieties of bread: wholemeal, harvest grain and a white bloomer. Naturally, she wouldn't let them leave until she had secured firm confirmation of Maggie's intention to stand for the Parish Council.

'Just to be sure, dear,' Angela drilled, 'are you on the ballot paper? I never bother with all that voting malarkey, but if it's you, Maggie, I'll make the effort and put my cross next to your name.'

'I'll be very grateful, Angela,' Maggie beamed at her. 'I have indeed put forward my candidacy.'

'I always knew you'd get into politics one day. You'll give that stuck up Henry Oopsy-Poo a run for his money.' A few Bishopians had started calling his Right Honourable Henry Hopps-Wood MP *Oopsy-Poo* behind his back after the worst kept secret of his affair with the late Penny Ruta had leaked into the public domain. Jokes had been flying around for months on end about his prowess in bed and insatiable sexual appetites. Just imagining Henry's awkwardly elongated physique *in flagrante delicto* made people holler with laughter.

'I wouldn't go as far as competing with Henry,' Maggie giggled, 'but I want to get on the Council to sort out the funding for the Stone Circle.'

'Oh, yes! I know all about it. That new vicar – what's his name – has been making changes to how things are. I never liked the man. Or his wife. She tried to get me on one of her charitable committees, as if I had the time to amble about the town, rattling a money box in people's faces. I told her as much – *I am a busy woman, Mrs Magnebu*, I said, *I've got a bakery to run, unlike some ladies of leisure with time on their hands.* Apparently she bakes her own bread,' Angela snorted.

Maggie expressed her commiserations to Mrs Cornish and thanked her again for her support. Sam was impressed. She already sounded and acted like a true politician.

At the butcher's shop, as bags of bacon, sausages and pork chops were being carefully selected by Maggie, Robert Kane, the proprietor of Kane & Sons, waved his butcher's knife in the air and declared, 'I couldn't believe me eyes when I saw what that good-for-nothing Isaac Wotton done to your wall!'

ANNA LEGAT

'You should've seen what he did to his leg!' Maggie exclaimed.

'Serves him right. That boy ain't nothing but trouble. Twas him that broke into the off-licence and got away with nothing other than the suspended sentence.'

'His father has paid for the damages. The wall is as good as new. We've put the matter behind us,' Sam felt obliged to point out. Mr Wotton was dead keen to have it hushed up.

'Old Harry can't be bailing him out forever, you know.' Robert Kane handed over the chops to Maggie. 'Will there be anything else, Miss Maggie?'

Luckily there wasn't and Maggie, followed by Sam laden with her shopping, proceeded towards the pink-and-cream stall of Kev and Jane Wilcox. The expedition couldn't be complete without the obligatory Rum & Raisin Extravaganza. Sam watched with horror as two pounds of fudge made it into Maggie's basket, followed by six brioche rolls – 'Just in case Mrs Rotich likes those for breakfast' – and finally a coffee-and-walnut cake the need for which Maggie did not bother to explain.

'Stocking up for a rainy day, eh? A wise move,' Kev approved. 'It may be a while before we can set the stall again. That wretched virus is spreading like wild fire.'

'That's what I was thinking,' Maggie concurred. 'You see, Samuel? I was right. Better safe than sorry.' Sam didn't even try to fathom how "safety" featured in the acquisition of fudge.

The last item on the agenda for the day was coffee-and-cake (more cake!) with Maggie's school friend, nurse Kylie Pearce, at the Old Stables café. Sam tagged along not because he was keen on the catch-up, but because he had no energy to resist. He knew that resistance would be futile. Saddled with countless shopping bags, he shuffled meekly behind Maggie. She was bristling with vigour. Carrying her little basket that rippled with lettuce leaves and celery sticks, she strode towards the Arcade.

Kylie was already there. She looked almost unrecognisable. The haunted and tired face Sam remembered from the hospital was nowhere to be seen. She looked pretty with makeup on. Her hair was loose, sitting in coils on her shoulders. She waved to them from her table.

They ordered their tea and cake, and joined her. Sam drew the line on exchanging hugs and kisses with Kylie. He nursed his double expresso and drifted into a world of his own while the two ladies caught up on the last forty years.

'You bet it did!' Kylie's amplified voice cut through his musings. 'We knew it was coming – 'course we did – but what good was that, you tell me! We had sandbags, and all. Anyway, the water just— I don't know how it got there. I suppose it seeped through. It was up to my knees in the cellar. We had a pump going day and night.'

'Oh dear!' Maggie commiserated. 'I always said Holbrook Estate shouldn't have been built right by the river.'

'It's a flood zone!' Kylie banged her fist on the table, evoking a few alarmed looks from the neighbouring tables. 'What this is going to do to our insurance premium bears no contemplation. Jack says we ought to sue the County Council for giving the developer permission to build there in the first place.'

Maggie saw an opportunity to do some voter canvassing. Sam was impressed. She said, 'I think the Parish Council should look into building flood defences, don't you?'

'I can't make them, can I?' Kylie sighed. 'Anyway, let's face it – they're a bunch of old farts. Totally out of touch. What was that all about those bridleways? Not even Lord Philip rides his horse anymore. He's too old, and that white mare of his must be dead by now.' Kylie was referring to a new initiative by the Parish Council to develop a network of bridleways exclusively for foot- and horse traffic. A few lanes and dirt roads had been repurposed, resulting in hefty fines for many unsuspecting motorists who had innocently strayed into them.

'Well, I'm hoping to get on the Parish Council,' Maggie struck while the iron was hot. 'My name is on the ballot paper. It's time to give them a bit of a shake-up, make a few changes and bring the lot of them into the twenty-first century.' That was rich coming from Maggie, Sam pondered, considering that her first objective was for the Council to invest in a five-thousand-year-old pile of stones.

Kylie clasped her hands. 'That's the best thing I've heard all week! I'm going to get the whole of Holbrook Estate to vote for you, Maggie.'

Demurely, Maggie bowed her head and said, 'Thank you, Kylie. I won't let you down.'

Sam's expresso was long gone as were the two ladies' teas and cake. He fidgeted in his chair and gave a little cough. Kylie's gaze swooped upon him.

'And how is Mrs Dee?'

'Recovering nicely, thank you.'

'That's good to hear,' Kylie rejoiced, but soon her face dropped. 'I can't say the same for poor Indira Edmunds. You know, I mentioned her to you the other day – Dr Edmund's wife.'

'Yes, we met her when we visited Deirdre in hospital. Such a sweet, beautiful woman. Did she take a turn for the worse?'

'Unfortunately. It was touch and go, but we brought her back. Still,' Kylie sighed, 'she won't last long. Everyone knows. Jonas – Dr Edmunds – is beside himself with grief.'

'That would explain why he couldn't see Deirdre. She had an appointment with him but was seen by someone else.'

'Oh yes, Jonas has taken a few days off to be by Indira's side.'

'It's so unfair. He must be devasted that he can't do any more for her. Being a doctor and knowing it's out of his hands ...'

'Can't cheat death,' Kylie said.

It was past 6 o'clock when Maggie and Sam finally made it home. Sam had bravely endured their strenuous shopping expedition followed by a flurry of activity at Badger's Hall in preparation for the arrival of their first guest tomorrow. He was exhausted.

He brought the rest of the shopping to Maggie's and together, they unpacked it. Maggie offered to whip up a quick pork chop with mash for dinner. While she occupied herself in the kitchen, Sam went to fetch his mother.

He found her in her bedroom, poised by the open window. She was hunched with her head inclined. Before he spoke, she pressed her finger to her lips and hissed. She beckoned him and pointed towards something outside. Sam tiptoed and gingerly peered over the windowsill. His nostrils were assaulted by the distinct odour of weed and his ears wilted at the fruity language expelled by two young male voices. The swearing was unrepeatable. The two youths seemed to be having a debate about their ungentlemanly intentions towards a girl with such physical attributes that the young men found it impossible to contain not only their language but also their hormones.

'Blimey!' Deirdre mouthed.

Sam closed the window and puffed out his cheeks. 'Let me deal with it.'

He headed for Maggie's. It was clear that Deirdre had discovered the intruders who had of late been camping by Maggie's back gate under the holly bush and generating a rising pile of beer cans, confectionary wrappers and expired joints. He informed Maggie of the discovery and together they crept outside.

Armed with a potato masher (which she happened to have in hand when Sam arrived), Maggie charged ahead. She probably regarded herself as adequately protected. She reached for the latch and swung the gate open with the words, 'And what do we have here?'

Two hooded figures scrambled to their feet. One of them took a panicked look at the potato masher and scampered. The other tried to follow suit but had a pair of crutches to reckon with. He grabbed one, tripped over the other, and landed on the ground with a groan. His cast-encased leg sprung up over his head.

'Young master Wotton! Why am I not surprised?' Sam stood over him with his hands on his hips, ready to catch him if the boy tried to run for it – although the chances of that were very slim. Isaac failed to stifle a curse. Sam shook his head disapprovingly. 'My mother's confined to her bedroom up there,' he spun his head towards the top window. 'You realise she had to listen to the two of you spewing profanities all day? It's not fair on an old lady, is it now?'

'We only been here ten minutes,' Isaac had the nerve to counter.

Maggie meantime pressed ahead amongst the tombstones, bellowing after the escapee, 'Thomas Moore, come back here this minute!'

Having been recognised, Thomas Moore stopped in his tracks and stood there with his back to them, probably contemplating his next move: should he stay or should he go now?

'Come back here! Don't be a scumbag!' Maggie drilled into his conscience. 'Don't leave your friend in need! I thought you were better than that!'

He hesitated for a few seconds but in the end turned to face Maggie, and dragged himself back to the scene of the crime. Like Isaac, he was a pimply teenager, perhaps a year or two younger than Isaac – eighteen at best. Unlike Isaac, he was bulky, with a fiery shock of red hair and a lazy demeaner.

'Hi, Miss,' he addressed Maggie sheepishly.

'Hello Thomas. A right mess you two have made on my doorstep.' She pointed to the undeniable evidence of alcohol and drug use in their den.

'It wasn't us, was it?'

'You tell me.'

'You can't prove nothing, Miss.'

'We caught you here red-handed, so I say it was you.'

Sam had to admire Maggie's composure. Then again, she was a teacher and had been trained in handling the explosive material of hormonal youths as high as kites. He would be inclined to call the police and distance himself from the matter as quickly as possible, but Maggie had other ideas. 'I want you to clean the mess and stay away from my property. And from the communion wine! Especially you, Isaac,' she rounded on him with a stern glare. 'You've done enough damage without adding more to it, I should think.'

'Yes, Miss,' Isaac agreed and kicked Thomas in the shin, 'Go on, mate!'

'Yes, Miss,' Under duress, Thomas concurred.

'Right, I'll get you a bin bag and you can start the clean-up,' Maggie declared.

'You won't tell me Dad,' Isaac gazed pleadingly at Sam.

'This is the last time,' Sam warned him. 'And Miss Kaye is right about the communion wine. It was you two, wasn't it? Don't try to deny it!' Sam raised a forbidding finger as soon as Isaac began to open his mouth. 'Just stay away from the church and the graveyard, and from our walls. That's a good boy.'

'And what's with the amulets you

keep hanging around the cemetery?' Maggie demanded. 'The vicar is none too pleased about all that voodoo on his doorstep.'

'What amulets?' The boys asked simultaneously, both with the most innocent – and baffled – expressions.

'Charms, pentagons, bird feathers, I hear,' Maggie elaborated.

'That wasn't us, Miss! Honest!' The boy called Thomas Moore protested.

'It'd better not be you!' Maggie wagged her finger at him. 'And maybe it wasn't you, but I bet you know who it was.'

'Dunno, I swear!' Thomas shook his head.

'But we can keep an eye out for them,' Isaac offered.

'No, don't worry. Just stay away from the graveyard,' Maggie decreed. 'You've done enough. And all that mess,' she swept her arm across their camp, 'Get on with it! You don't want me to find a single loose cigarette butt when I come back later.'

Over the pork chop dinner, Maggie explained to Sam and Deirdre the hold she seemed to have over Thomas Moore: 'He was my student a couple of years ago. Only briefly, but he stuck in my mind. He was in year 10 and I was covering the class for their English teacher. Off on sick leave, poor chap. They'd driven him to a breakdown. Thomas had probably had his hand in it. He isn't an easy young man. Anyway, he and I managed to sort out our differences and by the end, believe it or not, he gave me flowers.'

'That's a result!' Deirdre was impressed.

'Well, it was only a twig of lilac he'd probably snapped off from someone's front garden, but it's the thought that counts,' Maggie chuckled.

CHAPTER 9

Maggie's Journal

We had been waiting for Mrs Rotich since noon. By four o'clock we had lost the will to live.

'Why didn't you ask her what time she'd be here?' Samuel sounded a little harsh. We were bored out of our skulls having spent hours playing Snakes & Ladders behind the reception desk and jumping to our feet every time the cuckoo clock struck another hour.

'Would you have asked?' I demanded to know. 'Would it be even polite to ask?'

'It would've saved us lots of time wasted waiting,' he said grumpily.

'Maybe she's not coming?' I hunched my shoulders in defeat. 'Maybe the whole booking was a prank.'

'She gave you her credit card details, though.'

'True.' I mulled over various other possibilities. We knew that lockdown was imminent. It was to be announced on Monday. Maybe our guest had changed her mind about travelling. 'She's probably not coming and forgot to cancel.'

'All those cheeses,' Samuel sighed.

I felt responsible for the fiasco and, of course, for the copious amount of cheese, sausage, brioche rolls and fudge I had purchased with Mrs Rotich in mind (well, *primarily* with her in mind). I resolved to make it up to Samuel.

'Why don't we test the hot tub?' I suggested. 'Just to see if it's in good working order.'

'We may as well,' Samuel brightened. 'I'll set it up.'

I offered to fetch our swimming costumes from home, and departed. In my bedroom, I donned my one-piece swimsuit and checked myself in the mirror. I was pleasantly surprised to discover that it fitted me well and no bits of me wobbled as I strolled up and down. All that power walking on the cruise liner was paying off. I discarded my formal attire and dressed in my casual tracksuit. Since our first paying guest had failed to show there was little point in remaining in the straitjacket of a tight bodice. I dashed in to next door. It took Deirdre fifteen minutes to locate Samuel's swimming trunks. She handed them to me with a wink.

'We're testing the hot tub,' I explained.

'Of course, you are,' she said.

When I returned to Badger's Hall the hot tub was fully operational and the water bubbling joyously. I dipped my finger in to find that the temperature was just right. Samuel changed into his costume and I poured us two glasses of wine. We had a bottle of Australian Shiraz left over from our engagement party three weeks ago. We wrapped ourselves in towels and, wine in hand, padded across the patio. The air was cool and the flagstones felt chilly, but the moment we jumped into the tub we were enveloped in relaxing warmth. The bubbling water tickled my armpits and made my swimsuit swell over my bust creating the illusion of my breasts being the size of two mature melons. We had a good laugh about that and clinked our glasses.

'I love you, Maggie Kaye,' Samuel declared out of nowhere. That made my heart skip a beat.

I was just about to declare my undying love for him in return when an intruder gave a loud cough, followed by, 'I'd like to check in. There's nobody at the reception.'

It was Mrs Rotich.

She stood there holding a small travel bag. She was a tall woman with an ample bosom and equally ample hips, and a narrow waist in between. Her hair was picked up tightly into a topknot which burst into a frizz of tight curls like a huge black chrysanthemum. She was in her mid-forties.

'Mrs Rotich!' I exclaimed in shock and looked at Samuel to check that he was seeing her too. For a split second I thought she may be a ghost. Samuel's face told me that she wasn't. We scrambled out of the hot tub, climbing over each other and performing all sorts of contortions to wrap our bodies in towels without exposing ourselves to our guest.

'We'll be with you in a moment,' I managed to stammer. 'If you wait in the reception, please.'

'Yes, I will,' said Mrs Rotich and made a U-turn. She disappeared behind the sliding door.

We climbed out and followed her, our feet flapping over the flagstones and leaving a wet trail. There was no time to change into more conventional garments. We couldn't possibly keep Mr Rotich waiting.

'I hope you had a pleasant journey?' Samuel asked politely.

She nodded, 'Very nice, thank you.'

'Where did you park? I can't see your car outside. I hope you haven't left it out in the street. Not a good idea, I'm afraid. It's only double yellow lines around here – you might get a ticket from the tireless Mr Worsely. He's Bishops' traffic warden. We only have one though he is omnipresent. The man lurks in the shadows and pops out when least expected,' I blabbered mindlessly.

'Maggie is right,' Samuel said. 'Bring your car on site and use the space by the entrance.' He looked comical making those helpful suggestions while standing in front of her half-naked, dripping with water. I didn't look any more professional.

'I came by train to Sexton's Canning, then I took a bus. I don't drive,' our guest informed us as soon as she was able to get a word in edgeways.

'Oh, I see ...' Samuel breathed out and, bereft of ideas, just stared at her.

I pushed the Guest Register in front of her and presented her with a complimentary pen. 'Could you please sign here, Mrs Rotich,' I pointed at a blank page.

'It's Miss Rotich, actually.' Her dark skin coloured a little when she added, 'But not for long. I will be Mrs Jackson later this summer.'

'Getting married?' I rejoiced. 'What a small world! We're getting married in August.'

'How lovely!' Her face cracked in a wide smile.

We had found common ground and the ice was broken. We chatted about weddings, churches and honeymoons. By the end of it, we were the best of friends and moved swiftly to a first name basis.

I handed her the key to her room, and Samuel offered to carry her bag.

'Don't worry about the bag. I can manage. There is hardly anything in there,' she held on to it.

'Why don't I show you to your room, Daisy?' Rather me than Samuel, I decided. At least, I was covered in my towel from my armpits down. He, on the other hand, was flashing his chest and displaying an outbreak of goosebumps.

On the way to her room, Daisy confessed to be being starved and I recommended Rook's Nest. 'The best homemade food within ten miles.' Terrence Truelove would owe me big time for all the custom I'd be sending his way, starting with Miss Daisy Rotich.

'Will you be here when I get back?' she asked.

'No, we don't live at the lodgings. But don't worry – the second key on your keyring is to the front door. You'll be able to let yourself in at any time.'

The next morning Samuel and I descended upon Badger's Hall at 6:30am. I was not used to getting up at such an early hour. It surprised me that it was still pitch-black outside. The streets were eerily empty. One car went past, its headlights blazing. The only consolation was that it wasn't raining. We'd had three days of no rain. The flood waters on the plains along the Avon were beginning to recede. The residents of Holbrook Estate could breathe a sigh of relief.

We were in good spirits. Samuel suggested that while we waited for Miss Rotich to rise, we could have a nice English breakfast to start the day on a high note. I couldn't think of anything better to do so we rolled up our sleeves and started cooking. Division of labour came naturally to us: I focussed on grilling and Samuel took charge of frying. The prospects for our married life together looked very promising indeed. In no time, we were seated in the dining room, relishing our full-English culinary masterpiece.

Miss Rotich came down from her room, full of smiles and compliments. 'Mm ... the yummy smells woke me up. I'll have what you're having,' she said.

'Fried egg, bacon, two Cumberland sausages, hash brown, mushrooms and grilled tomato,' Samuel listed all the delicious ingredients.

'Sounds great.'

'White or brown toast?'

'Would you have any harvest grain?' Miss Rotich inquired and my chest swelled with pride.

I gazed pointedly at Samuel when I answered, 'Of course, we do. Fresh from our village bakery as it happens.'

Miss Rotich looked pleased.

'Would you care for some cheese?' I ventured into the contentious cheese territory.

'No, thank you. I'm allergic to dairy. Unless you have goat cheese?'

No, we didn't have that. We had everything else, but no goat. I felt slightly deflated. I decided to add a box about allergies to our booking form.

Samuel finished his breakfast and withdrew to the kitchen to get Miss Rotich's ready. I stayed behind to entertain her with conversation – immediately after I found out everything there was to know about her. Her background was as exotic as her appearance promised it to be. She was a born and bred Kenyan from a small village north of Mombasa, the unpronounceable name of which escaped me as soon as I heard it. Her father used to be a wealthy farmer. He ran a herd of three hundred head of Boran cattle. He also kept goats. Daisy was one of the very few lucky girls from the village to go to Mombasa to train as a teacher.

'I'm a teacher, too,' I was delighted to find we had something else in common.

'My fiancé always says it's the most noble profession in the world. But he would say that – he's the headmaster of the private school where I teach. That's where we met three years ago. But we're now moving to the UK. He's been offered a position in a secondary school in London.'

Samuel entered enveloped in wonderful aromas of fried bacon and grilled tomatoes. Daisy welcomed her breakfast with a squeak of joy and tucked in. It was my turn to do all the talking so that she could do the eating, which was a pleasing spectacle to behold. She praised Samuel's cooking no end. He was glowing.

I gave Daisy a short exposé on the proud history of Bishops Well and pointed her towards our main attractions: 'The Early Celt Museum is not to be missed. It's out of town. You'll need to take Fields Pass towards Sexton's Wood. The road will fizzle out towards the end: the main route would take you to the Weston Estate, but that is still inhabited by Lord Philip and his family and closed to the public. I really think they should open parts of the estate to visitors, but Lord Philip is a stubborn old man. I'm sure James – that's his successor – I'm sure he'll make some changes when he inherits the title. He's a progressive man, and a friend,' I warbled.

I didn't realise I had strayed off course until Samuel interjected.

'You were telling Miss Rotich about the Early Celt Museum.'

'Oh yes! Well, take the slip road behind the huge elm tree. The path is signposted. You can't get lost. You'll go through the wood. It's a pristine ancient woodland – you'll love it. Don't stray from the path – there are pockets of marshes around it. But if you stick to it, it's an easy enough footpath and it'll lead you directly to the museum. We've excavated most of the ancient settlement and burial grounds. By we, I mean Bishops Archaeological Association. Samuel and I are members. Anyway, wait till you see it. You'll be amazed.'

Daisy Rotich nodded her enthusiasm but couldn't express it any other way as she was busy stuffing her mouth with sausage and egg.

'And of course, there is the Stone Circle,' I continued. 'It's closed to visitors at the moment, but give it a go. It's just down the road from here if you head south. If you're approached by a farmer in a funny hat, that'd be Mr Harry Wotton, the man who owns the fields, just tell him Maggie Kaye sent you. He'll let you through.'

I think I may have talked Daisy Rotich into submission for she finished her tea rather hurriedly and refused a brioche roll, quoting her dairy allergy.

'I've got something to attend to first,' she said. 'I'd better be on my way.'

'Enjoy your sightseeing. We'll see you tomorrow morning at breakfast.'

'I wouldn't miss it for anything,' she beamed.

Unfortunately, she did miss it. On Sunday morning, we repeated the ritual from Saturday, arriving at Badger's Hall at 6:30am and starting our busy day on a full stomach. Now that we knew Daisy's preferences, we had everything ready for her. All that was left to do was to fry the egg and toast the harvest grain.

Samuel and I finished our breakfast and settled for morning coffee and a small piece of fudge. We finished that and we waited. And we waited some more, but there was no sign of Miss Rotich. At eight-thirty (when, according to our B&B policy the last breakfast order would be taken) and after some lively deliberation, we resolved to knock on Daisy's door to wake her. We were keen to avail her of breakfast (for which she was paying) before she started packing to leave. Our check-out time was 10:30am.

Daisy didn't answer the door so, again, we deliberated and agreed to use the master key to get in. By this time, we had serious concerns about her wellbeing.

'What if she is dead?' I whispered, the horror of such a possibility making my lips dry.

'You'd be seeing her spirit, Maggie,' Samuel sounded calm. 'Are you?' Even he was having doubts.

'No, but then I don't always.'

'Okay, let's do it.'

We opened the door and shouted her name from the threshold just in case she was a sound sleeper. Nothing. We entered and found the room empty. I sighed in relief. At least, she wasn't dead and sprawled on the bed with a knife in her chest and a puddle of blood soaking our brand-new bedsheets.

Her bed had not been slept in. Her travel bag was on the floor. She hadn't taken it with her. Samuel checked the bathroom. 'Her toothbrush is here.'

We sat on the bed, stumped. I peered into her bag. There was very little inside it: just her pyjamas and a small toiletries pouch. I fumbled amongst the contents and discovered a necklace with a figurine of a native woman carved from dark reddish-brown wood, possibly mahogany.

'This looks like an African amulet,' I showed it to Samuel.

He turned it in his hands, examining the worn leather strap and the figurine. 'Yes, some sort of Mother Nature deity.'

'Maybe it was Miss Rotich who was hanging all those bizarre amulets around the graveyard?'

'I don't think so, Maggie. She arrived in Bishops only this Friday.'

'True. I've never seen her before,' I nodded, 'and she would be difficult to miss.'

'I can't help wondering what she's doing in Bishops.'

'Me too. Somehow, I don't think she's here for sightseeing. She wasn't much interested in our local attractions. And then she said she had somewhere to be. Where?' I pondered.

'Wherever she went, she didn't come back last night,' Samuel stated the obvious.

'What do you think has happened?' I was at a loss. My usually fertile imagination was momentarily barren.

'Maybe she did everything she wanted to do yesterday and decided to go home instead of spending another night in Bishops. There's been talk about lockdown. It's definite now, starting tomorrow. She may've heard on the News.'

'Yes, she probably panicked and took the first train back to London. Maybe she got a lift from someone. There's almost nothing in her bag, just her PJs.'

'And the toothbrush in the bathroom,' Samuel added.

'I always leave my old toothbrush behind in hotels.'

'Yes, there must be a perfectly innocent explanation,' Samuel stood and zipped up the bag. 'We'll keep it in case she comes back to reclaim it, though I doubt she will.'

'You never know. Somehow I don't think she would've left that necklace behind.'

'It does look valuable,' Sam agreed.

'Our first lost property,' I reflected. I was feeling overwhelmed with sadness. Our first guest left without a word. It was strange and inexplicable.

'We could try to get in touch,' Samuel had the bright idea. 'She completed the Guest Register, remember?'

We dashed downstairs to the reception. Indeed, Miss Rotich had scribbled down her mobile phone number next to her name. We dialled it and instantly listened to a pre-recorded message informing us that the number did not exist.

'It looks a bit short,' Samuel observed. We counted the digits. One digit was missing. We could try to guess it. After all there are only ten digits to choose from, but we had no guarantees that the digit was missing from the end. She could have omitted it from anywhere, or she could have made the whole number up. We admitted defeat. There was no point trying zillions of different number combinations of what could possibly be a random sequence of digits.

As we were going into lockdown from tomorrow, we cleaned her room and collected perishables from the fridge. Samuel diverted the Badger's Hall phone to his mobile in case Miss Rotich tried to get in touch. Then, at noon, we locked up and went to Priest's Hole for lunch. It was going to be Cumberland sausages with brioche rolls. And a particularly diverse cheeseboard.

We took the shortcut via the cemetery to check if Isaac and Thomas (and whoever else they fraternised with) were staying away from the church grounds, as promised. We considered it our civic duty to patrol our locality and deter all forms of vandalism. The graveyard appeared quiet and undisturbed. There was still a film of morning mist lying on the ground, but it was beginning to lift. A faint gust of wind ruffled a budding shrub and in the corner of my eye I caught a juddery movement behind it.

'What's that clicking noise?' Samuel asked.

We spotted the charm at the same time. It was hanging from the lowest branch of a silver birch. Samuel pulled it down and we examined it. A bunch of sticks was tied together in an elaborate arrangement. The wind made them rattle as they rubbed against one another.

'It must be one of those amulets the vicar was on about,' Samuel commented.

'I can see why he'd find it unsettling. It smacks of witchcraft.'

'Look there!' Samuel gave me a start. I followed his gaze towards the far end of the cemetery. There, vanishing into the fog, was a hooded female figure.

'Hello! Hi there!' we called out, but she didn't seem to hear us. Then she was gone. We heard the creak of the unoiled hinges of the West Gate that led into Parson's Lane.

'Was it Daisy Rotich?' Samuel blinked at me.

'I don't know,' I blinked back at him.

'Nah! What would Miss Rotich be doing in the graveyard?' Samuel reasoned.

'I wish it was her, but you're probably right,' I sighed. Short, slim and shrouded in her black cloak, the mystery woman didn't look anything like the flamboyant – and rather large – Miss Rotich.

I spent the night tossing and turning. I was worried about Daisy Rotich. I didn't know her, of course, but speaking to her I had formed the impression that she wasn't the sort of person to leave without a goodbye. And she had been looking forward to her Sunday breakfast!

What if she had strayed into a bog in

Sexton's Wood? It had been raining for days – the marshes would have turned into a treacherous terrain. The idea made me break out in a cold sweat. I rationalised with myself: the footpath was well signposted and gravelled, and there was a bridge over the most dangerous swamp. Unless Miss Rotich waded into it on purpose, she wouldn't have drowned on the path. She may not have even ventured into Sexton's Wood. I recalled her saying that she had something to attend to. It was a strange choice of words for a tourist. A tourist would have said that they had places to visit or things to see, not matters to attend to. On the other hand, her odd turn of phrase could be due to English being her second language.

I analysed everything that she had told us. Perhaps there were some clues there as to who we could contact to inquire after her. Her father was a farmer from a small village whose name I couldn't remember. She had mentioned her fiancé, a man going by the name of Jackson – a very common name. I despaired. He used to be the headmaster of a private school in Kenya. I considered contacting the Kenyan Embassy. I resolved to suggest that to Samuel the next morning. Slowly, I drifted into an unsettled slumber.

Bizarre noises awoke me in the early hours of the morning. With my eyes closed, I listened to an odd spell of scratching under the floor or possibly in the chimney breast; then there was a thud and everything went quiet. I sat up in bed and tried to penetrate the darkness that filled my bedroom like black ink. I pricked up my ears but could hear no suspicious sounds. The silence was absolute. It occurred to me that I may have been dreaming. I strained my brain for shreds of that dream, but nothing came to me. I checked my bedside clock. It was half past one. My eyes began adjusting to the darkness and soon I could identify outlines of furniture and a dim square of moonlit sky behind the curtains. I scanned the room gingerly for any ghostly presence. The spirits do tend to turn up under the cover of night. I crossed my fingers and prayed to the Lord Almighty that I wouldn't find Daisy Rotich's spirit sitting at the foot of my bed. To my relief, I found nothing and no one. I was alone in my silent bedroom.

Still, I could not settle back to sleep for a long time. I went downstairs and made a mug of hot chocolate. I drank it straightaway. It burned my lips. Hot chocolate never fails to put me to sleep, but on this occasion I continued to struggle with insomnia. I counted every sheep imaginable and tried to think positive thoughts. I meditated in the lotus position, but even then I was unable to clear my mind. It was oppressed by images of Daisy Rotich drowning in a murky swamp. When I banished those, the figure of a woman clad in a black hooded cloak floated before my eyes and vanished as if dissolved in a thick mist.

In the end, I fell asleep. By then, birds had already begun their dawn tweeting. I was so tired that I slept until noon when I finally rose from bed, feeling wretched. I switched on the News, subconsciously expecting to hear something about a Kenyan lady found dead in a boggy woodland on the outskirts of a small town called Bishops Well. Instead, I was confronted with the announcement of the draconian lockdown we had been expecting for weeks.

'She probably ran back to London before getting stuck in Bishops for months to come,' I explained to myself to put my mind at ease.

CHAPTER 10

A few days into lockdown, Sam and Maggie commenced their joint power-walking exercises. They would assemble on the driveway at eight in the morning, warm up with a few star-jumps and embark on a circular route around Bishops. They would traipse along the High Street westbound and then slip into Badgers Crossing, passing by Badger's Hall and Mr Wotton's farm. From there they would take Salisbury Road to the left and continue past Bishops Fire Station until they reached Fields Pass. That pleasant country lane framed with hedgerows led them back into town. They would emerge through the Arcade, going past the Old Stables Café, and back onto the High Street. Upon crossing the Market Square they'd take a shortcut through the cemetery to reach Priest's Hole. They favoured hard-surface roads over fields and woods – the ground off the beaten track was still too soft and soggy to facilitate a brisk walk. As usual, Maggie led the way and Samuel contented himself with trailing behind while enjoying the views of her shapely posterior being flung from side to side in her unique rendition of a power-walk. Sometimes he would rest his eye on a clump of trees in the distance or the carving of the White Mule in the chalk hill towering to the east.

These walks were their only moments of togetherness in the time of lockdown. Sam did his best to extend them as much as possible, often suggesting detours into Sexton's Wood or up towards the White Mule Hill. (Despite a few dissenting voices claiming that the carving was that of a donkey, the common consensus was that it was a mule although Maggie swore blind it was a horse and no one would convince her otherwise. Still, whatever it was, it constituted a uniquely Bishopian landmark).

'How did you sleep?' Sam asked Maggie as they crossed the High Street. He was concerned about her. She had been complaining about some mysterious noises coming from behind the chimney breast. He and his mother had heard nothing of the kind. This could mean that Maggie was drifting into a fantasy world and letting her imagination run riot. She was on her own, trapped in her house with nobody to talk to. What that did to her mental wellbeing bore no contemplation. Maggie was a people person – a social butterfly. She needed human interaction as much as Sam needed his privacy.

'Much better, actually. I slept right through the night – like a baby.' Maggie sounded surprised.

'No funny noises then?'

'No, not last night. Come to think of it, not a peep during the whole of yesterday.'

'It was probably a bird trapped in the flue. We'll get a chimney sweep to check it out after lockdown. When was the last time you had the chimney swept?'

'Never,' Maggie said. 'I didn't know I was supposed to have it done. I didn't even know chimney sweeps existed any more. I thought they were gone, like steam trains.'

'For as long as there are chimneys, there'll be chimney sweeps. It has to be done – you could have a serious fire hazard on your hands.'

They were passing by Badger's Hall.

'Should we go in and check that everything's in order?' Maggie asked. She had said that every day since they'd started on this route. She held the irrational hope that one day they may discover Miss Rotich waiting for them to reclaim her possessions and to explain her sudden departure. Sam decided to humour Maggie on this occasion.

'Okay, let's do it. The place could do with some airing once a week.'

As anticipated, they did not find Miss Rotich on the doorstep. Maggie went up to her room to double-check.

'You realise she still has the keys?' She justified her actions. 'She could come back at any time and let herself in.'

'She's long gone, back to London,' Sam shook his head.

'We don't know that for sure. She could be dead and buried under the floorboards,' Maggie countered.

Sam wanted to question which particular floorboards she was referring to, but bit his tongue. He already had to dissuade her from telephoning the Kenyan Embassy to inquire about Daisy Rotich's next of kin, one Mr Jackson – if Maggie had heard his name correctly in the first place. Sam's explanation that a person would have to be reported missing before it was appropriate for a total stranger to call a search party, fell on deaf ears.

'I'm not comfortable, Samuel,' she persisted. 'I've a feeling that something is wrong. Do you know that little niggle at the back of your mind?'

Sam knew what she meant but, being a man of reason, was reluctant to make a fool of himself by ringing alarm bells without justification. He pursed his lips and scratched his head to show that he was at least considering Maggie's words.

'We really ought to do something!' Maggie stomped her foot, her face puckered with anxiety.

Sam had an idea. 'Why don't we charge her

credit card for the two nights she booked with us? We should've done it anyway.'

'That's not what I meant,' Maggie scowled.

'It's a way of testing the waters,' Sam elucidated. 'If she's indeed missing and someone is looking for her, they will be keeping an eye on her credit card transactions. If we charge her, they'll know where to come. It's a subtle way of doing it – like sending a smoke signal without starting a fire.'

'I see. Let's do it, Samuel!' Maggie clasped her hands. 'It's a good start.'

After putting the charges through, they locked up and resumed their exercise. They carried on along Salisbury Road. It was winding, with ditches on both sides, but the hedgerows were well maintained so that visibility on the road was good. Not a single vehicle went past. Maggie commented on the benefits of lockdown for the environment.

'At this rate, Samuel, we'll reverse global warming. How long, do you think, it'd take to get there?'

'Do you mean for how long would we have to stop using cars?'

'And planes and everything else?'

'I don't know. I'm not an expert.'

'A year of lockdown? Two years? Ten perhaps?'

'Do you really think you'd survive living on

your own, in solitude, without contact with your friends for that long and not go mad?' Sam truly doubted it. He would manage, but Maggie Kaye? Not a chance.

She knitted her brows, contemplating the prospect. At last she spoke: 'You may have a point. I could try and make a sacrifice for, say… a couple of months. As long as you and I can have our walks and my supplies don't run out.'

'You do have at least two months' worth of Rum and Raisin Extravaganza,' Sam recalled the bulk of fudge Maggie had acquired a week ago at the Thursday Market.

'That is a distant memory, Samuel.' She picked up her pace. Sam gave a wolf-whistle. The woman was a scream.

They continued in silence for half a mile before taking a sharp turn behind the fire station. It was a purpose-made building erected in the mid-nineteenth century after the original fire station had burned down. It had been an accident – a drunk fireman had fallen asleep and left his sausages to burn. The whole station had gone up in smoke. When that happened Bishops Well had become the laughing stock of the whole county. The jabs and jeers had gone on for years.

The new station was apparently fireproof.

They were on Fields Pass by the time Maggie opened her mouth again: 'You know, Samuel, I've been thinking about something these last few days.'

'What is it, Maggie?'

'Now that we're getting married, we're practically a family, don't you think?'

'We definitely are.'

'So we don't need walls between us. Priest's Hole used to be a single dwelling.'

'So I understand.'

'Then I had it subdivided and you bought your half, but now ... I don't know ... It feels strange being right next door to you, but feeling like we are miles apart. If we took down those walls we would be in the same household and not breaking any lockdown rules. The thing is, Samuel, that I've been missing you a tiny little bit.' She crinkled her nose charmingly.

'And I'm missing you a great deal,' Sam admitted. 'This is a brilliant idea. I'll just have to think about how to demolish the internal walls without demolishing the whole house.'

'I can show you the plans that were drawn up for the builders to carry out the works. There was an arched door between our kitchens – well, your kitchen used to be a dining room. That door was bricked up. Perhaps we could start there?'

'I'll look into it,' Sam promised. He liked the idea but doubted that they would be able to get builders to do the work in lockdown. But at least, he could start making plans.

'I have a great big sledgehammer in the shed, if you want one,' Maggie offered helpfully.

As they entered the cemetery through the East Gate they simultaneously noticed a figure of a man slumped on the ground. He was lying on his side. They hurried towards him. It was Isaac Wotton!

The white cast on his left leg and a discarded crutch a couple of yards away from the body confirmed his identity. His arms were outstretched over his head and there was a track of flattened grass and smudged mud indicating that someone had been dragging Isaac across the graveyard only to abandon him halfway through.

'Isaac!' Maggie and Sam fell to their knees next to the youngster. As there was no response, Sam turned him by the shoulder. Isaac groaned faintly and slumped on his back. There was a bloody gash on the side of his head, a couple of inches in diameter. The wound was fresh – blood was oozing from it.

Isaac's eyelids flickered. He managed to keep his eyes open just long enough to whisper, 'Don't tell me Dad. He'll kill me.'

'What happened?' Sam shouted, but Isaac was no longer responsive. Sam shook him to bring him back, but it was no use. Isaac was limp like a rag doll.

Maggie lowered her ear to his lips. 'He's still breathing. Call an ambulance.'

Sam dialled 999. As soon as he was put

through to the operator, Maggie took over: 'We have a head injury. He is unconscious but breathing. Losing lots of blood from a head wound. Yes, it's a gash. We're in the cemetery, St John the Baptist, Bishops Well. How long? Okay. Yes, I know how to do that.'

When she rang off, she said to Sam, 'They'll be here in twenty minutes. We must put him in the recovery position and stem the flow of blood. Help me here, Samuel.'

Even though she had asked, she didn't look like someone who needed help. Expertly, she bent Isaac's knee and placed his hand under his cheek. Then she rolled him over onto his side. There was another weak moan but he didn't open his eyes. Maggie unzipped her tracksuit top and pulled it off. She bundled it into a ball and pressed it against the wound on Isaac's head.

'I'll wait here with him. Get his father.'

Sam broke into a sprint, weaving amongst headstones and statues of stone angels, jumping over a broken cross and landing in a fresh arrangement of flowers on the neighbouring grave. He looked over his shoulder to check on Maggie before leaving the graveyard. She appeared well in charge of the situation. He dismissed the niggling thought that whoever attacked Isaac may still be lurking in wait and could pose a danger to Maggie. They wouldn't risk hanging about the place to be recognised, Sam told himself; the assailant had long gone.

The Wottons' farmhouse was a modern barn conversion, single storey, stretching along a muddy driveway. Sam banged on the door and burst in without waiting for an invitation. He staggered from room to room, through the lounge and into the kitchen, but he couldn't find anyone. He ran out to the back door and headed for the outbuildings. There he spotted Harry Wotton shoving manure from the stables onto a trailer.

'It's Isaac!' Sam exhaled and squatted down to catch breath.

'What's he done now?'

'He's been ... He may have been attacked or just fell and hit his head. He's unconscious. We called an ambulance.'

Harry Wotton dropped his shovel and together they ran to the cemetery. Just as they approached so did the ambulance.

'Oh my God,' Harry mouthed as he took in the lifeless body of his son with a blood-saturated lump of fabric being pressed to his head by Maggie.

She moved away only when the paramedic told her he would take over from here. He examined Isaac and attempted to talk to him, but received no reply. He dressed Isaac's head. Then with his colleague he put Isaac on a stretcher and carried him to the ambulance parked in Market Square. Maggie, Sam and Harry Wotton followed.

Harry stepped forward as the paramedic was

about to shut the door.

'I'm his father. I'll go with him.'

'I'm sorry, sir, that's not possible. And you won't be able to visit. COVID regulations, I'm afraid. You can inquire by phone.' The paramedic smiled sympathetically.

'Is he ... Will he be all right?'

'I'd say so but I can't give you a diagnosis. He'll get a CT scan, but at first sight it looks like a superficial wound. There's lots of blood but that isn't the worst that could happen.'

'What could be worse than that?'

'If there was swelling of the brain. Here, you have an open cut – no pressure on the brain. Call the hospital in an hour or so.'

'The RUH, in Bath, is it?'

'Yes.' The medic shut the door and the ambulance left with flashing lights and blazing sirens.

Harry Wotton stood motionless with his arms dangling by his sides, watching vehicle disappear and listening to the last of the siren. When he could hear it no longer, he squeezed the bridge of his nose, pushing back tears. He turned to Maggie and Sam who stood behind him in numb silence.

'Bloody hell!' he puffed his cheeks and blew out the curse. 'It's always something with that boy! I'd better tell his mother. She'll be beside herself with worry.' He started on his way back to the farm.

Maggie stood shivering in her flimsy t-shirt. Sam took off his hoodie and wrapped it around her shoulders.

'You all right?'

'I'm fine,' she blinked at him. 'I don't think it was an accident. Someone smashed him on the head and tried to drag him out of there.'

'I got the same impression.'

They started back home, taking the route via the cemetery. They paused briefly where they had found Isaac. His crutch was still there, lying on the ground.

'We'd better not touch anything,' Sam said. 'It's a crime scene. I think I ought to call the police.'

'It could've been Isaac and Thomas fooling around – Isaac slipped – hit his head. Though, I don't think Thomas would've just taken off and left him for dead,' Maggie looked puzzled.

'Maybe he did when he saw us. He knew we'd take care of Isaac. Assuming of course Thomas was involved at all.'

'Isaac should be able to tell us soon enough. The medic said it wasn't serious.'

CHAPTER 11

Maggie's Journal

I could hardly complain of boredom in the twenty-four hours that followed our discovery. The cops arrived before lunch in full force. It had taken them less than two hours to respond, which was rather impressive. It wasn't just Samuel who had reported the incident – the hospital had done the same as they had reasonable suspicion that Isaac Wotton was a victim of a grievous assault.

I watched from my bedroom window as a Crime Scene Investigator went about exploring the area. He packed away Isaac's crutch which we had left undisturbed. He took photos of the marks imprinted into the soft ground by what I suspected was the assailant dragging Isaac's body a few yards towards the church before abandoning it. After examining the marks on the ground, the investigator crouched over the concrete base of one of the graves and ran his finger along the ragged edge. He took a photograph of it. Even from a distance I could see a circular discoloration indicating that something that had once stood in that spot was now gone. That empty spot seemed to have intrigued the forensics man. He scanned the immediate vicinity of the grave. His eye was caught by something hanging from a tree branch overhanging the grave. I strained my eyes to see what it was as he pulled it off and examined it. It seemed like another of those eerie amulets: it was in the shape of a star and made of crossing sticks bound with string. I was sure the fluffy white matter attached to the star was a bunch of feathers. The man showed his find to his colleague who shrugged his ignorance of the origins or purpose of the object. The amulet was bagged in an evidence pouch.

After a short conversation, the second investigator joined the first in searching the undergrowth. They were methodical about it, using sticks to part bushes without having to tread on them. They combed through until the first man stood up, holding up a stone vase shaped like an upturned bell. The base of it was stained red. Blood.

I was by then hanging out of my window with my camera-phone, trying to zoom in on the investigator's find and take a clear picture of it. No doubt he was holding a weapon. And there was no longer any doubt that Isaac's head injury wasn't accidental.

Vicar Quentin hurried from the vicarage. He approached the uniformed officer who was keeping guard by the police tape encasing the crime scene.

'What on earth is going on here?' the vicar thundered. 'All those tapes! This is sacred ground!' He tried to push past the officer.

'Please, don't cross the line, sir. Stay where you are.'

A plain-clothed detective who I had met previously walked towards Vicar Quentin. He had a memorable face because of his bulbous red nose that invariably brought to mind Rudolf the Red-Nosed Reindeer from my Christmas dress.

The detective flashed his ID card, 'DC Whittaker. There has been a serious incident – a young man was grievously assaulted at this spot this morning. He's unconscious in hospital. We're securing evidence. Are you the vicar?'

'Yes – Quentin Magnebu. When did it happen? I've been away since seven o'clock this morning – just returned from St Anne's in Parson's Combe and saw the police car. Oh dear Lord, who's the unfortunate young man? Is he all right?'

'Isaac Wotton. He should be fine, we're told, but he suffered a nasty blow to the head. So, you haven't seen anything?'

'No,' the vicar shook his head, his expression bewildered.

'And when you left at seven this morning, did you see anyone hanging about the graveyard?'

'I wouldn't have seen anyone even if they had. My car was parked on the other side of the vicarage. I got in and drove off. I didn't leave via the cemetery.'

'Quentin, what's going on!' Leanne Magnebu emerged from the church. She too had a wild and confused look in her eyes and a rather wild hairstyle by her standards.

'There's been an accident... crime, actually,' the vicar pointed towards the cordoned cluster of tombstones. 'Isaac Wotton is in hospital with head injuries. It's unbelievable that someone'd do such a thing – here, on sacred ground!'

'As if that would make a difference to a thug.' I heard that sentence being uttered from very close by. I looked up and only now did I realise that both Deirdre and Samuel were also watching the events unfold from their upstairs window.

'DC Whittaker,' the detective introduced himself to Leanne. 'Can I have your name, madam?'

Leanne informed him that she was the vicar's wife and added indignantly that what had just happened *on the church doorstep was inexcusable and beyond the pale.* I had no idea who precisely her accusation was aimed at.

'Yes, madam, crime usually is,' said DC Whittaker drily. 'May I ask whether you saw anything, or anybody, around here this morning? Were you at home?'

'I should've been in church cleaning as I normally do on Fridays, but I had a terrible headache, so I stayed in bed after Quentin left,' she replied. 'No one would've gone into the church, I can tell you this much. It is locked. Out here, I don't know … You can't see from my bedroom window into the cemetery unless you come out, which I didn't. I was incapacitated – didn't see anyone or heard anything.' Leanne gave a shudder and seemed to stumble. Her husband steadied her by putting his arm around her.

'You all right, dear? It's such a shock – it happened right under our noses and to a young man we actually know. Poor lad. I'll pray for his swift recovery.'

'Is he going to pull through?' Leanne asked the detective.

'We certainly hope so, madam. We'd like him to answer a few questions about his attacker.'

'For your information, DC Whittaker,' the vicar said, 'we've been having problems with the local youths. They always hang around – Isaac and his mates, youngsters with nothing better to do. You may want to talk to them. They may be able to tell you more than we can.'

'Any names?'

'No. I'd recognise them if I saw them, but I wouldn't know their names. Not your regular churchgoers.'

'They're no saints,' Leanne added with a note of anguish in her voice. 'We've had a couple of break-ins and an attempted arson. The church is now locked to keep it safe from vandalism.'

'Did you report any of that?'

'No,' Vicar Quentin said firmly. 'I don't wish to get those youngsters into trouble with the law. They need support, something to do with their time, a place to go for entertainment. There's nothing here for them. They're bored, but I don't think they mean harm.'

'Well, no harm intended, I'm sure,' DC Whittaker spoke cynically, 'until serious crime happens, like what we have here.'

The forensics man approached the detective. 'I'm done here, Gary. I think we may have the weapon.'

'A result, then.'

'And we found this,' the forensics man presented the star-shaped amulet in a transparent evidence bag.

'What do we have here?' DC Whittaker turned the object in his hands.

'Ah!' Vicar Quentin cried. 'That'd be the witchcraft goings-on. We've been removing these ... charms, or whatever you want to call them, for a month now. Someone keeps displaying them all over the cemetery: on gates, trees, headstones – you name it. We take one down, another two turn up in its place!'

'I pulled one down from the church door,' Leanne added.

'They are everywhere. I wouldn't be surprised if it's the same youngsters who broke into the church.'

'Pranksters, you think?' Whittaker said dismissively.

'Oh no, those talismans aren't just pranks. There's more to it – much more!' The vicar shook with fury, 'I recognise Satanist insignia when I see them! And that's what it is – satanism!' A note of dread quivered in the vicar's voice.

'Satanism, you say?' DC Whittaker raised a doubting eyebrow.

'Yes!' Vicar Quentin was emphatic. 'It starts with a few innocent rituals – charms and chants – but it may well end with sacrilege or even human sacrifice. I've seen it happen.'

'You must take it seriously, officer,' Leanne Magnebu urged Whittaker, seeing that he clearly wasn't.

'We will, madam. A serious crime has been committed. We're taking every piece of evidence very seriously indeed.'

The detective handed the evidence bag back to the forensics man. 'I'll see you at HQ, Bobby. I still have to interview the people next door. They reported the incident.'

Everyone's eyes travelled in our direction. I waved from my window. 'Where do you want us, detective? We could have a nice cup of tea while we tell you what we know.'

Samuel murmured something and looked embarrassed for some reason, He promptly withdrew inside his house, pulling his mother with him. Their window was shut with a shudder of its glass panes.

We gathered in my garden – DC Whittaker felt that an outdoor location would best comply with the new social-distancing rules. I served coffee (by popular demand) and Rich Tea biscuits (I was down to my dry foods reserves). Although, strictly speaking, Deirdre wasn't a witness of any kind, she tagged along with Samuel. I spread the chairs out on the patio allowing the legally-prescribed 6-foot distance between them. DC Whittaker invited us to describe *in our own time* what we knew about the incident, so between us, Samuel and I took him through the events of the morning from the moment we'd left Priest's Hole for our morning exercise.

'So at that time,' DC Whittaker interrupted before we even started, 'you didn't see Isaac Wotton or anyone else near the graveyard?'

'We didn't go via the graveyard,' Samuel clarified. 'We only came back that way, and that's when we found him. We saw no one else.'

I described our route to the good detective, and he took notes. Evidently, our exercise route was of some importance. 'We didn't meet anyone along the way,' I elaborated, 'but one car went past, didn't it, Samuel?'

Samuel nodded.

'Do you recall what model, colour?'

'A white estate – Hyundai or maybe Honda,' Samuel said. I was impressed. Personally, I couldn't remember anything beyond the fact it was a car. Cars all look the same to me.

We described finding poor Isaac slumped on the ground, him begging us not to tell his dad, and my valiant efforts to keep him comfortable until the ambulance arrived.

'I fetched Harry Wotton, Isaac's father,' Samuel added. 'He lives in Badger Crossing, some fifteen minutes on foot from here. He and I got back in time for Mr Wotton to have a word with the paramedics. It's fair to say that the man was shell-shocked.'

'That's to be expected,' DC Whittaker nodded pensively. He made a brief note in his book. He peered at us from above it and sucked his lower lip, thinking.

'Any other observations? No matter how small...' He encouraged us gently.

'It looks to me like someone may have tried to drag Isaac across the cemetery. There were marks on the ground,' I pointed out.

'Yes, we did notice them.'

'And you seem to have found the weapon,' I fished for information.

'Too early to say, madam, but it looks like it. We shouldn't really be talking about this. Please do not share these speculations with anyone.'

'I wouldn't dream of it!' I swore and, just in case, crossed my fingers behind my back.

DC Whittaker stirred sugar into his coffee and drank it. He refused the biscuits, 'Watching my waist, madam. I have a medical coming in July.' He patted his rounded belly affectionately.

'Right then,' he was raring to get on.

'About those youngsters running loose around the cemetery,' Deirdre spoke, 'we've seen them around, smoking drugs and swearing like troopers. Maggie knows who they are – from the school, you see. She was their teacher.'

'Only briefly,' I recoiled at the idea of betraying Thomas Moore, who I knew for a fact would have never hurt Isaac or anyone else for that matter. I remembered from our first prickly but non-violent encounter in the classroom of Bishops Well Academy that his life's motto was to do no harm, and he stuck to it no matter what.

'Oh, that's good news,' DC Whittaker perked up. 'Who would they be, Miss Kaye?'

'Well, Isaac, of course, and … well, his good friend Thomas Moore. He lives on Holbrook Estate, but let me assure you, he isn't the thug material you're looking for. I don't know any other names, but I'm sure there are others.'

'We've only seen Isaac and Thomas hanging around Maggie's back gate,' Samuel expounded unhelpfully.

DC Whittaker recorded Thomas's name in his little black book and thanked us for our co-operation. He saw himself out.

Since we were already in my garden on the pretext of official police business, I suggested we have lunch together. It was nearly one o'clock. We all deserved refreshments after the grilling by DC Whittaker and I really missed the company of friends. Deirdre and Samuel were quick to accept the invitation. I made cheese and pickle sandwiches (a great variety of cheeses was deployed, I should add) and put frozen scones into the oven for later. Unfortunately, there was no fudge left other than my emergency reserve for a very rainy day.

We chatted about the events of the past few hours but none of us had any bright ideas about what had happened to Isaac and why. He definitely hadn't tripped and fallen by accident. The stone vase had been used to render him unconscious, and was then discarded. I wondered why the assailant hadn't taken it with him. Leaving it there meant it would be found. Maybe it had all happened seconds before we'd arrived – maybe we had surprised him and he panicked. Maybe he was planning to come back for the vase after he'd dragged Isaac away from the crime scene. The most puzzling question was where was he planning to move the body. Was there a destination? Did he believe that Isaac was dead? Had he intended to kill him in the first place? At face value, it seemed like there had been no plan. It all looked a right mess with no rhyme or reason.

'My bet is on an argument gone wrong,' I concluded. 'People do stupid things in the heat of the moment, especially if they are young and full of testosterone.'

'Then they panic, try to hide the body, fail and run away. And hope things blow over somehow,' Samuel expanded on the idea.

'We'll soon find out from Isaac – when he wakes up,' Deirdre said, then pinched her lips and frowned. 'It's so damn inconsiderate of them, come to think of it – with the pandemic raging out there, we need every ambulance and every medic on standby. Hospitals are bursting at the seams and here are the blinking thugs smashing each other's heads in and hogging hospital beds.'

Samuel and I looked at each other, bemused. Deirdre, like most her generation, didn't mince her words. And there was no arguing with her – she was right.

'I wonder if those charms scattered around the graveyard are in any way related to what happened to Isaac,' I mused.

'Who knows,' Samuel frowned, thinking.

'Do you think there's anything to the vicar's allegations of satanism?'

'Is that what he said?' Deirdre, being a bit hard of hearing, had not heard Quentin's accusations.

We repeated what he had said to DC Whittaker.

'Poppycock!' Deirdre summarised her views on the matter. 'The boy was clobbered on the head with the first heavy object to hand – he wasn't crucified and hanged from a tree upside down!'

'I agree with Mum – it doesn't look like a ritualistic killing.'

'But he could've witnessed some unsavoury ritual and had to be silenced,' I speculated. 'There might be a connection. If only we knew who is behind those amulets...'

Samuel put on a mysterious smirk. 'There's a way to find out.'

'Go on!' Deirdre pressed him. 'Don't keep us in suspense.'

'You know the CCTV camera we've got set up at Badger's Hall? We could take it down and instal it under Mum's bedroom window, facing the cemetery. With any luck we might film those supposed Satanists.'

'Samuel, you're a genius!' I declared earnestly, even though I was a little put out that it wasn't me who came up with the idea.

'I'll sort it out tomorrow,' Samuel smiled

modestly.

A whiff of vanilla from my kitchen window reminded me of my baking.

'The scones will be ready,' I left for the kitchen.

As I juggled the hot scones onto the platter, I heard an urgent knock. To my surprise, I had a visitor. I left the scones to rest and dashed for the door. There stood none other than DI Marsh, known to us locals as Gillian, Michael Almond's girlfriend and a thoroughly prickly individual at that.

'DCI Marsh,' she presented her ID card to me as if I was a total stranger. 'I need to talk to you and Mr Dee. He didn't answer his door.'

'He's here. I mean, not in my house, of course! He's in my garden where we're adequately distanced,' I explained just in case she was here to fine us for mixing with each other. It'd be a lowly task for someone holding the rank of detective chief inspector, but no job was too small as far as Gillian Marsh's knack for making people's life miserable was concerned.

'Good. I need both of you,' she replied.

'DC Whittaker already took our witness statements,' I pointed out to her. 'He left an hour ago.'

'Whittaker has already been here?' She gawped at me, clearly befuddled. 'We've only just got the request from the Met...'

I was intrigued to discover that Scotland

Yard were interested in the assault on Isaac Wotton. The plot, as they say, was thickening fast.

'Come in. We're all in the garden,' I invited the waspish detective. 'We're about to have scones and tea. Fresh from the oven. Would you like to join us?'

Her quick, hard eyes softened at the prospect. 'If you have one spare...'

She helped me carry the jam jar and butter, which was astonishingly nice of her.

'DCI Marsh is here to talk some more about Isaac,' I shouted from the sitting room to warn Samuel and Deirdre. Marsh's arrival into anyone's meal time required a prior warning, especially for the weak-hearted, like Deirdre.

'Isaac who?' She fastened her beady eyes on me.

'Why, Isaac Wotton, of course! You are here to talk about the assault at the cemetery?'

'No, I want to talk to you about Daisy Rotich.'

The pieces of the puzzle were beginning to fall into place, but there were too many of them to form the full picture of what had happened to Miss Rotich. All I can say, and I say that with a dose of satisfaction, is that I was right. Miss Rotich was missing.

I shot Samuel a smug look. He raised his eyebrows and nodded in acknowledgement of my superior judgment.

'Daisy Rotich was reported missing five days ago by her fiancé, Arthur Jackson,' Gillian Marsh illuminated us on the background of Daisy's case. 'They arrived in England from Kenya two months ago. Jackson was busy setting himself up in his new school in London and Miss Rotich decided to travel to the West Country for sightseeing. Apparently, on Jackson's encouragement. He didn't want her bored and moping over leaving her homeland. He suggested shopping and visiting places of interest in London. She thought about it and in the end, out of the blue, chose to go to the West Country – she said she wanted to see Stonehenge. Travelling just days before lockdown,' Marsh grimaced her disapproval, 'but who am I to comment. Anyway, she was expected back in London last Sunday. She didn't turn up. At first, she wasn't answering her mobile and now it is switched off, so we are unable to trace it.' Gillian Marsh fixed us with her unerring eyes, 'As you have just charged Daisy Rotich's credit card, it looks like your B&B was where she stayed. We need to know about your dealings with her, how long she was here, what her plans were – everything you know. If you could just take me through it.' With that, DCI Marsh selected a scone, piled butter, cream and jam, in that order, on top of it and let us take the reins of the interview.

Just as earlier with DC Whittaker, Samuel

and I described our contact with Daisy Rotich in full detail. Between us, we confirmed that she had pre-booked her stay at Badger's Hall.

'How much in advance?' Gillian Marsh asked.

'About a week,' I said.

'It was on the same day as we took delivery of the hot tub – that'd be Monday, two weeks ago,' Samuel elaborated.

'Interesting...' Gillian Marsh puckered her forehead. 'My understanding was it was a last-minute decision. Anyway, continue with your account. We can unpick details later.' She waved her hand dismissively and reached for her second scone. That woman could give me a run for my money. I quickly grabbed my first scone before they all vanished.

While I was temporarily occupied eating, Samuel continued with his account of Miss Rotich's movements, 'She arrived quite late on Friday. It was about six o'clock. We'd given up waiting; then there she was. She only had a small bag – travelled light. It was for two nights that she booked her room with us. We still have her bag in our lost property.'

'I'll need that bag, and everything she left behind,' DCI Marsh indicated. 'In fact, I'd like to see her room.'

'I'm happy to show you,' Samuel offered.

'Unfortunately, we cleaned the room and changed the sheets,' I felt I had to warn Ms Marsh. I anticipated that she'd be disappointed to find the room spanking clean and without a trace of anyone's DNA but ours.'

She proved me right when she groaned and glared at me with the full force of her dissatisfaction.

'I can tell you though that Miss Rotich did not sleep in that room on Saturday night,' I added to sweeten the blow. 'I made the bed in the morning, after she'd left for the day, and when we came looking for her on Sunday morning we discovered that the bed hadn't been slept in.'

'So when did you last see her?'

'Saturday, early morning – we had breakfast together,' Samuel answered while I opted for my second scone, not to be outdone by a woman half my size who was already eyeing her third one. I'm not the competitive type but I must confess I got sucked into this scone-eating race. There were seven scones on offer. Samuel and Deirdre had none. It was between me and Gillian Marsh. She snapped her third one. I devoured my second and reached for another one. That left the final deciding scone lying on the platter, begging to be had.

'Did she tell you what her plans were?' Marsh asked.

'She was interested in local history,' I said and wiped crumbs off my t-shirt. 'I told her about the Stone Circle and the Ancient Celt Museum in Sexton's Wood. I did warn her not to stray from the footpath.'

'Why is that?'

'It's a swamp. If you don't know your way around the wood, you could get … a little soaked.'

'It could be worse than just a soaking after the downpours of the last couple of weeks,' Samuel pointed out.

'That's true. With a bit of rain some lower-lying patches can turn into a river.'

'I see.'

'Oh, and something else,' I suddenly remembered, 'she said she had an errand to run. Her exact words were: *I have something to attend to first.*'

'What do you think she meant by that?'

'No idea. She put it oddly, but then English isn't her mother tongue. Anyway, we didn't drill her.'

DCI Marsh narrowed her eyes as she took in my innocent expression. 'It isn't like you Miss Kaye not to drill people for information.'

'Well, we didn't,' I said huffily. 'It wouldn't have been polite. She was our guest.'

'OK. If that's all you remember, I'd like to collect Miss Rotich's belongings and have a look around the B&B.'

'If I were you I'd take a good look at her necklace with a wood carving of an African idol. We've also been having creepy talismans distributed around the cemetery, and the vicar is convinced that there is a Satanist sect operating in Bishops. They may've had something to do with Miss Rotich's disappearance and maybe even with the assault on Isaac Wotton,' I subtly insinuated the potential link which had just occurred to me when I remembered the necklace amongst Daisy's possessions.

'It's the second time you mention the name Wotton. What's that about?' Marsh asked.

'Don't you people talk to each other?' I was surprised she didn't know about Isaac.

'He's a young man from Bishops. He was attacked at the cemetery earlier today. DC Whittaker is looking into it,' Samuel explained.

'Your forensics team found a star-shaped charm at the scene. Vicar Quentin claims it's a Satanist symbol,' I elucidated further, trying to steer her deeper into the potential connection.

'I see...' DCI Marsh cocked her head to one side. Then she seemingly lost interest in the supernatural, and beckoned to Samuel. 'Let's get Miss Rotich's stuff. Are you ready, Mr Dee?'

Samuel stood up, keen to offer his cooperation to the police. 'We can walk. It isn't far.'

DCI Marsh snatched the last scone from the plate and followed him. The greedy cow! I had to hold myself back from attempting to tear that scone from her clutches.

CHAPTER 12

The following morning, Sam and Maggie embarked on their usual power-walking routine at their usual time of eight o'clock. The sky was overcast and it was drizzling incessantly but that didn't deter them. Despite the rain the morning was warm and there was always hope that the sun may come out to play in the end.

As they took the sharp turn after the fire station, they spotted a police van and two unmarked cars parked near the entrance into Sexton's Wood.

'Oh my, do you think they've found Miss Rotich?' Maggie gazed at Sam round-eyed.

With their curiosity aroused, they broke into a jog. Soon they levelled up with the crew of seven hefty uniformed police officers led by the diminutive figure of DCI Marsh. DC Whittaker was there too, dressed for fishing. He was wearing wading boots and a waterproof anorak.

Gillian Marsh was pulling on her wellies. She wore a bomber jacket without a hood. Her fair hair was glistening with droplets of rain.

'Miller, de Witt and Whittaker, you take the area north of the footpath. The rest of us will head southbound.' She instructed her team.

Maggie greeted her, received no acknowledgement, but asked nonetheless, 'Are you looking for Daisy Rotich?'

'We are. We've no reason to believe that she left Bishops Well. The trail runs cold here, in this village.'

'Town, actually,' Maggie pointed out.

DCI Marsh didn't hear her. She chucked her trainers into the boot of her car and shut it. 'Okay everyone, let's go.'

'There's only nine of you,' Maggie shouted after her. 'You haven't got enough people to comb through this wood. You need local volunteers, like us. We know this place inside out.'

'I must make do with what I have, Miss Kaye,' Marsh spoke over her shoulder as she dived into the woodland.

DC Whittaker approached Sam and Maggie on the road, his wading boots squeaking unhappily. 'Too many complications getting volunteers in lockdown,' he told them, 'but we certainly could do with local knowledge.'

'Leave it with us,' Maggie winked at him. 'Come on, Samuel, we have troops to mobilise.'

As they jogged home, Maggie shared her

plan of action, huffing and puffing between sentences, but not slowing down one bit. 'We'll call the AA members – if anyone knows Sexton's Wood it's us. Everyone except perhaps Edgar Flynn. He isn't local. He could get fined for driving all the way to Bishops. I wouldn't put it past Gillian Marsh. She'll be mightily peeved when we all turn up. Anyway, let's worry about that silly woman later. For now,' she panted, 'I shall get Cherie and Lisa, Vera of course. Rumpole could be of great help. It's a pity we handed Daisy Rotich's bag to Marsh – if we'd kept any of Daisy's personal items, we could have used Rumpole as a sniffer dog.'

'I don't think Rumpole is that way inclined.'

'Every dog is, Samuel. That's why they're dogs.'

Rather than argue with Maggie, Sam chose to save his breath. He'd probably lose such an argument anyway.

'I'll phone Vanessa,' Maggie continued. 'I hope Alec doesn't answer. We don't need him interfering and calling the whole thing off.

'I'll get in touch with James and Michael,' Sam volunteered before Maggie took over the entire recruitment process. 'Should we direct them straight to Sexton's Wood?'

'I think so. The assembly point will be at the top of the footpath, where the police cars are parked.'

They parted on their driveway and agreed to

regroup in twenty minutes.

Sam was intercepted by his mother in the hallway.

'What's the hurry? Getting up to no good with Maggie?' Her sharp instincts must have deduced that trouble was brewing, only she had the wrong end of the stick.

'We're helping with the search for Daisy Rotich,' Sam explained, conveniently omitting to mention that their help was neither requested nor authorised by the police. 'I must call a few people to put together a search party.'

'Where are you looking?'

'Sexton's Wood.'

'I'll get you suitable clothes.' Armed with a clear purpose, Deirdre shuffled away.

Sam got on the phone.

'I'll be there,' James agreed eagerly. 'I could ask Gerard.' Gerald was the Westons' longstanding butler. He was a geriatric gentleman, but knew the area around the estate, including the woodland, like the back of his hand.

'The more the merrier.'

Sam dialled Michael Almond and again explained the emergency. Michael sighed heavily. Sam could hear his jaw crack. 'You know, Gillian told me nothing about it,' he said. 'She knows I live here, and she knows I'd be happy to help. But she told me nothing. I'll never understand the woman – any woman...'

'Yeah,' Sam agreed, 'their minds work in mysterious ways. So, I can count on you, then?'

'Of course. I'll make a stop next door, see if Kev Wilcox wants to join in the search.'

Deirdre returned with a set of clothes, including a thermal vest, a pair of long johns, a light woolly jumper and waterproof joggers. 'And wear your wellies – keep your feet dry,' she instructed.

Sam changed into the waterproof gear and went out. There on the driveway he beheld quite an apparition. It was Maggie, of course, but she was barely recognisable in her tight-fitting wetsuit.

'Wow!' Sam's jaw dropped to the ground. 'I didn't know you possessed a wetsuit!'

'There're lots of things you don't know about me, Mr Dee,' she grinned. 'I was into coasteering in my youth – every summer in Pembrokeshire. I can't believe I managed to squeeze into it!'

Squeezing into it was the correct expression, Sam mused inwardly. He could see the suit was bursting at the seams. 'You're sure you'll be comfortable in it?'

'Like a fish in water!'

When Maggie and Sam arrived at the top of the footpath that led to the Ancient Celt Museum, everyone was already there, including Rumpole. Everyone was dressed for the occasion, but nowhere near as adequately as Maggie.

Cherie and Lisa exchanged meaningful looks. James murmured something under his breath and tried – in vain – to steer his gaze away from Maggie's bust which was bursting out through the strained zip of her wetsuit. Sam wasn't surprised that another man would be slightly embarrassed. Maggie looked a picture in her clinging suit. Michael wore his forensic pathologist's boiler suit and James his bird-watching gear. The ladies came prepared in their anoraks and wellies. Old Gerard looked frisky for his age in a tweed jacket and flat cap. Kev Wilcox brought his wife, Jane. They wore matching fluorescent yellow Hi-Vis vests over their coats. Jane's wellies were – naturally – pink.

'Thanks for coming, everyone,' Maggie began. 'The police are searching north and south off the footpath. There're only nine of them and they don't know the terrain. They've set themselves up to fail.'

'They have! They should've come to us for help in the first place,' Cherie commented, 'We've been digging here for years. We know every square inch of these woods.'

'That's Gillian for you,' Michael smiled ruefully. 'On some obscure principle, she just doesn't ask for help.'

'But help we will!' Maggie enthused and raised a broomstick she'd brought with her. Pointing with it towards the trees, she dispensed instructions: 'I say we comb through eastwards, parallel to the footpath. If Daisy Rotich had come here, she would've started on the path and might've strayed at some point, but I can't imagine she would've gone far off the footpath. The police are meandering through the wood in random fashion. We should stay close to the path and be methodical.'

'Makes sense,' Vera concurred. In her tweed jacket and riding boots she looked like the master and commander of this semi-subterranean venture. Rumpole sat obediently by her heel. His black nose twitched with anticipation of the hunt. His long, matted fur dripped with water, but he didn't as much as shake a paw until the briefing was over.

They spread out along the edge of the wood and the search began. Sam kept Maggie to his right and kept checking on her every now and again, making sure he didn't lose eye contact with her. He regretted that he hadn't brought a broomstick. It was the perfect tool for feeling the soggy ground under water. Maggie was using it expertly. He cut himself a long, but a little gnarly branch, and tried that.

The company were moving painstakingly slowly. In this way, not an inch of undergrowth remained untouched. The ground felt like a sponge. Sam was glad of his wellies – he was already up to his ankles in murky water and was treading deeper yet. There were few patches of dry land underfoot. He poked and tapped the ground with his stick, pushing aside fern leaves and long grasses. A few times he hit something hard, fished it out and brought it to the surface of the bog only to behold a plain stone. He found two beer cans. He was surprised that there weren't more, but then who in their right mind would want to go drinking in a swamp full of mosquitos? Apart from the homeless folk, perhaps, but they were long gone.

The homeless camp that had once flourished in the wood was now just a memory. It had been demolished and its residents re-homed (at least that was the official version) after they had unwittingly given shelter to a marauding Afghan terrorist responsible for the Bath train bombing and for the death of Lord Philip's younger son, Joshua. Prior to that, Lord Philip had been trying to evict the squatters for years, but not even the best lawyers in the land were a match for the elusive drifters *what knew their rights*. It took a tragedy before the courts had come to the Lordship's rescue and authorised the eviction.

Meticulous in his search, Sam scrambled up a steep embankment to explore a cave hidden under an old oak. It was concealed beneath the jutting roots and it had once been used as a makeshift dwelling. Although the corrugated iron sheets and cardboard had been removed, the cavity was still there. It would make a perfect place to hide a body. Sam shone his mobile-phone torch into the hollow. The beam hit the moss-carpeted floor. It appeared undisturbed. Nobody had been here in months. Sam turned off the torch and left, stepping gingerly over the protruding roots as he negotiated his way down the slope.

Maggie stood at the bottom of it. 'And?' She pushed her fists into her hips, squinting at him curiously, 'Anything there?'

'Nope.'

'I didn't think so.'

'So why are you here?'

'It occurred to me that we should check out the travellers' site, by the Plains,' Maggie replied. 'I thought to myself: why don't I find Samuel and we can head that way to investigate. The travellers may have seen Miss Rotich. They may know where she is. They could even be responsible for her disappearance, not that I'm pointing fingers, mind.'

'Assuming that they're still there,' Sam said. The travellers' camp had sprung up soon after the homeless had been evicted. Sam had a sneaky suspicion that some of the alleged travellers were in fact the erstwhile squatters. Whoever they were, the travellers came and went as they pleased to Lord Philip's despair. They were a thorn in his side, or rather a whole army of thorns. He could never quite get them out from under his skin, or to be precise: from his land. Firstly, they were never there long enough for legal paperwork on trespass to be completed and served on them. Secondly, they would never set camp on the same spot. Sometimes they would sit squarely within the Weston Estate; on other occasions they would be wedged that little bit further into Salisbury Plain. The border between Sexton's Wood and Salisbury Plain was not clearly demarcated, and they knew that.

'Let's check, just in case. If they were there when lockdown started, they would've stayed put, like the rest of us,' Maggie speculated.

'I wouldn't hold my breath. They're not known for sticking to the rules.'

'Should we find out?' That question could have easily been a command. Maggie was determined to interview the travellers and Sam was determined not to let her do it on her own. They set off towards the south-east boundary of the wood.

They went past the Weston Estate to their left. As they were walking silently, the sounds of nature kept them company. Birds were twittering. The occasional cry of a fox and snap of a twig told them wildlife abounded in Sexton's Wood.

'You're lucky I'm not a betting woman,' Maggie peered at Sam with triumphant superiority when they emerged into the meadow to find no fewer than ten caravans. Most were motor campervans but two were of the wagon-and-horse variety. 'Because if I were one, you would've lost.'

Before Sam had a chance to retort, a black monstrosity of a dog set off towards them, its wide, burly frame growing in size as it approached with unforgiving speed. Two more canines followed the leader, one of them, a small but fierce Yorkie, yapping in bloodthirsty excitement.

'Don't run,' Maggie instructed Sam and took a few rapid steps backwards, oblivious to the fact that she was doing exactly the opposite.

Sam shoved Maggie behind him and swallowed hard as he faced the oncoming pair of toothy jaws that belonged to what appeared to be a purebred Pitbull. Within seconds the dog's purple gums undulated as it bared its teeth. Sam would have to confront the beast head-on to distract it from Maggie, but what of its second-in-command? It was an equally evil-looking demon of a dog, and it was catching up with the leader. Would it go for Maggie or would it join the Pitbull in mauling Sam? And then there was the fearsome Yorkie—

'Tyson! Fury! Heel!' A man shouted and the two beasts stopped in their tracks, turned tail and ran back to their master. The Yorkie went momentarily silent and halted, unsure whether to continue with a sole offensive or retreat. It gave the matter some thought and wisely trotted after its two big brothers.

The man walked towards Maggie and Sam, flanked by his dogs. He looked old but was probably in his prime, wiry and short, but with a menacing authority about him. His swarthy face was shaded under the floppy rim of his hat. He was wearing baggy navy-blue joggers, boots without laces and a sweatshirt with a Harvard University logo that spelled the word VE-RI-TAS across a red shield.

'What you want?' He greeted Maggie and Sam in a rather brusque tone. His voice was raspy as if there were millstones grinding in his throat.

Maggie stepped out from behind Sam's back. 'Oh, hello there! I'm Maggie Kaye and this—'

'I know who you are. I said, what you want.'

Maggie gaped at the man wide-eyed. 'You know me?'

'Mystic Maggie,' the man confirmed.

'Yes ... well ...' Maggie looked none too pleased, but rose above her displeasure. She pointed to Sam, 'And this is my good neighbour, Samuel Dee.'

Sam extended his arm to the stranger, hoping that he wasn't breaking any protocols. The man shook his hand readily.

'John,' he said.

A woman and another man stepped out of a campervan. He was skinny as a rake; she was short and stubby, with sizeable hips. 'You right there, Johnny?' the woman called.

'All good, Sally! It's only Mystic Maggie and that poncy bloke from Priest's Hole!' the man called John, or Johnny, replied, and returned his attention to the intruders, 'So, what can I do you for?'

'You see, Samuel and I – we own this B&B, Badger's Hall,' Maggie began.

'I know.'

'Of course you do,' Maggie nodded. 'A guest of ours, Miss Daisy Rotich, disappeared a couple of weeks ago. We were wondering if you might have seen her. She's a black lady, strikingly good-looking, in her forties.'

'Why would we, of all people, of seen her?' John furrowed his forehead to signal his puzzlement. 'No one ever comes this way.'

'I sent her this way, actually, to explore the wood and check out our excavation site by the museum.'

'That's a good couple of miles away from here.'

The stocky woman called Sally levelled up with Johnny. 'What they want?' she jerked her head in Maggie and Sam's direction without looking at them.

'They say we got something to do with that woman what gone missing.'

'So, you do know her!' Maggie peered at Johnny expectantly.

'What we know is that she gone missing – the coppers are banging about the wood, putting off game. Hard to miss!'

Sally bunched her fists against her wide

waist and clicked her lips. 'Why is it that they always come sniffing round here when there's trouble in town?' she asked Johnny pointedly, then fixed her gaze on Maggie, 'Are you pointing fingers, missy?' The menace in Sally's expression was not open to interpretation.

'Whatever gave you that idea, *missy*?' Maggie pushed her fists against her ample hips and met Sally's glare head on.

Johnny shifted the bulk of his chest forward. Tyson and Fury bared their canines. The little yorkie emitted a growl.

Sam felt compelled to step in to defuse the situation. 'Maggie and I were just passing and we thought we'd just ask on the off chance that you may've seen something. We've been asking everyone, everywhere. No offence. You didn't see the woman – we'll take your word for it and be on our way.'

'That's right – you'll be on your way,' Johnny pulled back and the dogs lay down by his feet, relaxed, 'but be sure you understand this: when I say we didn't see no black lady round here, that's because she wasn't. If she'd been here, we'd of known. We know everything what goes on in our wood.'

'Technically speaking it is Lord Phil—' Maggie started clarifying the legal status of Sexton's Wood, but Sam grabbed her arm and turned he around swiftly, speaking above her, 'Thank you both for your time. Have a good day!'

Maggie wiggled trying to break free from his grip but Sam would have none of it.

'If you finished that sentence, Maggie,' he hissed, 'Sally there would've silenced you with a single punch between the eyes and Johnny would've fed us both to his dogs.'

'Don't be silly, Samuel. They look worse than they really are. In fact, they are excellent carpenters, and very reasonably priced at that!'

'That may be, but we weren't offering them a building contract, were we?' Sam snapped. 'We were implying that they knew something about Miss Rotich's disappearance. I'm not surprised they didn't take kindly to such an implication.'

Maggie gazed at him, baffled. 'Maybe you were implying that. I did no such thing!'

Samuel knew when to capitulate. He had already lost this battle of wills.

'Of course, you didn't,' he nodded. 'Shall we carry on?'

At last they arrived at the excavations of the Celtic settlement. The round building of the museum and souvenir shop stood on stilts at the entrance. It was locked due to the pandemic. The police officers were already there, sharing two outdoor benches. They looked tired and miserable. Clearly, they had not found Miss Rotich or anything that could give them some indication whether she had come here at all. The volunteers too had nothing to show for their efforts.

Gillian Marsh marched past Maggie and Sam, heading directly for Michael Almond. 'What are you people doing here?'

'Helping you lot,' he shrugged, none too pleased with her reaction.

'Trampling over the evidence isn't very helpful,' she countered.

'There's nothing there, Gillian. We were very thorough.'

The volunteers stood with their heads down and shoulder's rounded, all resigned to the fact that it had been nothing but a wild goose chase.

'At least we know now for a fact that Daisy Rotich hasn't drowned in the bog, which is a good thing, isn't it?' The glass half-full person, Maggie Kaye, could always find something to celebrate.

'It doesn't mean she hasn't drowned – maybe she has but not here,' Gillian Marsh poured a bucket of cold water on Maggie's eternal optimism. 'We'll have divers check the river tomorrow morning. I don't want you people anywhere near the banks of The Avon, or I'll have you arrested.'

Soon Marsh and her troops departed from the scene. Cherie magicked out of her pocket the key to the building. 'We all deserve a cuppa, and we have rations of crackers on the premises, for an occasion such as this.'

'We can't all go inside,' Vanessa objected

weakly. 'The rules …'

'I wouldn't dream of breaking the rules,' ever the military type Cherie reposted. 'Lisa and I will go in, make the tea and bring it all out here into the fresh air.'

'Sounds perfect!' Maggie beamed. She was the least bothered by the unrelenting rain as her wetsuit comprised a hood that neatly encircled her face, keeping her dry and cosy throughout.

The volunteers made themselves comfortable on the wooden decking, sticking to their household bubbles. The refreshments arrived within minutes. A conversation about the possible whereabouts of Daisy Rotich fizzled out before it even started. People were knackered and could think of nothing else than going home. One could only speculate so much about potential hiding places around a town the size of Bishops Well.

'She's long left the town,' Vera concluded.

'But where did she go?' Maggie asked.

Vera shrugged her shoulders, 'Your guess is as good as mine.'

'Well,' Maggie began sceptically, no doubt convinced that her guess was incomparably better than Vera's, though she didn't say so out loud. Instead, she changed the subject, 'By the way, thanks a million to everyone who gave their vote for me. I've done it!'

'You're in? Well, well, our new parish councillor – Maggie Kaye,' James nodded appreciatively.

Maggie was radiant inside her rubber hood.

'Well done!' Kev and Jane gave her the thumbs up.

'Bravo!' Vanessa clapped her gloved hands, and everyone joined in the applause.

Maggie delivered an enthusiastic bow, although she was restricted in how far she was able to bend her body.

'So, my first Parish Council meeting is on Tuesday, at seven pm. It's a Zoom meeting, of course. I'll need you all there.'

'I don't think we can gate-crash a meeting, Maggie,' Sam said.

'Of course, you can. I checked: members of the public can attend as observers,' Maggie corrected him. 'Please do come! I'll forward you the invitation. You see, I'm planning to go into that nest of smugness, all guns blazing.'

'Oh dear,' Old Gerard muttered. Having spent all his working life in the service of Lord Philip and fancying himself the guardian of etiquette, he had a natural aversion towards trouble makers and rule breakers.

'It has to be done. Right from the word *go*. They need a proper shake-up. My first objective is to have Harry Wotton's funding cut reversed.'

'That's a worthy cause. I'll be there, in the gallery, waving my fist,' Cherie smirked.

'Me too,' Vera backed her up, and soon everyone came to their way of thinking.

CHAPTER 13

Maggie's Journal

I was humbled by the turnout. My computer screen teemed with dozens of tiny faces of all the people who had joined the meeting at my behest. I had to put on my glasses (I hardly ever need them – only to read the smallest of print) in order to identify my friends and foes alike.

The flushed, chubby face endowed with thinning, greying hair was that of the Chair, Howard Jacobsen. He had the image of the Palace of Westminster behind him – a bit of an overstatement, I thought. He used to be the headmaster of Bishops Lord Weston's Primary School and although he had retired years ago, he was still in the habit of looking sternly at the unruly crowd of faces and trying to clap his hands to bring us to order. Unfortunately, his clapping and his high-pitched voice were lost in the general cacophony.

I also recognised Agnes Digby, a gentle and kind-hearted soul, if marginally doolally. Her computer was clearly set on mute while she engaged in crocheting. She was utterly unfazed by the high turnout. A lady in her seventies, she was narrow-shouldered and slightly hunched. Her grey eyes, when she raised them to the screen from time to time, seemed enormous, magnified by her powerful spectacles. Her background was her own living room, cluttered with many framed photographs and trinkets.

Unlike Agnes, Councillor Aaron Letwin appeared agitated. He was scowling at his screen, muttering curses of astonishment which fortunately were also muted. By day, Mr Letwin was the CEO of Bishops Rugby Club, the image of which was unsurprisingly in his background. His competitive, overtly misogynistic nature was something I was acutely conscious of. If anyone was to make trouble, apart from Quentin Magnebu of course, it would be Aaron Letwin. I expected him to throw obstacles in my way and object to everything I proposed just for the heck of it. For the reason of his obnoxious personality, Mr Letwin and I didn't mix in the same circles.

I was also dismayed to note the overwhelming presence of Vicar Quentin. The vicar held a place on the Parish Council by virtue of his office, and it was common knowledge that he was behind the withdrawal of subsidies for the Stone Circle. It followed therefore that he would try to derail me in my efforts to reverse that decision. I'd had a sleepless night, anxious about what he might do or say. My proposals to reinstate funding for the Stone Circle would deliver a fatal blow to his campaign of rooting out paganism. I didn't expect him to just roll over and let me get on with it. Vicar Quentin was a modern-day crusader; hellbent on upholding Christian values and eradicating heathens from our small community.

The heaving mass of tiny faces on the screen was called to order by a woman with an unmemorable face hiding behind designer horn-rimmed glasses. These glasses were her only distinct feature – everything else was dull, starting with the bob of iron-grey hair and ending with her pale, thin lips. When she raised her voice to shush the audience, I surmised that the woman was our temporary Parish Clerk – a replacement for George Easterbrook who was galivanting in the Himalaya.

'Order! Order!' she bellowed. Voices subsided in response. 'Thank you. I'm Claire Thackery, the Parish Clerk. We have a large audience in attendance tonight. I must ask everyone, except for the members of the Council, to mute their microphones and switch off their cameras.'

Rapidly the little faces started vanishing

from sight. In the end, only Claire Thackery, Howard Jacobsen, Aaron Letwin, Vicar Quentin and Agnes Digby shared the screen, with my tiny image cowering in the bottom right corner. I felt bereaved and momentarily overwhelmed by the task that lay ahead of me.

'Thank you,' Claire Thackery continued, her voice authoritative and deep. 'I call the third Parish Council meeting of two-thousand and twenty—'

She was interrupted by Aaron Letwin, 'The Chairman opens our meetings, always. You've no authority, Claire Thackery.'

'I am the Parish Clerk, sir,' her tone was stone cold.

'Exactly. Know your place, missy,' Aaron snorted. 'You've been getting ahead of yourself since you parachuted up on us two months ago. I should remind you you're here only temporarily, until Easterbrook comes back.'

'This is preposterous,' Ms Thackery blinked her indignation. 'You, sir, ought to watch your language – how you address people, especially women.'

I must say that I wholeheartedly supported Ms Thackery on this point, but at that moment I would have preferred the impromptu agenda item on gender equality to be postponed until the next meeting. I had my own agenda to stick to and it had to be addressed today, whilst I had a sympathetic audience behind me. Fortunately,

Howard Jacobsen recovered his wherewithal and intervened.

'I'll take over from here. Thank you, Ms Thackery,' he said in his falsetto. 'Welcome everyone. It's great to see so many residents join the proceedings. It's unprecedented.'

'It must be the boredom of lockdown,' Letwin commented. He had something else coming, I smirked under my breath.

'And a special word of welcome to our new councillor, Miss Margaret Kaye.'

'*Maggie* is fine,' I said.

'Welcome. Great to have you on board, Maggie. Would you like to tell us something about yourself, your goals and aspirations for your term in office?'

I straightened my back and pushed my chest forward. This was my moment in the spotlight. I removed my glasses. I wouldn't be reading – I had the whole speech in my head.

'I'm Maggie Kaye. Most people in Bishops know me well. They knew my father who was the village constable for many years. Some people may still remember my Grandpa Bernie, but they probably remember him as Vicar Bernard. He was the vicar as St John the Baptist's as was his father before him.' I was laying thick before them my ancient Bishopian lineage, not because I'm a snob but because they had to see that I was an established and well-connected keeper of Bishops Well's identity and customs.

'Don't forget your grandmother Edith was in the Wrens in the War,' Agnes Digby piped up from above her crocheting.

'That too,' I saluted towards good old Agnes. 'Thank you, Miss Digby.'

'Your pedigree is undeniable, Miss Kaye,' said Jacobsen. 'We're lucky to have you on board.'

'I'm glad you think that because I joined this council on a clear mandate from all the residents who voted for me and who are here, listening to us tonight.'

'Hear, hear!' a voice from the zoom gallery chipped in. I think I recognised Dan Nolan. If there was any trouble brewing, Dan Nolan wouldn't be far away. He was drawn to public disorder like a cat to a mouse.

'Order! Order!' shouted Ms Thackery.

'And my objective is to protect the longstanding traditions and monuments of this town. I wouldn't have bothered putting my candidacy forward if it hadn't been for the withdrawal of Parish funding for the upkeep of the Stone Circle – our Bishopian pride and joy as it happens to be.'

'You go, Maggie Kaye!' another voice became momentarily unmuted. I was sure it was Robert Kane. 'We're all behind you!'

'You have our backing, girl! Waiting for your signal!' That was definitely Dan Nolan.

'Order!' Ms Thackery repeated her threat. 'The next person to interrupt the proceedings will be removed.'

Aaron Letwin snorted, but said nothing. He had seemingly decided to hold his breath until he knew where his loyalties lay in this debacle.

I wasn't finished yet, so I went on, 'Just like the Stone Cross in the Market Square, the Celtic Settlement in Sexton's Wood or the White Horse on Weston's Hill,' I threw the White Horse into the mix to add some weight to its significance even though, theoretically speaking, it wasn't that ancient seeing that we had only carved it there two years ago, 'the Stone Circle is one of our local treasures. It dates back to the early Bronze Age, but it is still in use today. We celebrate our births and marriages there, the summer and winter solstices, and we cherish it because it is part of who we are.'

Spontaneous applause erupted from the not-so-muted gallery. It stopped as suddenly as it started, shut down by Ms Thackery. She must have gagged the lot of them by pressing a single button on her computer. 'I did warn the room,' she said firmly. 'Continue, Miss Kaye.'

I wasn't happy about her draconian methods, but this wasn't the time to say so. I had momentum and public support. I carried on, 'A few months ago, I'm told, this Council voted unanimously ...' I paused to emphasise the weight of their collective responsibility, 'to cut the funding that Mr Harry Wotton had been receiving for the maintenance of the fence, the grounds and the access footpath to the Stone Circle. Apparently the Stone Circle flies in the face of our Christian values, which as we all know is utter hogwash—'

'That coming from you, Miss Maggie!' Vicar Quentin bellowed, his eyes bulging with indignation. 'You – a granddaughter and great-granddaughter of respectable local clergy – you should know better than question our faith!'

'I don't,' I retorted quickly. 'I just can't see how our ancient monuments stand in the way of Christian values.'

'Don't you?' he seethed. 'Have you already forgotten about the town's youth committing sacrilege and acts of violence – playing Satanist rituals on the sacred ground of our Church? Their souls are already corrupted. What more do you want before you can see the light!' The vicar hit his customary oratorical notes.

If everyone else wasn't muted, we would have heard a gasp of stunned disbelief. As it were, it was just me and Quentin on loud speakers tearing each other to shreds.

I maintained perfect composure. 'I think you're getting carried away, Vicar. Just because you've had a couple of bottles of communion wine nicked from the vestry—'

'And what about those evil charms, huh? What about the burning of holy books? What about the young man bashed unconscious at the cemetery?'

'The police are looking into it,' I countered. 'Theft, arson, even violence do happen even in such sleepy places as Bishops Well, but it's a huge leap of faith to blame such crimes on ancient monuments!' I may have raised my voice beyond what one would consider reasonable, but I was incensed. I despise all forms of fanaticism, and frankly the vicar's attitude smacked of just that: religious bigotry. 'What next? Witch hunts?'

'I do not wish to persecute anyone. It's the harmful, unholy practices that I fear,' he spoke back, now with a faint note of sadness to his voice, 'and those monuments you're trying so hard to protect, Miss Maggie, give those practices legitimacy.'

'You can't blame monuments for people's actions, Vicar. The Stone Circle stood here for millennia, causing no harm. It is our heritage. It's our duty to look after it, as generations of Bishopians did before us.'

'It represents paganism!'

'So what if it does? Christianity and paganism are intertwined on many levels, and practically inseparable. There's no conflict there whatsoever, and never was.'

'Never was,' Agnes Digby echoed my words, and without further ado resumed counting stitches in the new row of her crocheting creation; her lips continued to move mutely.

'All right, I've heard enough,' said Aaron Letwin grimly. 'We reversed the funding for

Wotton because we thought you, Vicar, had it on a higher authority that it had to be done. I'm not so sure anymore.'

My eyes widened – it appeared that the vicar had lost his one and only ally on the Council.

Quentin Magnebu went as pale as his mahogany skin allowed. His lower lip quivered for a perplexed, embarrassed second, but he said nothing.

'Indeed,' Howard Jacobsen confirmed. 'The Parish of Bishops Well has tight links with the Church of England. We did not wish to tread on the Church's toes, so to speak. We voted as Vicar Magnebu recommended.'

'Right pickle we got ourselves into,' Agnes muttered.

'That vote was unanimous,' Mrs Thackery pointed out, unhelpfully in my opinion.

'Can we un-vote it?' I stepped in. After all, this was my show. 'The Council was misled and I challenge the validity of the original vote.'

'Who is in favour of reinstating the funding to Mr Harry Wotton for the upkeep of the Stone Circle? Can I have a show of hands?' Ms Thackery took the reins of the process into her own hands.

Four – virtual – hands shot up.

'Motion carried,' Ms Thackery validated the vote.

'On your heads be it!' bellowed the vicar and left the meeting.

I dropped my shoulders, relieved beyond

words. All that nervous energy had evaporated from my body. I wanted nothing more but to curl up in a bundle and fall asleep. My mission was accomplished. By gods, I had won! I didn't relish entering the collision course with Vicar Quentin, but it had to be done. I wasn't going to let any individual dictate to our community or change our ways, no matter how holy, and well-meaning, he may be.

I sat through the rest of the meeting, numb and brain-dead. If anyone had asked me what the remaining items on the agenda were about, I wouldn't have had a clue. I drifted into my own world, dreaming of gin-and-tonic and wondering what was on telly at nine o'clock.

Two hours later the meeting was closed. By then most of our audience had crumbled away and it was just the four of us councillors ploughing through the daily trivia of Bishops' public life. At long last, Claire Thackery advised us of the date of our next meeting. I said my goodbyes and clicked on the LEAVE button. My laptop screen went black.

I stood up and stretched my stiff limbs. To restore the blood circulation in my body I performed ten star jumps and five, slightly wobbly, sit-ups. Today's triumph called for a celebration. Due to lockdown I'd have to celebrate on my own. I checked the contents of my drinks cabinet to find a half-full bottle of gin.

It was a promising start. Tonic however might prove elusive. There was none in the fridge. I had a fumble in the pantry and uncovered the second-best mixer after tonic – lemonade. I poured my drink and settled on the sofa in front of the TV.

A repeat of *Vera* was about to start on ITV. I have a poor memory for plots but I enjoy detective series tremendously, so although I must have seen it at least once before, I was looking forward to a real mind-bending case. It wasn't meant to be. My phone ringing its lively tune made me jump and spill my G&L.

I cursed into the receiver.

'Miss Maggie? It isn't a bad time, eh?' I recognised the sonorous voice of Harry Wotton.

'Oh no, not at all. I just spilled my drink, but there was hardly any left in the glass. Now I've an excuse to have a second one and pretend the first didn't happen. What can I do for you?'

'Ah that, I'm calling to say thank you from me and Mrs Wotton. She's sat here by me side chewing me ear off, telling me to ring you this minute and say our thanks. For the Circle funding, that is.'

'Not at all, Mr Wotton. You don't owe me any gratitude. It's the other way around. You keep the Stone Circle in good order for all of us. You don't charge for people trampling over your fields. You don't complain. The least we can do is to cover your out-of-pocket expenses.'

ANNA LEGAT

'You are right there, Miss Maggie. You put up quite a fight against the mighty vicar, I say! Well done, you, for putting him in his place. Accusing me Isaac of Satanism, I never! The man's one straw short of a coocoo nest. Me Isaac and the rest of them boys wouldn't know Satan if he bit them on the arse, excuse me French.'

'And how is Isaac?' I felt obliged to inquire. I paused *Vera* on the first scene. I wasn't planning to miss the start of the film.

'Still sleeping it off,' Harry Wotton's voice softened, 'in an induced coma, like. But it's all good. The swelling's gone down. He'll be having surgery tomorrow morning to–' I heard him exchange whispers with his wife. 'Yeah right, it's to release pressure on his brain. It sounds dire but the doctor says it's a routine procedure.'

'Thank goodness for that,' I cheered.

'You can say that again! But I tell you, Miss Maggie, the little devil's been driving me and Mrs Wotton to our early grave with his antics. When he gets home, I'll have his guts for garters, and that's just for starters.'

'Go easy on him, Mr Wotton. We don't know yet how he came by that bump on his head. He may be an innocent victim in all of this.'

'Innocent, my arse!' Harry Wotton exclaimed, and was quickly pulled in line by Mrs Wotton. Her small voice lectured him in the background – something about minding his language. Harry spoke over it, 'Excuse me

French, Miss Maggie. It's just that the little shite makes me see red. All right, all right, I hear you, woman!' He was speaking away from the receiver. At last, his attention returned to me, 'Well, I'll bid you goodnight, Miss Maggie.'

'Goodnight, Mr Wotton.'

While Vera Stanhope was waiting patiently on pause, I made myself another gin-and-lemonade.

CHAPTER 14

Their morning power walk on Friday was dominated by the subject of toilet paper and self-raising flour. As much as, in any other situation, Bishops Well was a perfectly self-contained town, in lockdown severe shortages started appearing like cracks in a load-bearing wall. With the Thursday Market cancelled and most of the shops closed until further notice, such necessities as toilet paper and self-raising flour rose to the top of the shopping wish-list. One could easily get fresh bread, cake, meat and eggs in the many Bishops essential supplies outlets; a leg of lamb was on offer at all times from Mr Wotton's farm and greens could be cultivated in one's garden (although those would take time and patience). However, toilet paper supplies had dwindled to nothing.

'I suppose we'll have to venture into Sexton's Canning,' Maggie puffed, resigned to the inevitable. She was pumping her elbows energetically as she powered across Market Square.

'Isn't there one of those discount superstores in Sexton's?' Maggie asked.

'They have ALDI if you want a real bargain.'

'I do. I need to watch every penny. I'm flat broke, if truth be told. But what do you expect? Schools are closed. I haven't done a day of supply teaching since before Christmas. And Badger's Hall is generating no income.'

'And we don't qualify for the government loans.' Sam sighed and pondered. Surely, his wife-to-be didn't need to rely on government loans – she had him. He squared his shoulders and said, 'But that doesn't matter. We don't need loans when we have each other. We're family, aren't we?'

'We almost are,' she smiled that lovely dimpled smile of hers. 'But how does that relate to the state of my finances?'

'I'm happy to tide you over until you can stand on your own two feet. It's not a problem. Mum and I have no money worries.'

'That's very kind of you, Samuel. I'll keep it in mind, of course I will, but I'm used to fending for myself. For now, I'll just have to be careful with my money.'

They entered the cemetery through the gate from the Market Square. It was dead quiet. Snippets of the police tape had come loose from the cordon around the crime scene. The light springy breeze scattered them around the graveyard. A ribbon had become trapped in the rails of the fence. It was fluttering, desperate to fly away. Next to it was another one of the mysterious amulets, complete with colourful strings and feathers. They decided to let it be – it was doing no harm.

'It'd be good though to know who's doing this,' Maggie said. 'Have you had a chance to instal the camera?'

'I'll do it tomorrow,' Sam promised.

Maggie's mind returned to daily trivia. 'I may have to give up on luxuries. This is a good time to give up alcohol and chocolate,' she was musing aloud, 'but I need my Weetabix and the toilet paper goes without say—'

She paused mid-word. She stood, frozen to the spot, her eyes arrested on the very area where they had found Isaac Wotton on Monday. Her cheeks drained of colour. Sam followed her gaze but saw nothing except the cluster of three headstones overgrown with moss, the still fresh indentation where Isaac was dragged on the ground and the same evergreen shrub where the forensics man had found the stone vase that had been used to bash Isaac's head in. Maggie was evidently seeing much more than he was.

Sam's heart gave a thump. He did not wish to contemplate what she was looking at.

'Maggie? Are you all right? What is it?' He

asked though he already knew the answer.

'Isaac,' she whispered. 'He's dead.'

Their first instinct was to run to see Harry and Elsbeth Wotton. The thought that they would be breaking the social-distancing rules didn't cross their minds. It was the shock of Maggie's discovery, and her conviction that Isaac was dead, that drove them.

'I only spoke to Harry Wotton on the evening after the Parish Council meeting,' Maggie was panting as she broke into a jog. 'He said Isaac was fine – was going to have a routine procedure on Wednesday. My God, what happened?'

'Maybe he isn't dead. Maybe he's still in a coma,' Sam tried to reason. 'Remember, you used to see Ivo's sister, and she was alive.'

'Yes, you're right. She had locked-in syndrome, didn't she?' There was a tiny flicker of hope in Maggie's eyes as she looked up at him.

They arrived at the farmhouse. Maggie banged her fist on the door. Silence answered her.

'No one's home,' Sam speculated. 'They're probably at the hospital, visiting Isaac.'

'No, they're not. No one's allowed visits during lockdown. They're home,' Maggie insisted and knocked again.

Elsbeth Wotton answered the door. Her blood-shot, puffy eyes said it all without the need for words.

'I'm so, so sorry!' Maggie blurted out and

pulled the grieving mother into her arms. Elsbeth expelled a deep, hollow sob into Maggie's shoulder.

'This shouldn't have happened – it makes no sense,' Maggie was trying to solve an unsolvable puzzle. 'He was getting better.'

'Come inside,' Elsbeth motioned towards the kitchen.

There Harry Wotton was seated at the table, his hands clasped over his face. When they entered, he lifted his head and said, 'You knew straight away, Miss Maggie. If anyone should know, it'd be you.'

'Yes, I … It just hit me that he was … that something had gone terribly wrong,' Maggie stammered. She would never officially admit that she could see the stranded souls of the dead, but it was common knowledge around the town. Usually people joked about it, calling her Mystic Maggie and taking her supposed gift with a pinch of salt. But deep down, they knew and believed it. Bishopians were a superstitious lot, though they preferred to call themselves *spiritual*.

'It's gone real bad. He's gone.' Harry Wotton squared his shoulders and wiped his face with the back of his hand. 'The hospital called last night. The doctor said… What did he say, Elsbeth?'

'That it was a medical misadventure.'

'That's it – a mishap, he said. He said there's never a hundred per cent guarantee when it comes to surgery – always a small chance something may go wrong. So it went wrong for our Isaac.' Harry snuffled and tugged at his nose.

'He didn't respond as they expected, as—' Elsbeth added. Her voice trailed off.

'But what went wrong?'

'They didn't say. Or maybe they did … But I didn't register. My mind wasn't there.'

'I can't even begin to imagine.' Maggie sat in a chair next to Harry and lightly touched his shoulder. 'I'm so very sorry.'

Sam remained standing. He too murmured his sorrow.

'Thank you,' Harry Wotton jerked his head backwards, fighting tears. 'The only good that came out of it was that they could use his heart for someone that badly needed a transplant. He had a strong heart, our Isaac. They asked our permission – we said yes. What else was we supposed to say? His heart was no use for Isaac no more. They said he was brain dead.'

'My God, how could it have gone so wrong?' Maggie could not let it go.

'They'll be looking into it. There be an autopsy on Isaac – it's why we can't have his body for burial. We must wait.' Pain quivered in the father's voice.

'It's all the same. Any which way you look at it, we couldn't have a proper funeral. Not with people coming to church or anything like that. It's lockdown rules, Maggie.' Elsbeth wrung her hands and gazed vacantly into her lap. A tear trickled down her cheek and dropped onto her hands. She wiped it with her thumb, surprised to see it.

'We'll wait. We called Rose – she knows. She was in tears that she couldn't come home, but I said to her "It don't matter a jot – we can't see him either."' Rose was Isaac's older sister. She studied at a uni in Scotland and that was where the lockdown caught up with her and held her confined.

'Thank you for coming, Miss Maggie, Mr Dee. You've been so good to our Isaac,' Elsbeth looked at them warmly.

'If there's anything we can do,' Sam started but didn't quite know how to finish that sentence. There was nothing that could be done for Isaac – not anymore.

But Maggie felt quite the opposite: 'I can promise you this,' she clenched her fists on the table. 'This is now murder and I won't rest until I find out who did it to Isaac. I'll rip the bastard's heart out with my own hands.'

CHAPTER 15

Maggie's Journal

'See you tomorrow morning, Samuel,' I shouted from my porch and pretended to roll the terracotta pot to fetch my key from under it.

'Same time, same place,' he smiled and disappeared inside his house.

I waited for a couple of minutes to make sure that he was gone, then crept across the driveway towards the main road. My plan was to take the twenty-five minutes' walk to Holbrook Estate where I was hoping to accost Thomas Moore. I knew he lived there with his mother and younger siblings. I had the image of their terrace house in my mind. The house was located in a residential lane at the back of the primary school. I didn't know the street name or the house number, but I would find it. I was planning to camp there and sit in wait until Thomas emerged from his home. I would have to cross my fingers that Master Moore wasn't taking lockdown too seriously.

It was half past nine in the morning. I was wearing my comfortable power-walking gear. The sun was hovering over the horizon, still pale and a bit hazy but fully in charge of the sky. Not a cloud scudded by. It was promising to be a lovely day. I marched at a good pace, inhaling the uplifting aromas of the blooming spring. Yellow daffodils swayed in a gentle breeze by the side of the road. The hedgerow on the other side was swelling with fragrant white flowers. Finches, blue tits and cantankerous sparrows dive-bombed into the shrubs and burst out of them like pebbles from a catapult. The world seemed a beautiful place this morning and totally oblivious to the tragedies that went on behind people's closed doors. Isaac Wotton's death was one of those tragedies. It was man-made. It wasn't an unfortunate accident or a random strike of the indiscriminate virus, but somebody's premeditated action that had killed Isaac. I would find and expose that somebody. My starting point was Thomas Moore. He was Isaac's closest friend. He was bound to know something. I was determined to extract that knowledge out of him.

I arrived at Holbrook Estate a few minutes

past ten. I wasn't concerned about the time. The likelihood of an eighteen years old youth getting out of bed before ten was slim. I located the lane and the row of five terrace houses with no difficulty. The Moore family lived in the second one from the top of the road. They were only small, two-bedroom, two-storey dwellings with shallow front gardens. Most of them featured nothing more exciting than gravel and weeds. One had a campervan parked right by the house; its back was protruding into the road and taking up most of the pavement. In front of Thomas's front door lay the skeleton of a motorbike with no wheels.

I crossed the road towards the school and stooped behind a lilac bush. It was a perfect hiding place – it smelled divine. All that remained was to sit tight and wait. The school grounds were empty as it was the Easter holiday. Even the keyworkers' children were at home. Cars were parked in an uninterrupted line by the kerb. A few sandbags were abandoned in some people's gardens. They were no longer needed. The river had receded three weeks ago, leaving behind some sediment on the ground and those unwanted sandbags. Holbrook Estate seemed like a ghost town.

A long and tedious half-an-hour into my wait I was rewarded by a blind being pulled up in the top window and the midriff of Thomas Moore appeared. Although his face was obscured by the blind that hung askew with one side drooping, I was no doubt that the torso belonged to Thomas. His t-shirt was black and displayed a rot-green skull with some long and windy lifeform crawling out of its eye socket. It could be a venomous snake or a harmless earthworm, I couldn't tell. Thomas lifted the hem of his t-shirt and scratched his abundant stomach. For his age, he was seriously overweight. A bit of power-walking would do him a power of good.

After a brief scratching session in the window, Master Moore withdrew into the dungeon of his bedroom. I assumed that he would now indulge in an unhealthy, sugar-infused breakfast. My educated guess was that it would take another half-an-hour. I decided to take a walk around the block. The estate was slowly coming to life. A group of children congregated in a playground despite there being a public notice stuck to the gate, informing the residents that due to COVID the facility was off limits. The children were young – five to eight years of age – and maybe they weren't the sharpest of readers. Maybe they thought the notice didn't apply to them. After all it had no illustrations. If I were to write a public announcement of this kind, I would make it into a work of art with speech bubbles. I picked up pace as one of the little ones attempted to push another one from a swing, and the latter one, clinging on for dear life to the chains, told the former *to piss off or his dad would beat the shit out of him.* There, I thought – survival of the fittest in action. I turned a blind eye to the swing squabble and carried on my way. On a patch of grass a group of older boys were playing football. A dispute erupted over a disallowed goal. The language I witnessed is unrepeatable.

I turned a corner and was back in Thomas's lane. I squatting behind a wheelie bin. Fingers crossed I wouldn't have to squat for too long. My knees wouldn't be able to take it.

My prayers were answered as Thomas Moore emerged from his house, slamming the front door behind him with gusto. His skinny jeans quarrelled violently with his meaty backside. He waddled across the street and, with an agility I'd never suspect him of, jumped over the school fence. I had no choice but to trespass on the school grounds. Luckily I was dressed for the occasion. Scaling fences in my Sporty Spice outfit would be a piece of cake. I kicked my leg up and hooked my foot over the ledge. I pulled myself up and heaved my body over it. I didn't land gracefully. My spine took some beating. Swiftly, I rose to my feet and rubbed my back. It seemed unbroken. I located Thomas. He was heading towards the PE shed at the back of the mobile unit. I ran after him and only when I almost had him in my clutches did I shout:

'Thomas Moore, I need to have a word with you!'

He stopped dead in his tracks and turned slowly to face me. 'Miss? What you doing here?'

'I could ask you the same question, Thomas, but let's pretend we're not trespassing here at all,' I was saying as I strode towards him. Soon we stood face to face, but with the obligatory two metres between us. Thomas's expression was that of a cornered fox, which went well with his red mane.

'What the—' he intoned.

'Isaac Wotton is dead.'

'I know – I heard.' His was contrite. I could see the grief in his eyes.

'I'm going to find out who clobbered him in the cemetery that day, and you're going to help me.'

'I didn't do it, Miss.' His wariness returned. 'And I don't know shit.'

'I know you didn't do it, but he was your friend and you do know something. You owe it to Isaac to tell me. His family are in pieces. You owe it to them.'

'I didn't see nothing. I wasn't even there!' He was backing off towards the hedge.

'Just stop and listen, Thomas!' I shouted and pinned him with my best penetrative glare. 'I'm not saying you were there and I'm not saying you did anything wrong. I just want to know why he was there so early in the morning.'

'He was meeting someone,' Thomas mumbled.

'Who?'

'I don't know, do I!'

'But you knew he was meeting someone and that something fishy was going on. Was it something to do with the voodoo charms hung all over the graveyard?'

'Voodoo?' He gaped at me, incredulous.

'Maybe not voodoo – maybe Satanism,' I floated the idea even though I didn't believe in it. Still, if I were to conduct an objective investigation, I could not discard any possibility.

'What you on about, Miss? I don't know nothing about no Satanism, or voodoo, or whatever.' He knitted his pale brows and peered at me with concern. 'You all right, Miss?'

'I'm not hunky-dory, no!' I snapped. 'A young man was lethally assaulted on my doorstep. I want to know how it happened, and I want to catch his killer. You must help me. So Isaac told you he was meeting someone that day. He must've told you what it was about.'

'He just said he was going to the graveyard to —' Thomas got stuck. He furrowed his freckled forehead. I urged him mutely to go on. 'I don't know!' he shouted, frustrated. 'He said he was gonna make some dosh. He was like, *I'm gonna swim in it, bro...* Someone had a job for him, I reckon. I didn't ask becouse I didn't want to know.'

'Why? I thought you did everything together,' I probed.

'Not everything – not that shit. And I don't mean no stupid Satanism.'

'So, what do you mean?'

He compressed his lips mulishly. 'I don't want nothing to do with his crowd. I reckon it was to do with them lot.'

At last, we were getting somewhere. I pressed him further: 'What sort of crowd are we talking about, Thomas?'

He glared at me defiantly from under his freckles.

'Come on, Thomas, you can't be covering up for them. It's like being an accessory to murder, you know.'

His lip went slack. 'I got nothing to do with them. I told Isaac to stay clear of the lot of them. They're bad news, Miss.'

'I imagine they are. There's a chance they had something to do with Isaac's death, so you must help me find them. Who are they? Give me names.'

'I don't know their names, Miss, I swear. They are a crowd from Sexton's. They're into theft, robbing people of their mobiles, electronics, bikes – all sorts of gear, depending on demand. That's why Isaac broke into the off-licence. They told him to do it. It's gone tits up for him but he was in.'

'In?'

'Part of the crowd, I mean.'

I reflected. We were onto something. Maybe

the crowd had a new job for Isaac. Maybe it had something to do with the church. Didn't Vicar Magnebu say that he'd had a few break-ins of late? It could well have been Isaac acting on the instructions of *the crowd*. Maybe that morning he had changed his mind and said no.

'Thank you, Thomas. Sexton's, you say? Will that be Sexton's Comprehensive. Isaac went there, didn't he?'

Thomas nodded, then said, 'You didn't hear it from me, Miss,' he fixed me with anxious eyes. 'If someone asks, I told you nothing. I'll deny it.' He followed that with an expletive, turned on his heel and started across the playground, towards the river. There, he vanished from sight.

I felt a sense of accomplishment. I had my first lead. I checked the school building for any CCTV cameras (it would take some explaining what I had been up to here harassing a former student), but I couldn't see any. Our secret trespass would hopefully remain between us. I jogged back to the wall on the estate side and negotiated it in style, by which I mean without landing on my backside and dislodging any of my discs.

CHAPTER 16

'And how is Grandma doing?' Abigail asked. A note of concern rang in her voice. Abigail and Deirdre had grown close after Alice's death. Deirdre had adopted the role of mother on top of her grandmotherly duties. She was generous to a fault with the twins. When they were at uni, both Abigail and Campbell had learned to milk it for all it was worth. At some point Sam had to tell them to stop bleeding their grandmother dry and to start earning their own living. Campbell complied, but Abigail remained comfortably wedged inside her grandmother's pocket. Deirdre insisted she stay there. The girl needs to focus on her studies, she would point out, and live a little while she's still young. Work can wait. Besides, I can't take my money to my grave, can I? Who was Sam to argue with his mother? Giving to her grandchildren was what made her happy. And they gave her so much back, in kind.

'She's fine – going from strength to strength,' he told Abigail. 'She hasn't slowed down for one day since she came back from hospital. Still as loud and as bossy as ever.'

'Talking about me?' Deirdre shouted from the kitchen where she was busy (against the doctor's orders) whipping up a full English breakfast.

'Yes, Mum. Who else do we know that's loud and bossy?' Sam jested.

'I could think of at least one person – your loud and bossy fiancé,' Deirdre stood in the doorway, a tea towel thrown over her shoulder and an upright spatula in her hand. She gave a wink, 'but then they do say that men marry their mothers. There's lots of truth in it.'

'Maggie isn't bossy,' Sam protested, at the same time conceding the fact that she was pretty loud.

Deirdre chuckled, 'Just wait until you're married. But don't you worry about that – you need a strong woman to keep you in line.'

Sam could hear Abigail giggle inside the phone.

'Do you want a word with Grandma? That will force her to sit down and rest while I finish cooking our breakfast.'

Abigail was only too keen. Sam confiscated the tea towel and the spatula, and ordered his mother to put her feet up on the sofa. She may be bossy but he was stubborn. Deirdre

187

ANNA LEGAT

took the phone and began jabbering about the latest dramas and misfortunes that had befallen Bishops Well, 'Oh, I'm tickety-boo, not dying for a while yet, but we've had a young man, no more than twenty, murdered on our doorstep a week ago. And, if that wasn't enough, Sam and Maggie's first paying guest vanished without a trace after just one night at Badger's Hall. Well, if you ask me, the accommodation wasn't up to scratch. She upped and left,' Deirdre's low chuckle rattled in the air. 'My thinking is that this hospitality business isn't for the pair of them. What does your dad, or Maggie for that matter, know about guesthouse keeping? You tell me? Still, he keeps himself – and me – amused.'

Sam shook his head with ostentatious dismay and ran to the kitchen to salvage the bacon rashers from burning to a crisp.

Armed with his mother's mile-long shopping list, Sam knocked on Maggie's door. They were planning a joint escapade into Sexton's discount supermarket. Sharing a lift wasn't exactly following lockdown rules, but Maggie wouldn't let him do her shopping for her – she insisted on being there in person, *to feel her own melons*, as she had so eloquently put it.

'I'm ready!' She announced from behind her front door. 'Just getting my gear on!'

Two minutes later she emerged wearing surgical gloves and a handmade facemask featuring a catface with a wide smile which gave the illusion that Maggie had two sets of eyes and an unusually toothy grin permanently plastered onto her face.

'Great mask,' Sam commented wryly.

'Do you like it? Made it from a t-shirt. I can make one just like this for you and Deirdre.'

'You're okay, Maggie. I prefer dogs anyway.'

'I do have an old t-shirt with an image of a dog I could use. Only he isn't smiling.'

'A cat and a dog? We wouldn't be compatible, would we now?' Sam observed.

'Nah, we're made for each other.' Maggie hooked her arm over his bent elbow and they walked towards his car. 'And just remember this – opposites attract.'

The supermarket car park was full to the brim. Sam cruised around looking for a space and ended up waiting for an elderly gentleman to reverse out of his parking bay, which took several failed attempts and nearly five minutes. At long last Sam had a space which he shot into like a bullet before someone else tried to beat him to it. He and Maggie picked up their bags for life and joined the queue of shoppers interspersed outside the store in two-metre intervals. The queue weaved around the corner of the store and extended into the loading area. It seemed like everybody in Sexton's Canning and the surrounding villages had decided to go grocery shopping at this very hour. It was possible – Easter was just around the corner.

'Maggie! It is you, isn't it?' A shrill voice addressed them from behind. Since they were all wearing face coverings, recognising familiar faces wasn't what it used to be. It took some detective work to put together all the clues of someone's identity: their height, weight, the way they moved and the sound of their voices. People's hairstyles were no longer distinctive – everyone carried a full thatch or a bird's nest on their head with wisps of hair, like dry twigs, jutting out in all directions. A lot of men, but not Samuel, lived in the shadows of their bushy beards. As if by prior agreement, almost everybody had stopped caring about what they wore: dishevelled old sweatshirts and uniformly grey joggers had become the universal fashion trend. After all, there was little point in dressing up if you only nipped out to get bread and milk. The whole local population had descended into shabbiness.

Maggie spun on her heel and took in the masked face of the owner of that voice. Her eyes smiled brightly. 'Kylie! So good to see you! How are you?'

'Run off my feet, Maggie, to be honest. Intensive Care is busy like hell – almost everyone there is in with COVID. We've got critical patients in corridors and sent everyone else home. It's a nightmare.'

'Oh dear, that's awful!' Maggie gasped. 'How are you coping?'

'I don't know, Maggie. One step at a time, I suppose. Twelve-hour shifts, then you drag yourself home. Sometimes I can't remember how I got to my doorstep. I take a long hot shower and just go to sleep. Thankfully, Jack is there for the kids. He's been furloughed.'

'Are you managing – moneywise?'

'Just about. It's not easy but at least Jack's there to hold everything together. He's going mad, mind, cooped up at home, with nothing to do, but I say to him, "Be grateful. At least you aren't staring death in the eye day in and day out."'

'We've no idea what really goes on out there. We stand on our driveway once a week, clap for the NHS and all that, but we don't know how bad it is, do we?' Maggie peered at Sam. There was sadness and even guilt in her eyes. 'The worst is that we can't do anything to help.'

'Just staying at home helps,' Kylie's brow lifted. 'And it isn't all doom and gloom. We have little miracles every now and again. Remember Indira Edmunds?'

'Dr Edmunds's wife?'

'Yes, her. She was on her deathbed – living on borrowed time. And then last week she received a new heart. The surgery went well. She's recovering – will be going home after Easter. Things like that make you realise it is worthwhile to keep going.'

'Was Isaac Wotton the donor?' Maggie asked exactly what Sam was thinking.

'Yes. It's dreadful what happened to him, but at least Dr Edmunds was able to salvage his heart, and Indira got it. Dr Gupta performed the transplant, and it looks like her body accepted it.'

'You could say Isaac Wotton saved her life. It's ironic, isn't it? Someone like Isaac had to lose his life for Indira to keep hers,' Sam said.

'The thing is, it was a one in a million chance.'

'What do you mean?'

'Well, Indira has been waiting for a heart for so long because of her very rare blood type,' Kylie explained as they shuffled closer to the shop entrance. 'But Isaac was a match. Honestly, it was a miracle. I say it even though I don't believe in miracles.'

Sam and Maggie were directed by the store attendant to go inside. Before pushing their respective trolleys through the door, they paused and waved goodbye to Kylie. She sent her love and an air-kiss for Deirdre.

'We must meet up for coffee when it's all over,' Maggie said.

They were navigating food aisles in compliance with the yellow arrows on the floor that directed the one-way traffic. With near military precision, they ticked items off their lists as they went. They each succeeded in acquiring a six-pack of toilet paper for their respective households. Although she claimed to operate on a strict budget, Maggie managed to smuggle two packs of Jaffa cakes into her trolley, plus three giant Easter eggs and a bottle of red wine (the latter being on special offer and therefore, according to Maggie, it did not count). Overall, the shopping expedition was a triumph.

They were proceeding towards the checkout when someone rammed their trolley into Maggie's and sent it veering out of her hands and down the aisle. Maggie dashed after her trolley, squawking in panic. A large woman with a round face and eyes narrowed into slits by her meaty cheeks puffed like a locomotive and charged after Maggie with her trolley aimed at Maggie's back. Sam abandoned his shopping and hurried in pursuit of the attacker. The woman's strawberry blond knot of hair wobbled ominously on top of her round head. Her massive thighs were forcing her legs wide apart as she ran. This slowed her down considerably since she seemed to be executing side steps rather than forward strides. Despite this handicap she did catch up with Maggie and her trolley in no time, screaming, 'It's you, Miss-bloody-Kaye! I recognise you! It's been you harassing me Thomas!'

Maggie stopped dead in her tracks and glanced over her shoulder, an expression of utter incomprehension in her eyes. Quickly however, that expression morphed into a grimace of sheepish discomfort. Maggie executed a U-turn with her trolley, ensuring that it stood between her and the would-be assailant.

'Mrs Moore, I presume?' Maggie squeaked weakly.

'Don't you Mrs me, Missy,' the alleged Mrs Moore thrust a wagging finger at Maggie. 'I seen you in the school field chasing after me Thomas!'

Other shoppers paused in the wings to watch the spectacle. Maggie flushed crimson – even the whites of her eyeballs were red.

'I wasn't chasing after your son. It wasn't – it wasn't what you think,' she stammered.

'It looked awfully like it was what I think!' Mrs Moore stomped her foot petulantly. It hit the floor with a thud. 'You was harassing an innocent teenage boy, Missy! You call yourself a teacher? Bah!'

'Mrs Moore, calm down,' Maggie was wriggling like a worm on a fishing hook. Whispers of condemnation and disbelief rippled through the onlookers. Maggie's voice started to tremble, 'I was simply asking him a few questions. About Isaac. Isaac was his friend, Mrs Moore, and Thomas knows more than he's letting on.'

'Are you now accusing my Thomas of killing his friend?!'

'I'm doing no such thing. I just wanted to ask —'

Mrs Moore pushed her trolley out of the way, then did the same with Maggie's, only more fiercely. The thing rattled and squeaked, finishing its fateful journey jammed into a shelf with Special Offers. Breaking the two-metre social distancing rule, she bulldozed into Maggie and pushed her face right at her.

'You stay away from me son, Missy, or I'll have you!' she hissed.

Fortunately, both women were wearing their masks, otherwise it would have been COVID transmission in the making.

The shop's security guard was hurrying towards the small crowd. 'Please disperse,' he wailed. 'Keep your distance!'

Shoppers began to shuffle away. The security man approached Sam. 'What's going on here?'

'I've no idea,' Sam said honestly.

The man fixed Maggie and Mrs Moore with a reproachful glare, 'Are you causing trouble, ladies?'

'No, it's okay,' Maggie mumbled. 'Just a small misunderstanding.'

Mrs Moore begged to disagree. Once again, she punched her finger into Maggie's grinning catface mask and reiterated her earlier point, 'I told you! Stay away from me son! Don't let me catch you again.' And on that final note, she reversed her trolley and waddled away, cursing under her breath. The security man followed her warily.

'That was close,' Maggie exhaled.

'For a second I thought she was going to tear into you. It can't have been without a reason. I think you have some explaining to do,' Sam spoke sternly.

CHAPTER 17

They paid for their groceries and departed from the store as quickly as their feet could carry them. A few critical looks trailed behind Maggie like a nasty odour. It bore no thinking what those random bystanders had made of the confrontation. Maggie's name had been cited in full and her position of trust as a teacher thrown into the mix for good measure. When they finally sat in his car, Sam could see that Maggie's hands were shaking. The grinning catface of her mask looked ghoulish.

'Let's get out of here,' she said in a low, clenched-teeth voice.

Sam started the engine and reversed. He drove through the car park slowly while Maggie's fingers tapped the dashboard, urging him to hurry. Nobody was paying any attention to her anymore, but she acted as if she was being hounded. Sam joined the traffic on the main road. It was moderate at first but quickly thinned down to almost nothing. The inhabitants of Sexton's Canning were soon all left behind and there was just Sam's Jag sailing along the windy country road that would become School Lane as soon as they crossed the bridge over the river Avon. Maggie began to relax. The intense crimson subsided from her cheeks. She wound down her window. The fresh afternoon breeze swirled inside the car.

'Okay Maggie, let's talk,' Sam afforded her a cursory glance, and then kept his eyes on the road. 'What have you been up to with that woman's son?'

'Thomas Moore?'

'If that's the boy's name.'

'Yes, it is, Samuel. You know Thomas – we caught him and Isaac getting up to no good at the cemetery, remember?'

'Ah, him!'

'Good,' she enunciated primly. 'So you should know he isn't a boy, strictly speaking. He's eighteen.' Maggie elucidated and jerked her head up haughtily. As if it made a jot of difference that the young man was an adult - just about an adult, at that! Sam dreaded the thought of what outlandish conspiracy she and young Thomas were up to. Why the hell was it imperative for her to meet him? In lockdown!

'He may be eighteen, Maggie, but you and him... pretty weird. What did that poor mother mean by saying you'd been chasing after him?'

'Hardly!' She puffed out her cheeks indignantly. 'If you must know I went to see him about Isaac. I knew there was more to that day – that morning when Isaac was attacked.'

'You accused Thomas?'

'No! No, quite the opposite. I only questioned him—'

'Interrogated, more likely,' Sam sighed.

'I know Thomas a little, and I know that if you talk to him nicely, he'll cooperate. His heart is in the right place, Samuel. So he and I—'

'Co-operated?' Sam sneered.

'In a way, yes. No need to be snooty,' Maggie slapped him on his thigh. 'You see Isaac was meeting someone at the cemetery that morning and he was expecting some windfall to come out of it. According to Thomas, Isaac was mixed up with a bunch of petty thieves from Sexton's Comprehensive – they're the sort that steal things to order. It's possible that morning Isaac was meeting one of them and possibly they were about to… well, I don't know what, but it can't have been praying. I need to speak to them, find out what really happened and if they were in any way involved in Isaac's death.'

'You will do no such thing! Have you lost your mind?'

Sam was livid. Regrettably, Maggie had little sense and a great deal of faith in people, even if she didn't know the first thing about them. Having lived all her life nestled in a small village, she hadn't experienced the gritty reality of the city: gangs, drugs and deprivation. She would have waltzed into the mouth of the criminal underworld of Sexton's without a second thought. And she would have paid a high price for it. She was like a big child who would always need looking after.

'Maggie, you don't just go and have a casual chat with those people – they are hardened criminals. They run about town with knives and God knows what other weaponry, and they don't – I repeat – they don't give explanations to nosy little ladies from the deep country,' Sam lectured her patiently, though deep inside he was tearing his hair out in despair.

'Oh Samuel, I have to investigate this. I promised Harry Wotton that I would, and I will. And an investigation cannot be done wearing kid gloves. Sometimes things get ugly. I realise that, and frankly, I think you underestimate me. I know how to carry myself with mobsters.' She stuck out her bottom lip huffily.

Sam pulled up by the side of the road. He turned to face Maggie and gently removed her mask. He cupped his hands around her cheeks and spoke softly, 'I nearly lost you in St Petersburg. No way will I let you put yourself in danger ever again. You will not *carry yourself with mobsters*, Maggie Kaye. We have information relevant to the police investigation so we will share it with the police. And that's final.' On that last word he kissed her firmly on the lips in flippant disregard of her protestations and the social distancing rules.

Sam drove Maggie straight to the doorstep of Michael Almond's cottage in Fields Pass. He assumed that his girlfriend, detective Gillian Marsh, was staying with him during lockdown considering that prior to lockdown she had been virtually living there.

Michael's picturesque, thatched cottage was situated off the road and was embedded in a large garden that blended into the fields behind it. There was no fence to demarcate the grounds, though it was easy to tell where Michael's lawns ended. They were mowed to plush-blanket perfection. Further away, the fields buzzed with luscious abandon: nettles, wild blackberry bushes and knee-high grasses.

Sam ushered Maggie from the car. They put on their masks before knocking on the door. The absence of a dog barking on the other side was a telling sign. Gillian Marsh travelled with her dog, Corky (and a cat whose name Sam had forgotten) whenever she came to stay at Michael's. Sam's hopes at finding her here faltered.

Michael opened the door. He was a tall man – six foot at least. He was slightly stooped but that was due to his height rather than age. He was in his early fifties and quite fit. He looked surprised to see Maggie and Sam on his doorstep. His heavy moustache twitched. Michael Almond was famous for his moustache. He seemed to have a love-hate relationship with it: one minute there it was squatting over his upper lip like a red-squirrel's tail, the next it was gone and Michael's naked face struck everyone as something unnatural. It seemed that in lockdown the temptation to cultivate his facial adornment became irresistible. Michael's hair was also longer than usual and his sideburns appeared to spread across his cheeks like rampant ivy.

'Sam, Maggie – to what do I owe the pleasure?' He greeted them semi-enthusiastically.

'It's not you, Michael, we want to see,' Maggie said stiffly. 'It's Ms Marsh. We – I have information for her in connection with Isaac Wotton's death. May we come it, or perhaps she should come out and see us outside?'

'I'd invite you in, but she's not here. I haven't seen her since the lockdown began.' Michael's moustache dropped a fraction.

'Oh… We thought she'd have moved in with you,' Sam said.

'I'd have thought that too, but you know Gillian – she wouldn't have it. She said we couldn't be trapped *on top of each other* for God knows how long. Her words,' Michael puffed, his breath teasing his moustache into a brief, airborne flutter.

'Yes, it's not easy being stuck on your own.

I'm in the same boat,' Maggie sighed. 'Sorry to have bothered you. We'll just have to deal with it on our own.' A tiny note of joy tinkled in Maggie's voice.

Sam however was not going to let her run away with the idea of independent sleuthing. 'You wouldn't have Gillian's number? We could call the police, of course, but it may be more efficient to cut a few corners. It's urgent.'

'I'm sure she won't mind being contacted – if it's anything to do with a case she's on, she'll welcome a call at any time of day or night. Just try not to make it sound like a social call.'

'We wouldn't dream of it. It'd be impossible anyway,' Maggie scowled.

Before they parted ways, Sam made Maggie dial Gillian Marsh's number. She attempted to wriggle out of it, promising she'd ring from her landline, but Sam didn't believe her. Not for one minute. He knew Maggie would want to solve Isaac Wotton's murder all on her own and take full credit for it.

Peering at him petulantly from under her brow, she pressed the mobile to her ear.

'Oh, Ms Marsh, good afternoon. It's Maggie Kaye here,' she spoke in a formal tone. 'Yes, that's correct – *the busybody from Bishops Well.*' She rolled her eyes pointedly at Sam. He bit his lip to stop himself from laughing.

'Well, this isn't a social call, you'll be pleased

to know. I have some information for you. Yes, information. It's relevant to the circumstances of Isaac Wotton's death. Correct. Okay, so I had a word with Thomas Moore – yes, Moore. Isaac's friend. I did tell DC Whittaker to interview the boy. I can't be sure if he followed up on it. He did? Good. Still, I don't think Thomas would've told him anything. He told me however. I was his teacher – he trusts me. I taught him when he was in year 10. We have a bit of history, Thomas and I. Sorry, what?' Maggie frowned. 'Yes, I am getting to the point!'

She covered the phone with her hand and whispered furiously at Sam, 'Why did you make me call her? The woman is insufferable!'

Sam mouthed a heartfelt sorry.

Maggie returned to her call, 'Well, Isaac was meeting someone at the cemetery the morning he was attacked. He was expecting some sort of payoff. The point is that he was mixed up with a gang from Sexton's Canning Comprehensive – small-time thieving, burglaries, stealing things to order – that kind of gang. So, I think they were planning to break into the church or rob a grave – something like that. In fact, the church has been broken into on a couple of occasions recently. You can ask the Vicar. He suspects occultists. Yes, occultists – Satanists. That's right. We think it's absurd, too. What do I mean by *we*? I mean, Samuel Dee and I. Yes, *the two of us at it again...* We think it's all to do with Sexton's criminal ring.

I bet something went wrong – they quarrelled, fought, Isaac was clobbered on the head with that stone vase. Yes, I know about that – I saw DC Whittaker find it! No, I'm not interfering!' Maggie stomped her foot angrily on the gravel and a couple of pebbles shot out from under her boot. 'That is why I am ringing you, Ms Marsh! Okay, no problem. My absolute pleasure!' She spat out and rang off.

CHAPTER 18

Having installed the CCTV camera three days ago, Sam hadn't looked once at the recorded footage. He didn't expect to see much. Spying on the activities of the dead couldn't be that entertaining. However, yesterday Maggie had asked if anything new had transpired and Sam had to admit that he hadn't checked. He felt obliged to rectify the situation, not to mention that there was little else to do. Daytime TV wasn't his cup of tea and even if he were tempted he wouldn't be able to wrestle the remote control out of his mother's hand. Whilst recuperating, she had developed a fascination with places under the sun and homes under the hammer. Sam retired to his study to review the footage of the last three days.

He started diligently, watching every frame in real time, amusing himself with identifying bird species and other wildlife which seemed to abound in the absence of humans. Soon, the novelty wore off and he pressed the fast-forward button. The speed soon accelerated to x16 – clouds started shape-shifting across the sky. Twice a female figure shot across the screen. Sam paused and rewound only to discover that on each occasion it was Leanne Magnebu on her way to and from the church. Vicar Quentin was nowhere to be seen. That surprised Sam. He used to think that clergymen spent most of their time in prayer in the sanctity of their temples. Clearly not the modern-day clergy. Like the rest of us, they seemed to do their jobs remotely from home.

It was on Sam's third cup of coffee (he needed all the caffeine he could get to stay awake) that something worthwhile finally happened. The time was 6:12 in the morning and the sun was just rising in the east, casting long and flat shadows. A cloaked figure entered through the East Gate, her own shadow heralding her arrival before her image registered on camera. Sam sat up and narrowed his eyes, trying hard to decipher the woman's face from the thick mist of pixels. He was failing and the woman's hood pulled over her eyes wasn't helping. She veered towards the well (it was an ancient thing, ornamental rather than functional since everybody preferred to use the tap). From her pocket she magicked one of those charms that had recently plagued the cemetery. Sam knew instantly what it was although, due to the poor quality of the recording, he wasn't able to recognise its precise shape. She leant over the well and tied the charm to the rusty chain wound over the pulley. When it was secured, she peered furtively over her shoulder and moved on, heading towards the church. She took a turn behind the western elevation and disappeared.

Sam was ecstatic and keen to share his discovery with Maggie. He unplugged his laptop from the wall and carried it to the garden. There, he picked up a small pebble and threw it at Maggie's bedroom window.

'Maggie!' he shouted, but received no reply. No wonder, he realised when he came to his senses. She was probably in her sitting room, watching television, oblivious to little pebbles flying at her bedroom window. Luckily, he didn't break any glass. Like a civilised, twenty-first-century man he took his mobile phone and called her. She answered instantly.

'Maggie, come down to my garden. I've got something to show you.'

Within seconds she could be heard thrusting her patio door open and padding barefooted on her garden path flagstones. She was in her pyjamas. Sam noted that the elastic in her pyjama bottoms had snapped. Maggie's solution was to gather and clutch the excess fabric with her hand. Wisely, Sam chose not to comment. Instead he said, 'We've got the Satanist on camera. It looks like the same female we saw the other day, but I can't see her face. She's wearing a hood.'

'Show me.' Maggie kicked her foot over the wall. She started to climb it, pressing her stomach into the parapet and wiggling her legs in the air in an attempt to volley her bulk into Sam's garden.

'You're coming over here, I take it?' Sam watched her, bemused.

'Yes, as you can tell,' she managed to heave herself over the wall and landed successfully on her feet, never once letting go of the waist of her pyjama bottoms. 'I want to take a close look.'

They sat at the garden table. Sam navigated to the start of the section featuring the mystery figure. Maggie watched, raptured, frowning and cocking her head from side to side as the figure proceeded along the footpath and careered towards the well.

'You can't see her face,' she complained.

'I'm afraid not.'

'That's no good. Maybe the police experts could clean the images enough for us to see who it is.'

'That's if we share the footage with the cops, and I'm not entirely sure that it is within our right to record the goings-on at the cemetery. In fact, I'm positive that we've breached some privacy laws.'

'Hang on!' Maggie cried just as the woman raised her hands to fix the charm to the well.

Sam paused the recording.

'Can you zoom it, please? On her hands,' Maggie directed, and Sam did just that.

Maggie beamed and pointed at the screen, 'It's Sabine! I recognise those bracelets. Can you see – the whole lot of them on her forearm? It's Sabine.'

Sabine sounded neither defensive nor particularly bothered when Maggie called and confronted her about her distributing occult paraphernalia around the graveyard.

'Yes, I've been doing that,' she confessed readily (Maggie's phone was on loud speaker for Sam to tune in). 'What of it?'

'The vicar is convinced it's a Satanist sect intending serious mischief,' Maggie explained.

'And what's worse,' Sam added, 'he alleges that whoever's been doing it, is also responsible for breaking into the church, arson and the deadly assault on Isaac Wotton.'

'Blimey!' Sabine cried.

'Does that mean you had nothing to do with any of that?' Maggie sought definitive clarification.

'Who do you take me for!' Sabine sounded none too pleased with the insinuation.

'It's just that all of these... activities started at about the same time. The conclusion that they are connected seems inescapable,' Sam suggested as delicately as he could.

'Inescapable but wrong,' Sabine said. 'I'd hope you thought better of me than to suspect me of Satanism or, bloody hell, battering some poor sod to death!'

'I'd never think that of you, Sabine. You know that,' Maggie protested. 'It's the vicar.'

'A supercilious prig, if you ask me,' Sabine growled.

'Agreed.'

'Is that it, then?' Sabine sounded offish.

'Well, it's just... if you don't mind – just to satisfy our curiosity,' Sam stammered, 'can I ask —'

'Ask away: why I've been hanging charms around the cemetery, right?'

'Yes.'

'It's simple – to contain Death.'

'To contain Death?'

'It's an old pagan tradition – in the time of plague, Death spreads like a wildfire. You have to contain it. Surrounding it with amulets is like building a fortification around it to keep it in one place. And what better place to contain Death than a graveyard, I ask you?'

'I couldn't think of any other if I tried,' Maggie conceded with genuine sincerity. Sam could tell that she considered Sabine's explanation perfectly plausible and logical.

'I could do with some help,' Sabine said. 'I've got other cemeteries to cover so if you two took over St John's, that'd be grand.'

'No problem at all,' Maggie enthused.

'Great. I will bring you the charms next week.'

'Vicar Quentin won't be too happy,' Sam observed.

'Who cares about that pompous buffoon?' Sabine asked, and neither Maggie nor Sam could think of anyone.

'Before you go, Sabine,' Maggie seemed to have something else on her mind, 'do you know a woman going by the name of Daisy Rotich? Is she one of your coven?'

'Coven?' Sabine chuckled. 'What else? A black sabbath? Come on, Maggie, I'm a pagan, not a witch!'

Maggie apologised unreservedly about the misnomer, but repeated the question about Daisy Rotich.

'No, can't say that I know her. Who is she?'

'She was our guest at Badger's Hall. She went missing.'

'What makes you think that I should know her?'

'An amulet we found in her belongings. It was a wood carving of a woman. Primitive art, sort of thing, but I think it had some special – supernatural – meaning. I thought maybe she was one of *you*,' Maggie was careful this time, 'and maybe she was meeting you? She was certainly meeting someone.'

'Nah, I never heard that name. Sorry.'

'Never mind. It was worth a try,' Maggie sighed.

'Describe that carving to me, though. I may be able to identify it – if it's a pagan talisman,' Sabine offered.

'It's made of dark wood, almost black; an inch and a half in size. And it's a woman – naked, with ample breast and a large, round stomach. The nipples are particularly prominent—'

'Say no more,' Sabine interrupted. 'That's a universal symbol of fertility. It's a fertility amulet. Maybe the woman was trying for a baby?'

'That'd be a bit premature. She's only just got engaged.'

'But she was at least forty,' Sam interjected, 'so maybe fertility was on her mind?'

'Very likely,' Sabine delivered her verdict. 'You say, she disappeared?'

'Just like that,' Maggie clicked her fingers. 'No one's heard from her. I'm really worried she may be dead.'

'I'll ask around in my circles. Daisy Rotich?'

'Yes. A Kenyan lady, only recently arrived in the UK,' Sam provided more detail.

'I'll let you know if I hear something, but don't hold your breath. She doesn't sound like anyone I should know. Many women wear native amulets without realising what they stand for. Maybe she just liked the look of it.'

CHAPTER 19

Maggie's Journal

I t was the evening of Good Friday. The day had been unusually hot for April and that heat had filtered into the evening. I had all my windows wide open, allowing fresh summery air into the house. Being rather ancient and built of stone with no cavity walls, Priest's Hole required frequent airing to keep the damp at bay. Even at the height of summer the house felt chilly. Usually, I would have the fire going in the grate well into late May, but not today.

After a satisfying supper of pan-fried bass, homemade chips and crisp greens, I went upstairs and sat at my bedroom window overlooking the cemetery. I watched a handful of people visit the graves of their loved ones and put flowers in pots. I promised myself that tomorrow morning I'd cut the best daffodils and tulips from my garden and take them to Mum and Dad's grave. Remembering them and the wholesome, buzzing household of my childhood, with Will playing heavy metal music in his bedroom, Andrea screaming her socks off and Mum sharing the latest village gossip with Dad, I suddenly felt incredibly sad and alone in this world. A small tear rolled down my cheek and strayed towards my lips. I licked it from my mouth. It tasted salty. It always surprises me how salty tears taste, even though I have swallowed them so many times. I really shouldn't feel sorry for myself, my head reminded me, but my heart had never listened to my head and it wouldn't start now. So, I had a little sloppy moment of self-pity, and cried, and cried some more.

Unsurprisingly, it made me feel better. I wiped my face and started thinking happier thoughts. I had a future to look forward to. It was a brighter future than ever before. I had a wedding to attend – for once it would be my own. It had taken me a while to get here – almost half a century – but then one shouldn't rush good things, I told myself. Samuel Dee wasn't just a good thing – he was the best. I truly loved that man. He had come from nowhere, when I had least expected it, and saved me – from loneliness, from emptiness and from myself. When I had lost Mum and Dad he had been there to catch me. He was God-sent. I'd forever be grateful to whoever it was that had orchestrated his arrival in Bishops Well. It can't have been accidental.

I had a reason to smile. I couldn't understand why I was still crying, until, combined with the smile, those tears revealed themselves as tears of sheer, unrestrained joy.

Even though it was Easter the church was closed. There was to be a virtual service, I'd heard, and I wondered how many of our elderly parishioners would be able to operate their electronic gadgets (if they had them in the first place) to join remotely. Still, better safe than sorry, I mused wryly; given a chance the virus would wreak havoc on St John's aged congregation.

My eye was drawn to the ethereal figure of Isaac Wotton. He'd left the cordoned area of the crime scene and was meandering restlessly amongst the graves. Even after death he retained his youthful, boisterous swagger. His shoulders were hunched a little and his head lowered, and in death, just as in life, he looked as if he had something to hide. I wished he could speak to me or simply gesture to point me in the right direction – towards his killer. I wished he would leave the cemetery and lead me to him, or her. I wished he were alive. He hadn't really had a chance to live. His death had squeezed the air out of his parents' lungs too. So much devastation caused by one ill-fated swing of a stone vase...

He paused and seemed to be gazing down the footpath leading to the Market Square. I followed his gaze to discover two detectives proceeding towards the vicarage: DCI Marsh and DC Whittaker. I was duly impressed by their dedication to their line of duty. After all, this was Good Friday – a bank holiday for most of us. There was no emergency – nobody, to my knowledge, had been brutally murdered in the last twenty-four hours in my immediate neighbourhood. I could safely speculate that they were here to follow up on my report about the thefts at St John's and their possible connection to Isaac Wotton's death. I punched the air in triumph.

I had every intention of spying on the two detectives, but I didn't want to do it on my own. I rang Samuel.

'Samuel, the police are here! No, not here – here, but I saw them heading for the vicarage. I'm off to eavesdrop. Are you coming?'

'Do I have a choice?' He gave an ostentatious sigh, but I could hear excitement in his voice.

We met at my back gate and, doubled-up, crept across the graveyard, using bushes and headstones as camouflage. DCI Marsh and DC Whittaker appeared to have gained no entry to the vicarage and were now on their way to the church. We ducked behind an old, moss-covered tomb just in the nick of time.

Fortuitously, we found ourselves at a perfect vantage point. From where we were squatting we had a full view of the façade of the church. As we were no further than twenty yards away from the entrance, we could also hear quite clearly the conversation inside. As much as I am a master squatter, Samuel struggled with crouching on his hinds so he adopted a kneeling position. In case we were discovered we could easily claim that we were here to pray.

The church door stood open. That indicated that the vicar or at least the vicar's wife were inside.

'Hello!' DC Whittaker bellowed in his low bass. 'Anyone home?'

I gave a low chortle, and whispered to Samuel, 'Is he talking to God?'

Samuel grinned.

God didn't answer, but sure enough, Vicar Quentin and his other half soon emerged to greet the detectives.

'DCI Marsh, DC Whittaker!' Quentin Magnebu opened his arms and smiled widely. 'It's lovely to see someone visit the church on Good Friday, but I'm guessing this must be police business?'

'It is,' Gillian Marsh said curtly. 'We have a few questions about your recent break-ins.'

'Ah that! We did tell DC Whittaker about that, didn't we, love?' the vicar looked towards his wife as if seeking her confirmation. She nodded. She looked a right mess, wearing an unflattering brown apron and yellow rubber gloves, not to mention a dreadful headband that pulled her hair from her high forehead and flattened it in a way that made her appear bald. Her strapped sandals looked at least thirty years old. Even I wouldn't be seen dead in those.

'That may be so,' Marsh replied, 'but we'd like more detail about what went missing and when.'

'We can certainly enlighten you on that front,' said the vicar. 'Forgive me if I don't invite you in, but we've discovered an unpleasant odour in the west nave. Probably a decomposing rodent or a bird stuck in the rafters. It'll pass but we're giving the church a thorough cleaning and airing.'

'It's been closed for so long that it needs it anyway,' Mrs Magnebu added and clasped together her gloved hands.

'I know the feeling,' I whispered to Samuel. 'I've had my windows open all day today.'

'It does smell a bit musky in our kitchen,' Samuel agreed. 'I thought it was the rubbish bin.'

'It's the old stone walls. If you want character you have to put up with the damp and the stink.'

'So, about the break-ins,' Gillian Marsh demanded.

'It was nothing, really,' Leanne Magnebu started, but was instantly interrupted by her husband.

'Don't say it was nothing, dear,' he countered. 'They stole two bottles of communion wine, and that's just for starters. We replaced them and within a week that was gone too. And lest we forget – the fire by the baptismal font!'

'Arson?' Marsh sounded incredulous. 'We have no report of arson.'

'That's because we didn't report it.'

'My good wife didn't want to get the Bishops' youth into trouble, and I agreed,' Vicar Quentin snorted. He was evidently in disagreement with his wife's stance on this issue.

'It wasn't worth the trouble. And it wasn't really arson, just horseplay by some teenagers, I am sure,' Leanne went on. 'They picked up some leaflets and hymn sheets from the back of the church and set them alight. All that was left by the next morning was a small pile of ashes. I swept them away and that was the end of it.'

'What about the hymn books? We counted three missing. They burned them, Leanne, and that's just plain sacrilege. What's next – the Holy Book?' His eyes flashed with holy indignation.

'Anything else?' Marsh inquired calmly, indifferent to the report of sacrilege.

'What else would you like, DCI Marsh!' Magnebu rolled his eyes at the detective in disbelief.

'I mean any electronic gadgets, valuables… I don't know what's worth stealing from churches these days – gold goblets?'

I knew instantly where she was going with it. According to Thomas, the Sexton's Canning gang operated on a steal-to-order basis and they specialised in electronic devices, laptops, smart phones and the like. A couple of bottles of communion wine didn't quite fit the bill. The link to Sexton's criminal world seemed very weak indeed. There could be no link here at all to Isaac's dodgy connections and, more to the point, to his death.

'No, God forbid, nothing of the sort!' Vicar Quentin exclaimed. 'We have two nine-carat gold communion chalices under lock, but then the key is left in the keyhole of the tabernacle. Not very smart, come to think of it. Nevertheless, they didn't touch that.'

'That's why I'm sure it was just a bunch of kids getting up to harmless mischief. We didn't report that, but we did take to locking the church doors, didn't we, Quentin?' Leanne hooked her arm over her husband's and inclined her head onto his shoulder.

'We did, yes,' he patted her hand, 'and there's been no trouble ever since.'

'How long ago was that?'

'In winter – three months ago. The church is under lock and key throughout the week and we only open the doors for services, except that of course since lockdown began there's been no services even on holy days. That's why the place needs airing.' The vicar steeped his fingers thoughtfully. 'I wish the pandemic was over and done with, so my flock could return to fill the church with song and prayer. Churches weren't built to stand empty.'

'Good luck with that,' Marsh responded. I wondered if she was being sarcastic even though sarcasm wasn't her thing. She was as straight and dry as a spent match – on the emotional intelligence front, I mean.

'Anyway,' she continued, 'on the morning of Isaac Wotton's assault, was the church open?'

'No. I was in Parson's Combe that day – left at seven am,' the vicar said. 'So no, unless Leanne?' He looked to his wife for further clarification.

'No, it wasn't open,' she said. 'I was at home – in the vicarage. I had a bit of a lie-in. Not that I usually indulge myself like that, but that morning I woke up with a headache.'

'Leanne suffers from debilitating migraines,' Quentin elaborated.

'So I took painkillers and stayed in bed with the curtains drawn. I got up around nine o'clock, give or take half an hour. I only noticed the commotion outside when the ambulance arrived. It was called by Miss Kaye and Mr Dee, I believe. They found Isaac.'

'We're being implicated,' I mouthed to Samuel.

'Not really. It's true – we did find Isaac and called the ambulance,' he pointed out in a whisper.

Something caught my eye behind Quentin Magnebu's back. It seemed as if a bird or a black shadow passed across the aisle. It was only fleeting and the church interior was dark anyway at this late hour, but the shape seemed darker than the night. I brought the interior of the church into focus and I could swear, but only for a split second, that I saw Daisy Rotich float across the aisle. I blinked, and the impression was gone.

'My God,' I hissed at Samuel, 'I think I've just seen Daisy Rotich!'

'Where?' He looked around him, alarmed.

'Not here. Inside the church. She just went past,' I was beginning to realise that it didn't make sense. 'No, forget it. I must have imagined it. If she were there she would've come out. In fact, she would've gone back to her fiancé in London three weeks ago. What am I like! I've been thinking a lot about her. Then again...' I paused to consider the matter in depth.

'I know what you're thinking, Maggie,' Samuel kept his voice down despite his excitement. 'You think it could be her spirit.'

'Exactly! Because I saw her and you saw nothing.'

'Of course not, but then, isn't Isaac Wotton somewhere around here? You said he was hanging around the graveyard.'

'He is – he's here right now.'

'So, even if Mrs Rotich was dead – which isn't a proven fact – but even if she was, she couldn't be here at the same time as Isaac, correct? You told me the spirits never rain on each other's parade – there are never more than one of them in the same place at the same time,' Samuel argued, I must admit, quite lucidly.

'Except that she is inside the church and he is out here, in the cemetery.'

I was about to deliberate whether the church and the graveyard counted as one and the same place when a deep bass disrupted my train of thought: 'Isn't that Miss Kaye and Mr Dee?'

It was DC Whittaker.

He and Gillian Marsh must have walked in on us as we were having our heated debate about the habits of stranded souls. My heart sunk into my stomach. I wondered how much they had heard.

'It's us, indeed,' Samuel rose from his knees and swiped grass and soil from his trousers. 'We've been paying our respects to...' His eyes swept over the inscription on the headstone we were hiding behind, '... to Jennifer Leroy here—'

'My great-great-grand aunt on my mother's side,' I lied smoothly having quickly established that the lady in question had died in 1821.

'If you say so,' Marsh raised a doubtful eyebrow. 'Don't let us disturb you. Let's go, Whittaker.'

They turned to leave when Samuel stopped

them. 'We couldn't help overhearing your conversation with the vicar and his wife.'

'I'm sure you couldn't. You hardly ever can,' Marsh retorted.

Samuel ignored the sarcasm. He went on, 'It's just that although it doesn't look like the Sexton's gang was involved in any of the petty thefts from the church, there's a possibility that they may've something to do with the disappearance of Daisy Rotich. Maybe even her death.'

'How so?' Marsh executed a U-turn and focused her attention on Samuel. So did I. Did he believe that I may have just seen her spirit inside the church? I rejoiced. It seemed that Samuel Dee was now my disciple. I felt a wave of warmth rise inside my body.

'Well, they specialise in gadgets – mobile phones, I understand. Maybe Miss Rotich was here – sightseeing in this historical cemetery. With the church locked she'd have been in full view and very possibly alone. It was an opportunity – easy pickings. What I'm saying is that maybe she was attacked for her mobile phone. I know it's missing. We – Maggie and I – tried to call her on it. It rang at first, and then it was dead. Maybe she fought back and something bad happened. The gang made away with her phone, but she was hurt – possibly dead. They'd have had to remove her body and dump it some place where she'd never be found. Or maybe she's still alive and they are keeping her because she could identify them? I don't know where, but my point is that perhaps Isaac stood up to them, threatened to go to the police?'

'He wasn't a bad boy,' I added. I recognised where Samuel was going with this, and I was a hundred per cent behind him.

'Just a prankster, but not a killer. So maybe he regretted what happened and a couple of days later he decided to come clean. The gang would have wanted to shut him up pretty quick, wouldn't they?'

'Oh yes! So they lured Isaac here a couple of days later. It was Wednesday morning, wasn't it?'

'Or Thursday?' I queried.

'Well, whichever day, they met again and Isaac threatened to talk. There was a scuffle. Isaac wasn't on top form – he had a broken leg so it wouldn't have been hard to overpower him. One of them hit him on the head with that vase... Maybe they realised what they'd done and tried to drag him somewhere, probably to some get-away car out in the Market Square – maybe they even intended to take him to the hospital, but we turned up and they fled.'

'There were drag marks on the ground,' I pointed out. 'They're still there.'

'So, what we're saying is, DCI Marsh, don't write off the link to the Sexton's gang. We have a young man dead and a visitor to our town gone missing. Nothing much happens in Bishops so if two tragedies happen almost back-to-back, you can't help but wonder whether they are connected.'

DCI Marsh tilted her head and narrowed her eyes to give the matter serious thought. She and DC Whittaker exchanged explorative looks. Then she gazed at Samuel with unprecedented respect. 'You may have a point there, Mr Dee. It is worth looking into. Thank you.'

I grabbed Samuel's hand and squeezed it, to hell with social distancing! I was so proud of him! He was almost as good as me at fitting bits of the puzzle together. And he believed that I had seen Daisy's apparition in the church.

Truth is, I didn't fully believe it myself. I was more inclined to think that it was just a trick of the dying daylight. And that was because I had just spotted Isaac Wotton entering the church. Two of them in the same place and at the same time - that just couldn't be true.

CHAPTER 20

Maggie's Journal

I spent the rest of Easter dwelling on the matter. There was little else to do. Apart from pottering about in my garden and making brief phone calls to my siblings offering season's greetings, I had no other engagements. My telephone call to my brother Will was brief because we don't really have much to talk about. I hardly see him these days, since Dad's death. I think Will is still smarting from the revelations about his parentage. My call to my sister Andrea was brief for entirely different reasons. She lives in New Zealand and although the two of us could blabber for hours on end given half a chance, I simply wouldn't be able to afford the resulting telephone charges.

I consoled myself with lavish home cooking

and demolished all the cakes and biscuits I still had lurking in my larder. Rum & Raisin Fudge Extravaganza was a distant memory. I was suffering withdrawal symptoms. Fortunately, I could steady myself with an occasional glass of red wine, but even the wine seemed to be evaporating faster than I could drink it.

Television was my only companion in the evenings. I dutifully watched the customary Easter offering of *The Sound of Music* and *Chitty Chitty Bang Bang,* and I danced to the hits of the eighties which I discovered on some obscure channel which I couldn't find again no matter how diligently I surfed. On Monday afternoon my attention was drawn to yet another repeat of *Miss Marple* with Joan Hickson. I watched it and all the other episodes that I could find, including variations on the same themes but with different Miss Marples. I still couldn't make up my mind which one of them was my favourite. My brain turned to custard and my eyes into squares. I decided to revert to some independent thinking and that was when the burning question of Isaac's heart ending up in Indira Edmunds's ribcage unsettled my mind.

I could not share my musings with Samuel. We still had our morning power-walks and they remained the highlight of my otherwise dull days. We never stopped talking about Isaac and speculated endlessly about the involvement of the Sexton's gang in his death and the disappearance of Daisy Rotich. However, Dr Edmunds did not – and could not – come into our conversation. I had my suspicions about him but I couldn't share them with Samuel. Because of Deirdre, he thought the world of Dr Edmunds. And so did I. After all, he had saved Deirdre's life and restored her faulty ticker to tip-top condition. It went without saying that he was a brilliant surgeon, but did that make him a saint? Did that mean that he was incapable of murder? I had my doubts. As Kylie had said, it was a miracle that at the last minute Dr Edmunds's wife had received a new heart – just as she was lying on her deathbed. And it was quite a coincidence that her and Isaac Wotton's rare blood group was a perfect match. I won't even mention the fact of Isaac's timely death – the idea sent a shiver down my spine. There were just too many miracles and too many coincidences, and I believe in neither. So the dilemma began to build in my gut: was the miracle-maker doctor responsible for Isaac Wotton's death?

I could not possibly suggest that to Samuel and his mother. Deirdre alone would bite my head off if she knew what sort of unsavoury ideas about the good doctor were passing through my head. I had to explore this avenue quietly and on my own.

I resisted acting on my suspicions for as long as I could, which was until Wednesday afternoon.

After lunch, I spent a couple of hours working in the garden. As I went about weeding, raking and planting, my eyes were constantly attracted to the figure of Isaac Wotton. He was wandering aimlessly in the graveyard, looking sad and lost. I could bear it no longer. I dropped my secateurs and fetched my face mask from the house. I was planning to pay Michael Almond a visit. He happens to be a forensic pathologist working for Sexton's Canning CID. I needed to run a few things by him.

On my way to his cottage, I passed by the cemetery to have a word with Isaac. It wouldn't be a two-way dialogue, I knew that. The dead don't speak. At least they don't speak to me. Maybe they have ways of communicating amongst themselves and perhaps some powerful mediums can hear them too, but they have no desire to converse with me. Still, I had a few things to say to Isaac. I caught up with him by the well. It is an ancient stone thing with a rusty old bucket hanging from a rusty old chain. Nobody draws water from it anymore as the cemetery now has a tap with running water. Isaac was seated on the edge of the well. He didn't acknowledge my arrival, but I was sure he knew I was there.

'I'm going to find out who did it to you, Isaac,' I told him. 'They won't get away with it. But I'd really appreciate it if you could give me just a tiny hint. Nod if I'm on the right track because, to be honest with you, I wouldn't want to upset good people. If I were wrong... Just a small sign, Isaac. I'd be obliged. Am I right in pursuing Dr Edmunds?'

Isaac did not nod to confirm my suspicions, and neither did he shake his head to deny them. He did absolutely nothing. He remained seated, dangling his feet and gazing blankly into the well.

'Maggie! Who are you talking to?' It was Deirdre. She was peering at me from her bedroom window.

I gave her a wave. 'Hi Deirdre! How are you? Should we have an afternoon tea over the fence tomorrow? I could bake some scones.' I did my best to distract her away from her query.

'It sounds good, but why are you talking to yourself?' She looked concerned. 'You know it's not a good sign when people talk to themselves.'

'I wasn't doing that,' I protested weakly. 'I was just... humming. Anyway, I must dash. Something to do!' And I took off without looking back.

Michael was at home as I expected him to be. He answered the door on the first knock. He must have seen me arrive from his kitchen window. He was wearing oven gloves. An aroma of vanilla and cinnamon wafted behind him.

'Maggie!' he put on a welcoming smile. 'Still looking for Gillian?'

'No, but I need to speak to you, Michael – in your professional capacity.'

'Wow, that sounds serious. Do you want to come in? Your timing is immaculate – I've just made fruit scones.'

I salivated at the mere idea. 'That'd be lovely,' I enthused. 'Would it be okay to sit in your garden? I'd rather not break any more rules today.'

'Yes, you're right. Come in through the side entrance,' he gestured towards a wrought-iron gate with spikes.

We sat on a swing bench fitted with cushions and a canopy. It overlooked the rolling fields behind Michael's cottage. I watched an abundance of insects buzzing and fluttering over wild flowers. Birds swooped in and out of the shrubbery. I even spotted a goldfinch.

Michael arrived armed with a proper Wiltshire cream tea, including a dainty teapot and cups. The feast began. I selected a scone and piled it up with cream and raspberry jam.

'From my own raspberries – last year's crop,' Michael pointed to a clump of raspberry canes which were already covered with bulging buds of fresh leaf.

'You make your own jam?'

'I do.'

Impressed, I scooped another teaspoon of jam from the jar and stuck it on my scone. I bit into it. 'Divine,' I complimented my host.

'So, what is it you'd like to ask me about in my professional capacity? I hope it's nothing to do with dead bodies?' Michael winked at me jokingly.

'Well...' I drew the word pointedly, 'it is and it isn't. It's about Isaac Wotton. His father tells me that he was having routine surgery and something went terribly wrong. Medical misadventure, I believe was the phrase the hospital gave him. Is that so?'

'Yes, in a nutshell,' Michael nodded. 'It was a very straightforward operation – more tiny bone splinters were found embedded in the tissue and had to be removed. But internal bleeding ensued and Isaac suffered a fatal stroke.'

'And who was the surgeon? Was it Dr Edmunds by any chance?' I asked casually.

Michael gazed at me, intrigued. 'Yes, it was.'

'And can you be absolutely certain that Isaac's death was unavoidable? I mean, could a different surgeon, for example, have carried it out successfully?'

'Well, you can never predict with absolute certainty what may go wrong during surgery. Why all these questions, Maggie?'

I put down my cup and looked Michael in the eye, 'Because I have serious doubts about Dr Edmunds's intentions.'

'Are you accusing him of incompetency?' Michael stared at me, incredulous. 'He is one of the best surgeons I know.'

'I don't question that, but like I said, I question his intentions. You see, his wife was dying of congenital heart failure. She'd been waiting for a new heart for years but because of her rare blood group, there were no donors. And suddenly Isaac Wotton turns up with his strong, young man's heart and a matching blood type...'

'It happens. It was a lucky break for Mrs Edmunds, I admit, but Dr Edmunds couldn't have magicked Isaac Wotton onto his operating table.'

'But the thing is that he could.'

'What are you saying, Maggie Kaye?' Michael compressed his lips and looked at me sternly.

'Let me explain. Isaac Wotton went to hospital with a broken leg a week or so before his death. Dr Edmunds operated on his leg and at that point he would've discovered that Isaac had the same blood type as his wife.'

'And what then?' Michael interrupted. 'He would've concocted to lethally injure the young man so that he could botch up the surgery and claim his heart for his wife? That's outrageous!'

'I realise it sounds outlandish and – and,' I stammered, 'and maybe the doctor didn't necessarily lure Isaac to the cemetery and clobber him unconscious... I am not saying that it happened that way, not exactly, but what I am saying is that as soon as Edmunds found Isaac on the operating table in front of him, the idea may have hatched in his mind to deliberately botch the operation so that he could… you know, snatch the boy's beating heart for his wife.'

There I'd said it! It felt good to get it off my chest. It had to be done. I just had to moot my theory with an expert. 'What do you think, Michael? As a pathologist, I mean. Could medical misadventure be the result of a deliberate action or omission on the part of a surgeon?'

Michael Almond sucked in his bottom lip and rubbed his chin pensively. His moustache rippled as he chewed his lip, thinking. 'I suppose,' he said at last, 'that it is possible for a surgeon to sabotage an operation. Mind, it's a very remote possibility. Dr Edmunds wasn't alone. He was surrounded by a team of other medical professionals: his junior, the anaesthetist, nurses. They watched and assisted him every step of the way.'

'But they may be covering up for him, or simply refusing to accept that he may have done something unethical. It wouldn't be easy for his colleagues to even imagine he was capable of such a thing. Even if they noticed something untoward, they might've dismissed it out of hand. The idea of Dr Edmunds killing a patient before their very eyes probably never occurred to any of them.'

'But I guess questions should be asked,' Michael concluded.

We sat silently for a while, gazing at the setting sun. Michael promised me he would consider this line of inquiry prior to finalising his report to the Coroner.

I was walking back home with a sense of accomplishment. I wasn't joyous about it – far from it. If Dr Edmunds was innocent, my accusation would cause him great pain and some damage to his professional reputation. But on the other hand, there was Isaac and his grieving family. They had the right to know what really happened. No stone should be left unturned, I reminded myself, no matter how many toes I had to tread on. I picked up pace. The sun was lying very low on the horizon, painting the treetops orangey-red. The air had finally begun to cool. Goosebumps appeared on my arms. I heard a stone rolling along the cobbled road and plopping into the roadside ditch. I spun on my heel, alarmed by some unidentified presence behind me. My heart was in my mouth. It was getting dark and I was alone in the middle of nowhere. Not long ago, a woman had gone missing here and a young man had been attacked...

I feared the worst and kicked myself for not bringing my mobile phone. Too late.

'Samuel?'

There he was, following me without revealing himself. What the hell, I thought.

'Maggie...' He threw his arms up in the air as if he was surrendering to the enemy.

'What are you doing here? Are you spying on me?' I demanded.

CHAPTER 21

'**S**amuel, come here! Hurry!' Deirdre shouted from her bedroom.

She sounded sufficiently alarmed for Sam to abandon his book and race up the stairs from the sitting room. Since his mother's heart attack, he had been living in a state of constant alert.

He burst into her room and found her leaning out of her window. 'Come, have a look!' she beckoned him. 'Maggie's been acting oddly, over there, by the well,' she pointed, 'talking to herself like a madwoman.'

'Oh, that's normal,' Sam relaxed.

'And now she's off somewhere – said she had something important to do. There, look,' Deirdre leaned further, 'off she goes.'

Sam and his mother watched Maggie march down the footpath leading to the Market Square.

'Did she say where she was going?'

'No. Just jabbered to herself for a while and

when I called out to her, said she had somewhere else to be. Isn't that odd? Don't you think we should—'

Sam was back on high alert. This time because of Maggie. 'Sorry, Mum, must go! We'll talk later, all right?'

He bounded down the stairs, hurriedly put on his trainers and shot out of the house. He sped over to the Market Square. Maggie was crossing the High Street, heading south towards Fields Pass. Sam crept behind her, keeping a safe distance. He did not wish to be discovered, but he absolutely had to keep an eye on his wayward fiancé. After her near-death experience in St Petersburg – all due to her unbridled sleuthing – Sam had promised himself to live up to his knight-in-shining-armour reputation and protect her from every peril she'd invariably wander into. He was under no illusion that once again Maggie Kaye was on a sleuthing mission. She would not rest until she uncovered Isaac Wotton's killer, and to achieve that she would probably put herself in danger. She was reckless and single minded. Sam's worst fear was that despite her promises she would attempt to track down and confront the mob from Sexton's. That could only end one way for her – badly.

He was puzzled that she was on foot (if she were heading for Sexton's Canning it'd be a five-mile trek each way) and even more confused that she was heading in the opposite direction (the county town lay to the north-east of Bishops; Maggie was proceeding southwards). Apparently today she had other plans than single-handedly bringing down Sexton's gangs. Nevertheless, Sam continued in pursuit. She was marching towards Sexton's Wood with a clear purpose to her long stride. Whatever are you up to, Maggie? Sam pondered as he dodged in and out of roadside hedgerows.

Within ten minutes, he had an answer. She turned into Michael Almond's driveway. Sam squatted behind the wall and listened. Maggie had barely knocked when Michael sprung out onto his doorstep, inviting her in. Had he been expecting her? If she went in, Sam would remain in the dark as to the purpose of their rendezvous. Fortunately, the gods smiled on him for Maggie said, 'Would it be okay to sit in your garden? I'd rather not break any more rules today.'

Michael told her to use the side gate to get into his garden while he disappeared back inside the house. Maggie walked in, and Sam followed. He tiptoed along the flagstones of the side path and concealed himself behind a sculptured bush to the left. It was the perfect vantage point. From there he could see them and hear their every word.

Maggie took a seat on a swinging bench, pushed herself against the bar and was rocking to and fro whilst sweeping her gaze over the fields. She seemed very much at home. Within a few minutes Michael arrived with a tray laden with scones, cream and jam. Sam could smell the enticing aroma of fresh baking from his hidey hole. He listened astounded as Maggie and Michael chatted about his homemade raspberry jam. They were way too familiar with each other for his liking. He was beginning to worry that something romantic was brewing between those two until Maggie started talking. Sam exhaled his relief. There was nothing romantic in Maggie's new theory about Dr Edmunds's involvement in Isaac's death.

Just like Michael, Sam considered Maggie's ideas and conceded that she had a point: there were too many coincidences. Maggie was onto something. *Sharp as a razor, that's my girl,* Sam thought, full of admiration for the crafty vixen. Soon however another anxiety began to nibble at the back of his mind: why hadn't she shared her theories with him? Why had she come to Michael Almond instead?

When the conversation between Michael and Maggie died out and they sat in a comfortably companionable silence, watching the sun drift on the horizon, Sam was battling his inner demons. The left side of his brain – the logical side – was reminding him that Michael was a forensic pathologist and it was only his expert opinion that Maggie was interested in. But on the other hand, the right hemisphere of his brain despaired that he himself had become irrelevant, unloved and unwanted. Wallowing in self-pity, he nearly missed the moment when Maggie rose from the swing and thanked Michael for his hospitality and his advice. She was about to leave.

Sam tumbled out from behind the bush and, doubled-up, skulked towards the road. There he hid under the parapet of Michael's stone wall, and waited.

Maggie waved goodbye to Michael from the driveway and strolled down Fields Pass. Sam set off after her. His progress however was erratic. Unfortunately, his left leg had gone to sleep when he'd been crouching in Michael's garden and he was now skipping clumsily on his right leg. A stone flew from under her his feet, rattled on the road and plopped into the ditch. Maggie stopped and turned.

'Samuel? What are you doing here? Are you spying on me?' She fixed him with an inquisitorial stare.

'No, course not. I was just...' He embarked on an impromptu lie but thought better of it. He raised his hands above his head and confessed, 'I was worried about you, Maggie, so yes, I've been following you.'

'Why would you worry? I am a big girl, you know.' She shrugged, but Sam detected a note of guilt in her tone.

'I was concerned you might go ahead with pursuing those hoodlums from Sexton's.'

'At Michael Almond's cottage?' Her eyes widened.

'Well, I didn't know that was where you were going, did I!'

'Oh Samuel,' she groaned, 'you have to trust me.'

'You don't trust me!' He pointed out. 'Why didn't you talk to me about your suspicions? I thought we were partners.'

'We are, but Michael has inside knowledge. I needed information, that's all.'

'Still, you could – should – have shared your theories with me. You left me out on purpose, didn't you?' He was unable to control the self-pitying tremor in his voice.

Maggie's chin dropped to her chest. 'I did, yes,' she admitted to Samuel's astonishment. 'But it was only to protect you and Deirdre. You think the world of Dr Edmunds. What if I am wrong? I didn't want to put you in an untenable position.'

'That's not good enough, Maggie. We shouldn't have secrets from each other. I can't deal with secrets. Not after Alice...'

'Yes, I see...' Her lips quivered and she pressed them together to stop it. 'I'm sorry. I didn't think.'

Sam walked towards her and pulled her into his arms. 'It's okay. Just let me look after you and we'll say no more about it.'

Deirdre was waiting in the kitchen and she

accosted him as soon as his foot crossed the threshold, 'So what's the story? What are you two up to? Enlighten me.'

'It's nothing, Mum. I'm just an old fool,' Sam dropped his shoulders.

'I already know that. Tell me something I don't know. Where did Maggie go? I assume you followed her?'

'I did, and she found me out.'

'Oh dear me!' Despite her exclamation, Deirdre did not sound sympathetic.

'I was worried she was going to do something stupid.'

'My sentiment precisely! She was rambling on to herself in the cemetery. You'd be excused for thinking the woman had gone barmy. So did you catch up with her?'

'She went to see Michael Almond.'

'The forensic pathologist? What the hell for?'

'She thinks – she suspects that Dr Edmunds caused Isaac's death.'

'My Dr Edmunds?' Deirdre gaped at him incredulously.

Sam had no choice but to take her through Maggie's hypothesis. Deirdre sat down, propped her elbows on the kitchen table and lowered her chin into the cup of her hands. She listened attentively without once interrupting him.

'...so she got it into her head that Dr Edmunds made deliberate mistakes during the surgery so that—'

'So that Isaac wouldn't survive and Indira could get his heart,' Deirdre finished the story for him. She gave the matter a little bit more thought before she finally said, 'Maggie may be right. If only you saw how much love Dr Edmunds has for Indira, you'd readily accept that he was capable of anything at all to save her life. I watched them for a week from my hospital bed – he was there by her side every day, talking to her, holding her, reassuring her and making her comfortable. He did all the jobs around her, even the lowly ones a hospital porter would be asked to do. And he kept urging her to hang in there because he'd get her a new heart. Yes...' Deirdre drew out her confirmation, 'yes, yes, he may have finished Isaac Wotton off. I wouldn't put it past him – with all that love he had for his wife...'

Sam sat staring at his mother, humbled by her unbiased assessment. She had more logical detachment from the matter than he had expected. The sober, non-sentimental pragmatism of the war generation was very much in evidence. He said, 'Maggie thought she couldn't share that with us – she thought it would upset us.'

'Bah! Silly girl,' Deirdre sighed. 'Dr Edmunds is a great doctor – a miracle maker, but he is also human. Only human. Even I can see that. I still hope she's wrong, but I won't hold my breath on account of his innocence. He would sell his soul to the devil to save Indira's life, and maybe he did.'

'We should know after the inquest.'

'Are you hungry? I've made ribs in barbecue sauce with chunky chips.'

Over the pudding of banoffee pie, Deirdre returned to the subject of Maggie's bizarre antics in the cemetery. 'I still don't understand what she was doing. She was talking out loud to herself. There was no one there – no one but Maggie. I fear she may be going barking mad,' Deirdre despaired.

'Don't worry, Mum. That's just Maggie,' Sam tried to mollify her.

'No, son. It's more than just Maggie being Maggie. It looked...' Deirdre frowned, '... unnatural. Speak to her, please. She might not see it for what it is. She may get angry with you when you broach the subject. But you should have a word with her – the sooner, the better. Break it to her gently, but you must get her to see a psychiatrist. Maybe that friend of yours – Edgar Flynn?'

'I can't do that!' Sam protested.

'You are to be her husband. If not you then who? Who else can take it up with her? Her parents are dead. She has no one but you.'

Sam had no choice. He had to level with his mother or she would never get off his back – or worse yet, she may approach Edgar directly and try to make an appointment on Maggie's behalf. Maggie would never forgive her, and Sam by association. Sam pushed aside his plate. 'Okay, Mum, you have to swear you won't breathe a word of this to anyone and most certainly that you won't let on to Maggie that you know.'

'Know what?' she blinked at him.

'What I am about to tell you.'

'Well, I can't promise anything until I—'

'No. You promise to keep it under your hat or I say nothing.'

'Blimey,' Deirdre rolled her eyes. 'Cross my heart and hope to die. Go on, then!'

'Maggie can see the dead.'

'Don't be ridiculous!'

'Not all of them and not all the time, but sometimes she can see them – the souls of those who can't pass over to the other side. They are held back here on earth, so she tells me, because their loved one can't let them go, or because they have some unfinished business on earth.'

'You don't seriously believe that gobbledygook, do you?'

'I do. Since Alice...' Sam inhaled deeply to steady his emotions and continued, 'Since Maggie saw Alice. She described her to me in fine detail, Mum. She knew what Alice had looked like when we had first met – thirty years ago. Maggie told me what Alice had been wearing that day. Only I knew that – only me and Alice. And then, there was more. There were other people that

Maggie knew had died before anyone else did. There is no other logical explanation. I believe her. She has proved it to me on many occasions.'

Deirdre gawped at her son, genuinely mystified. 'She can see the dead people?'

'Yes.'

'And she talks to them? You're saying that's what she was doing in the cemetery earlier today – speaking with a dead person?'

'Ah, that's different,' Sam stopped her. 'That's something new. She never used to talk to them. Apparently, they don't communicate with her. They're just there but they don't say anything and don't interact with her.'

'So, the fact remains that Maggie was talking to herself,' Deirdre triumphed. 'And that's not healthy.'

'I suppose you're right.'

'She was jabbering, waving her arms, and there was no one there. Just Maggie and a rusty old bucket. She's going bonkers, Samuel, and she needs your help.'

'It's this damned lockdown,' Samuel said. 'You and I, we have each other to talk to, we can do things together, share a meal, but Maggie is on her own, all day long. She must be very lonely even though she won't admit it. Our morning walks aren't enough.'

'Then perhaps we should ask her to move in with us,' Deirdre suggested.

'The other day Maggie had a better idea,' Sam

remembered. 'She said we could break down the wall between our houses. We would have one household – one home.'

'So what are you waiting for? Get on with it before she loses what marbles she still possesses.'

CHAPTER 22

Maggie's Journal

I saw Mrs Moore's chunky figure grow larger still as she approached. She was charging like a bull between the graves and brazenly walking over some of them. She had fire in her eyes. They shot out sparks visible from where I was. And I was in my garden tying the daffodils after they had flowered. I had a busy day planned: digging over the flowerbeds ready for summer bedding and sowing my marigold seeds in trays. I stood up to stretch my back and there was Mrs Moore storming towards me with murder on her mind.

She tripped over the low edge of an old grave which was sunk into the ground and almost invisible. Her huge bulk submitted to gravity and she fell with a fruity curse flying off her lips.

Something told me not to laugh – nor even smile. I bit my lip and waited. I knew she had a bone to pick with me – a great-big whale bone if her highly charged deportment was anything to go by.

'You!' She spotted me from the ground. 'It's you I want a word with!'

'Mrs Moore?' I lowered my trowel behind my back and dropped it discreetly. The last thing I wanted was to be accused of holding a weapon in my hand at the time of confrontation. And a confrontation was heading my way in giant steps. It was unavoidable.

Mrs Moore scrambled to her feet, pulled up her skinny jeans which seemed to have burst a button. She pressed her hand to her stomach and pointed at me with her other hand.

'You! You'll—' She started again, but could not finish the threat for she dissolved into tears. She clasped her hand to her mouth and gave a heartfelt volley of sobs.

I dismissed my fears and dashed towards her. My gate squeaked a warning, but I disregarded it. There was a woman in deep distress. She may have wanted to hurt me five minutes ago but now she needed a sympathetic person to pick her up.

Isaac's spirit appeared next to her. I had seen him earlier near the well, but now he was standing by poor Mrs Moore, sort of looking at her or through her. Although there was no expression in his ghostly face, I was in no doubt that he was there for moral support.

'Mrs Moore, what happened? Are you okay?' Then the worst possible thought occurred to me. This wasn't about Mrs Moore. It was about Thomas. 'Is it Thomas?'

She swooned off her feet and collapsed to the ground, weeping.

'Has something... has someone,' I stammered, standing over her on weak legs and feeling the blood drain from my body. My head went into a spin.

'They beat him up, didn't they! Because of you! Because you went after him, wanting to know things that were best left alone. And he gave in and told you. Did you think they wouldn't find out? Are you that stupid!'

My knees buckled under me and I also collapsed onto the grass next to Mrs Moore.

'I'm so sorry! How is he? Is he—' I couldn't bring myself to utter another word. What would that word be anyway: *hurt? alive? dead?*

'Not very good, is how he is!' She shot me a resentful look. 'Broken nose, beaten black and blue – that's how.'

'I'm ever so sorry,' I kept repeating, but I was painfully aware of how little meaning my sympathy really had. She was right. It was my fault Thomas was attacked. I would never be able to make it up to him.

'It's all my doing,' she cried, suddenly taking

the blame. 'If I hadn't made a fuss at Aldi the word wouldn't have got out, and my Thomas—' Here she wailed unable to say another coherent word.

I put my arm around her and helped her to her feet. 'No, Mrs Moore, it's my fault. I, I was so hell-bent on finding Isaac's killer that I didn't spare Thomas a second thought. I should've thought of his safety, his wellbeing... I really, really messed up. I'll never forgive myself. I know this is too little, too late.' My breathing became shallow. I was feeling lightheaded. 'If there's anything I can do?'

'I wanted to smash your head in, that's what I came here for,' Mrs Moore said, 'but not anymore. I need to go home, to Thomas.'

'Let me drive you. It's a long way to walk.'

She let me take her home but wouldn't let me see Thomas, citing lockdown rules all of a sudden. 'It's not allowed, don't you know? Anyways, he's most likely asleep. I'll tell him you're sorry.' Her anger had subsided and she looked exhausted. She stepped out of my car and dragged herself to the doorstep. There she paused and looked at me over her shoulder, 'Thanks for the lift.'

That was the last nail in my coffin. I screamed abuse at myself for being a self-absorbed and stupid woman, and not a patch on Mrs Moore.

The following day, I baked an apple and

blackberry pie and delivered it to the Moores. I left it on the doorstep, rang the bell and drove off without waiting for Mrs Moore to show up. I didn't want her to throw the pie in my face. For the next week I repeated my daily tributes, bringing offerings of cakes as well as hot meals. That was the least I could do to relieve Mrs Moore and let her focus on looking after Thomas.

It was on the sixth day that the door opened just as I deposited a chicken casserole on the step and collected my baking dish from the day before. Thomas stood in the doorway. His nose was still swollen and the colour of a rot-infested green apple. He looked awful but at least he was on his feet and clearly getting better.

'Thanks, Miss,' he muttered. 'You're a good cook, better than Mum.'

'Oh Thomas, so good to see you!' I melted into a wet puddle on the ground. 'Are you... better?'

'Yeah.'

'Please forgive me. I should've never pressed you for information.'

'It's okay, Miss. Not what you think,' he mumbled and lifted my pot from the doorstep. 'What is it today?'

'Chicken casserole,' I smiled through tears.

'I like chicken.'

I had cancelled my morning power-walking rendezvous with Samuel during that miserable week. I couldn't look him in the eye. He had been right – I shouldn't have bothered poor Thomas. I had jeopardised the young man's safety. I felt so wretched.

It wasn't just Samuel I was avoiding. In fact, I had cut all human contacts and focussed my energy on some well overdue soul searching. A few momentous truths had finally cut through my thick skull. One of them was the realisation that sleuthing ought not to equate to trampling over people's lives. The dead had their rights, and unmasking their killers was important to them, but not at the expense of the living. I chewed on those and other home truths during my many sleepless nights. Looking in the mirror in the morning to be confronted by my guilty face was a torture well deserved. I had a few strong words of chastisement to impart to myself too. I didn't mince those words. Sometimes, I raised my voice and screamed abuse at myself. It helped but only a little. I could now understand what self-flagellation was all about. If I had a whip with metal rakes, I wouldn't hesitate to use it.

I decided that the only person I would keep in touch with was Isaac. Though, of course, he wasn't a living person and he didn't engage with me. Still, he was there, unfailing and non-judgmental in his spiritual presence. I confessed to him about what had happened to Thomas because of my snooping. I ran by him the dishes I was planning to cook for the Moores. He didn't exactly approve of them, but I think he would've if he were alive. On the day I saw Thomas and spoke to him, I ran to the cemetery to report the good news to Isaac. He looked pleased, though I might have imagined that.

'I still want to find your killer, Isaac,' I told him. 'I made a promise to your dad.'

His apparition rippled with the setting sun whose weak rays filtered through it. It was as close as he would come to giving me his blessing.

'But I will be very careful how I go about it. No thoughtless accusations!' I vowed. 'Come to think of it,' I added, 'we might already have the culprit. What do you think about Dr Edmunds?'

Before he answered – which I knew he wouldn't – Deirdre's head popped out of her window and she shouted a cheery hello to me.

'Are you avoiding us, Maggie?'

'No, not at all. I'm just busy,' I replied without even trying to come up with something remotely plausible.

'This cannot go on,' Deirdre issued a sudden warning. 'You'll make yourself sick. We won't let you.'

'I'm fine – I really am!'

'No, you're not. You refuse to see Samuel. That's not fine. How do you think he feels?' Motherly concern rang in her voice. I could see I'd been wrong cancelling my walks with Samuel – wrong again! He probably took it to heart. I had hurt his feelings without a word of explanation.

I had been such a wretched cow!

'I've been a little under the weather,' that wasn't a lie, not entirely, 'Something I ate, I think.' That was! 'But I'm fully recovered so how about we resume our walks from tomorrow?

'It's a start,' Deirdre offered me a tight smile. 'I'll let him know.'

CHAPTER 23

E ven though Maggie had again joined Sam on their morning power-walks, she wasn't quite herself. She was subdued and deep in thoughts which she wouldn't share with him. On the rare occasions when she spoke it was only a throw-away comment about the weather being nice – or not so nice – or about the latest lockdown statistics. Nothing personal, not even a glimmer of a smile would as much as perch on her lips.

Sam fretted over Maggie's decline into a state that looked nothing short of depression. His mother was right: weeks and weeks of isolation had taken their toll on Maggie. Ordinarily, she was a jovial and gregarious person. Deprived of company, she seemed to be wasting away. Her little dimples had all but faded away from her face and she had become a woman who just wanted to be left alone. That wasn't the Maggie Sam knew. He decided to do something to bring the real article back.

They were going past Sexton's Wood, heading back home. The morning was wonderfully bright and full of birdsong. A few, featherlight clouds scudded across the sky. Dew glistened on the blades of new grass. Maggie would usually notice such tiny delights but not anymore. She was treading heavily; even the wiggle of her hips seemed to have abandoned her. A forlorn expression sat on her face like a boulder.

'Remember when we talked about breaking down the wall between our flats?' Samuel asked.

'Oh, that,' Maggie blinked, returning from some faraway land where she had absented herself. 'Yes, another daft idea of mine, I'm afraid.'

'No, not daft at all. I think it's a brilliant idea.'
'You do?'

'I wasn't confident about doing it by myself, but what the heck,' Sam flicked his wrist, 'the worst that can happen is that the whole house collapses on us!'

She didn't care for the joke. Sam's heart shrivelled by a fraction.

'We wouldn't want that,' she said half-heartedly.

'I'd rather that than spend another day without you, Maggie. I miss you and I think – without being too presumptuous, I hope – that you too could do with Mum's and my company.'

Sam grabbed her hand and forced her to halt. 'We need to be together for your sake, and mine. If you're still up for it, I'll borrow your sledgehammer and start bringing down those damned walls.'

'Oh, I don't know, Samuel... Right now, I'd be poor company for you.' She spoke faintly and without much conviction. She sounded ill.

Sam wasn't going to submit to her black mood. He was determined to pull her out of it. 'Even if you sat and didn't say another word, you'd still be the best company I'd ever wish for.'

Maggie pressed her lips together and blinked rapidly but could not stop a tear escaping and coursing down her cheek. 'I'm not a good person, Samuel. I don't think I deserve you,' she whispered.

'Now, you're being really daft. You're feeling low. It's normal in lockdown. It's driving many people insane. We just have to spend more time together and everything will be back to normal.'

She sniffled and jolted her head back. 'I'll think about it, okay? Give me a couple of days to sort myself out.'

He should have said no, but Sam didn't know how to say no to Maggie. He dropped his shoulders and sighed his agreement.

They carried on in a heart-piercing silence until he came up with another idea: 'How about afternoon tea later today? In our garden. Mum and I will get everything ready. You just need to turn up.'

'I'd love to but,' she looked apologetic, 'it's the AA meeting at four today. Didn't you get the Teams invite?'

Sam hadn't looked at his emails in days. He had no reason to. The invitation was probably languishing in his junk mail. He'd look for it as soon as he got home. The Teams meeting with all the old friends from Bishops Archaeological Association could be a blessing. It wouldn't be a face to face gathering at the Old Stables with a cup of steaming loose-leaf tea and the musky body odour of Rumpole lying under the table, but it would be a welcome distraction for Maggie.

'I completely forgot. I've been looking forward to it. It's been a while. I missed the last meeting.'

'You did, yes.'

'I won't miss this one. And we can adjourn the afternoon tea until tomorrow. But we aren't cancelling it.'

Maggie offered him a faint but encouraging smile in response.

Sam was pleased to see the familiar faces that began popping up on his computer screen. Over the last few years, he had grown fond of these people. They were an eccentric bunch of archaeology enthusiasts in general, and Bishops Well sworn loyalists in particular. And they were also thoroughly decent.

As it was a virtual meeting, there was virtually no excuse for anyone to be absent. In fact, this was one of those rare social opportunities in lockdown no one would miss out on. Maggie wasn't the only one confined to the four walls of her house without a soul to talk to. James Weston-Jones's wife and two boys had been in France when lockdown started and that's where they had remained. His step-mother, Lady Weston-Jones lived permanently in Switzerland, and his father Lord Philip was a recluse with the onset of dementia. James's only company were the birds he studied on the banks of the Avon. He was an avid bird watcher and a reluctant financial adviser. Edgar Flynn, just like Sam, had only his elderly mother for company, but it was common knowledge that living with one's mother wasn't without its own patience-stretching challenges.

Not everyone was alone, but that didn't mean they were happy. A change from her regular Westminster-widow status, Vera had Henry back at home. She claimed it was a cross she had to bear, but prayed it wouldn't be for much longer. She couldn't wait for Mr Bombastic (as she called Henry behind his back) to pack his trunk and return to the capital. He was apparently impossible to live with.

Vanessa endured her husband Alec working from home, and just like Vera counted the days until he'd don his Chief Superintendent's uniform once more and depart for Sexton's Canning Police HQ in the mornings and Horton St Anselm's golf course in the afternoons.

Cherie and Lisa had each other, and they appeared the least affected by the soul-destroying lockdown.

The conversation started with an assessment of everyone's new hairstyles and fluctuations in their body mass. Indeed, Cherie seemed to have expanded around her waist and her usually spiky, short crop of hair had morphed into a flamboyant wave. She had lost all her military deportment and seemed almost feminine. James's number two haircut had relaxed into a tuft of tight curls sprouting in all directions from the top of his head. Edgar's thinning wisps were beyond description and Michael Almond's moustache was about to beat its own record in bushiness. Sam had long lost his battle against the unruly mass of his hair. He now sported a long fringe reaching his eyes, and his ears and neck were covered too. Vera directed her camera at Rumpole who was seated by her legs. He looked shaggier than before, too shaggy even for an Irish Wolfhound which breed was famous for its unshorn hairiness.

'He hasn't seen the inside of a dog parlour for three months,' Vera lamented. 'His fur is so matted that I had to resort to snipping off the tougher knots with a craft knife.'

'It won't be a minute too soon when this

rotten lockdown is over,' James sniped, and everyone agreed.

The meeting assumed a more jubilant tone when the subject of Maggie's triumph over the wicked Vicar Magnebu came up on the agenda. The subject matter was of great interest to the Archaeological Association since it revolved around the preservation of the Stone Circle. The funding from the Parish Council had been secured thanks to Maggie.

'You wiped the floor with the lot of them!' Cherie enthused.

'I don't know that I did that,' Maggie said. 'I had the feeling their original decision didn't sit well with them and they all wanted it reversed.'

'Even the vicar?'

'Well, maybe not him.'

'A total religious fanatic!' Vera offered her evaluation.

'Not half as bad as his wife,' Vanessa said. 'I left the Women's Institute since she joined. It's always about her and her causes.'

'She is one weird madcap,' Vera pronounced. 'My cousin, Sabine, knocked on the vicarage door once, collecting donations for her shelter – it was before Christmas. She was counting on some festive goodwill and generosity – but the foul-tempered harpy sent her packing before Sabine so much as opened her mouth. And she threw abuse at poor Sabine and called her all sorts of names – a *witch* and *the agent of evil* being just some of them. Mad, absolutely raving mad!'

'I never saw her as such a bigot,' Sam raised a surprised eyebrow. 'She seems rather harmless.'

'Oh, she is harmless – until you cross her,' Vanessa said.

'We'll just have to stay out of her line of fire. And her husband's,' Edgar Flynn commented from his professional perspective. 'It's useless entering into any debates with people like that. Not only won't they listen – they become more radicalised in their views.'

'They won't terrorise me,' Cherie said.

'It'd be interesting to know what they make of the likes of you and me.' Lisa, her partner, pondered. They had been living openly as a couple for a while now and nobody in the rather conservative Bishops Well seemed to mind. Then again, Leanne and Quentin's opinion had not been sought on the matter.

'I don't know and I don't care.' Cherie shrugged and changed the subject to something more pertinent to the business of the AA: 'I was thinking about supporting Harry Wotton with the upkeep of the Stone Circle. We should make the Circle more prominent in our brochures. Anyone willing to do some research and write an article? And it'd be good to create a webpage dedicated to the Circle. Any takers?'

Sam and Maggie, simultaneously, put up their virtual hands: Maggie offering to write the piece and Sam to design the webpage.

'We'll take some photos of the Circle on our morning walks,' Sam suggested. 'We go past Harry Wotton's every day.'

'Leave it with us,' Maggie backed him up. He was pleased to hear her use the *us* pronoun. A joint project was exactly what they needed.

Further discussions were held about ways of fundraising for a circular footpath to circumvent the perimeter of the Stone Circle, using Stonehenge as a model. Community works would only be able to commence after lockdown, but firm plans were made and duly recorded by James in the minutes.

Before the meeting was called to a close, the unavoidable topic of Isaac Wotton's death arose. It was Edgar Flynn who asked the question, 'I hear the inquest has now concluded. What were the Coroner's findings, Michael?'

'Open verdict, actually. Listening to the witness testimonies, it was obvious that Dr Edmunds's hand may have slipped here and there on purpose. He was slow to act – dawdled, in fact, as one of the nurses had put it. He was sloppy, and that, apparently, wasn't the brilliant surgeon everybody knew him to be. The operation was not performed to his usual standards. With all those testimonies on record, a good prosecutor will be able to impute intent. It doesn't look good for Dr Edmunds.'

'He's been interviewed under caution and charged,' Vanessa said. She had first-hand intelligence from her husband DSI Alec Scarfe, but she rarely shared it. On this occasion, she chose to speak. The death of a young Bishopian played heavily on everyone's mind. People deserved to know. She added, 'DI Grayson from Bath CID is leading the investigation because the death occurred on his patch, at the RUH. Alec tells me Grayson may have enough to lay charges of medical negligence, but the CPS will make the final decision.'

'If there's sufficient evidence that Edmunds acted deliberately, they may be looking at murder, I guess,' Sam speculated.

'It's possible,' said Michael. 'And this is largely thanks to Maggie.'

Everyone's eyes focussed on the right-hand bottom corner of their screens occupied by Maggie. She peered at them bashfully, seemingly embarrassed about the attention.

'Has Maggie been sleuthing again?' Cherie inquired. 'Do tell, Maggie!'

'There's nothing to tell,' Maggie said modestly. It wasn't like her at all to be so humble.

'But there is,' Michael contradicted. 'Maggie made the connection between Isaac's and Indira Edmunds's rare blood types and the fact that Dr Edmunds knew about that, having operated on Isaac's leg a week earlier. Without that link we would've been none the wiser. It gave Edmunds a clear motive. The opportunity and the means were already there.'

'Clever cookie, our Maggie,' Sam beamed his enthusiasm at her.

Maggie puffed out her cheeks doubtfully and failed to acknowledge the compliment. If Sam wanted an indisputable verification of her poor mental health, he had it. The real Maggie would never miss an opportunity to take full credit for her achievements.

'Does that mean it was Dr Edmunds who attacked Isaac in the cemetery?' James asked.

'It would make sense, wouldn't it? The good doctor luring Isaac to a secluded place – where better than a graveyard! – and injuring him just enough to get him on to an operating table,' Michael said. 'But the police don't have any evidence to prove that Edmunds travelled to Bishops that morning. In fact, he was in hospital, seen by many – patients and colleagues alike. He can't have done that.'

'So it was just a lucky break for him when Isaac landed under his knife?' Maggie suddenly showed some interest.

'It looks like it.'

'So someone else bashed Isaac unconscious and left him to die...' Maggie was thinking aloud. 'This means that the Sexton's gang isn't out of the frame.'

'Gillian is investigating that link,' Michael confirmed.

'She'd better catch them and bring them to justice quickly. Those bastards have beaten up the boy who reported on them – Thomas Moore, my ex-pupil as it happens. They broke his nose, and… Oh God, they may not be finished with him! And I – it was me who told—' Maggie gasped. 'It'll be my fault if anything else happens to him, I will never… His mother will never—' she burst into tears.

Everyone started talking at the same time, trying to calm Maggie down. As much as Sam empathised with her burning guilt for what befell Thomas Moore, he at last achieved a sense of internal calm. He could now understand what had been gnawing at poor Maggie and making her unwell. She had been battling with her guilty conscience. That's it, then, Sam resolved, the wall was coming down and from then on he'd be there by Maggie's side to stop her from doing anything stupid, or dangerous, or as in this case both stupid and dangerous at the same time.

CHAPTER 24

Sam had to venture into Maggie's garden shed to find the sledgehammer. He might as well have travelled into a faraway galaxy. Maggie's shed was like the Tardis – small and unremarkable on the outside but astonishingly capacious within. It was filled with junk, some of it probably dating back to the Great Flood. There was a chance that it had indeed served as the prototype for Noah's Ark.

To get inside, Sam had to remove several items: Maggie's two bicycles (the smaller one still had stabiliser wheels), a manual lawnmower, three watering cans, a foldable workbench with clamps and a spherical barbecue grill with an accompanying bag of charcoal. Once he had created some room to manoeuvre, he swept away thick layers of cobwebs from the shelves which housed a multitude of gardening tools, nails, screws and assorted trappings, some still with their price tags attached. Now he could take a proper look.

'I didn't know I had a funny little table like that,' Maggie, who stood behind him idly, marvelled at the workbench. I could use it, you know, as my outdoor coffee table.'

'And why not. You can clamp teacups to it on windy days,' Sam smirked.

He was beginning to doubt whether Maggie possessed a sledgehammer. He checked all the shelves and found everything, including high precision surgical tools, everything but a sledgehammer.

'You're sure you've got it?' He asked, thinking that it had been a big fat waste of time looking for it and that now he'd have to find a way to shove the voluminous contents of the shed back into it.

'Yes, of course, I am. I have two, in fact. They're hanging on those big butcher's hooks on the back wall, behind that shelf,' she pointed casually.

'Of course, they are!' Sam exclaimed as his eyes followed Maggie's forefinger and rested on the two promised sledgehammers. He cleared his path towards the back of the shed from various items scattered along the way. When he finally reached the back wall he grabbed the bigger of the two sledgehammers and weighed it in his hands. It was heavy and unwieldy, but then it had to be to bring down a wall.

'I'll have the other one,' Maggie requested.

'You don't need one. I can manage on my own.'

'I can help with smaller bits,' she insisted. 'I always wanted to handle one of those big man's tools.'

'If you can lift it, it's yours,' Sam smiled, safe in the knowledge that the weight of the hammer would defeat her. He pulled it off the hook and handed it to her nonchalantly.

Maggie gripped it with both hands and, after an initial shock when her chin followed the sledgehammer on its unavoidable downward trajectory, she heaved it up into the air and waved it from side to side in a slashing motion. The velocity of that move forced her to perform a three-hundred-sixty turn whereupon she stopped and leaned on the handle with a triumphant grin. 'Piece of cake!'

Operation Sledgehammer was to be conducted on Maggie's side of Priest's Hole. Sam warned his mother that soon severe pounding, thudding and tumbling of bricks would be taking place, and advised her to stay out of the dining room until further notice.

'I'll be in my room if you need me,' Deirdre responded. The last thing Sam wanted was for his mother to start interfering and, God forbid, to wander into the midst of the precarious operation with sandwiches and tea.

'You're all right, Mum. Just stay upstairs.'

Maggie had a vague idea of where to strike the wall. 'There,' she pointed. 'I remember that stretch of the wall was the full width of the original dining room. It was open plan, all the way to the chimney breast.'

'Is here okay?' Sam double-checked before executing the first blow. 'There's nothing there? No structural—'

'Nothing at all. Just the new wall, and let me tell you, Samuel, they built it from wooden sticks, pink cotton wool and paper. It'll be child's play, trust me,' Maggie assured him, poised with her own sledgehammer for some action.

Sam stood with his feet wide apart to stabilise himself and took a wide swing. The head of his hammer cut through the wall like a knife through butter. Maggie was right – there was nothing to it. He would have that wall down without breaking sweat.

'Didn't I tell you!' Maggie cheered.

'You did. Now, step back. I wouldn't want to catch you on the head with this thing.'

She did as she was told, dragging her sledgehammer with her.

Sam rolled up his sleeves and, now with more confidence, began thrashing the flimsy structure with all his might. Although the hammer was heavy, he worked out his rhythm and the demolition work proceeded smoothly. The timber frame posts were cracking pleasingly and falling down taking with them the felt filling and membranes. The wall was tumbling down like a house of cards. He was so engrossed in his task that he didn't hear Maggie when she declared her intention to help. What he did hear a few seconds later was an almighty crash, bang and wallop. By the time he realised what was happening, it was too late.

Maggie, the delicate, five-foot-three Maggie, had somehow managed to crack open the side of the chimney breast and dislodge a huge oak beam which came crashing down to the floor and, if that wasn't enough, went right through it. A nasty, unbearable smell emitted from what seemed like an underground well.

'Oh dear,' Maggie pulled a contrite face. 'That wasn't the plan...'

Sam stood paralysed for a few seconds, fearing that the rest of the chimney, the wall and the roof of the house were about to fall down upon them, just as he had once jokingly prophesised. Although that did not happen, Deirdre descended from her bedroom and stood gaping on the other side of the partially demolished chimney.

'What the hell are you two up? The whole house is shaking in its foundations, for—' she started, but then screwed her face and said, 'And what in God's name is this vile stink?'

The odour was indeed unbearable. It filled the room and assaulted their nasal passages, acrid and suffocating like mustard gas.

'That's what's been stinking for weeks now,' Maggie commented, 'whatever it is – down there,' she peered towards the hole in the ground, holding her hand over her nose and mouth. 'It must be that bird stuck in the chimney.'

'What bird?' Sam and Deirdre asked together.

'Remember, Samuel, you said yourself that it had to be a bird trapped in the chimney? Remember? When I heard those scratching – squeaking noises, you said it was probably a bird. It must've died, hence the awful stink. At least now we can check the chimney – since it's been, sort of, opened by accident.'

It was very much like Maggie to see a bright side to the devastation she'd just caused.

'But that smell is coming from under the floor – from that hole,' Sam pointed and came closer to look at Maggie's inadvertent excavation.

He shone his mobile phone torch into it and was astounded to discover a flight of black-stone steps leading into the depths of the hole. 'Blimey, this is man-made. There are stairs down there leading to...' He leant over the edge, but couldn't quite see the bottom step, 'to a deep dungeon.'

Deirdre and Maggie were equally intrigued so they also approached the hole to have a look.

'Mum, please go back to your room. The floor may be unstable. I really don't want you here,' Sam spoke firmly. He would allow no opposition and no argument from his mother. 'Go now! Maggie and I will check this out.'

Deirdre snorted her displeasure, but turned obediently and shuffled away, repeating: 'You know where I am if you need me.'

'Yes, Mum. Off you go.'

'Ordering me around, I never!' her voice travelled gruffly from the hallway.

Maggie was peering over his shoulder. 'It's the long-forgotten priest's hole,' she declared at last. 'That's how this house got its name. It's just that nobody knew where it was.'

CHAPTER 25

Armed with torches and wearing multi-layered facemasks, Maggie and Sam climbed down the black stone steps into what seemed like an abyss. Sam had to tread sideways as the steps were too narrow to accommodate the full length of his size ten trainers. Maggie was right behind him, proceeding gingerly and holding on to his shoulder. She continued to enlighten him about the history of this and other priests' holes in a reverent whisper: '... and from then on Catholics took their worship underground, figuratively and literally. The nobility in particular didn't want to fall out of the king's favour, but not many could bring themselves to renounce their faith so they had those secret tunnels and chapels built. In case of a raid, the priest could hide away and lie low until the uninvited visitors departed.'

Sam knew all of that, and more, but didn't

wish to hurt Maggie's feelings by telling her so. While she babbled away, he reached the bottom of the stairs and stood in awe admiring the chamber. Its walls and ceiling were reinforced with timber joists. The clayish flooring was compressed and hard, having been trodden by many feet when it had been in use. On the wall Sam spotted an oil lamp suspended in a sconce against a circle of well-polished metal which must have acted as a mirror to reflect and distribute light within the vault. The chamber at the bottom of the stairs was approximately fifty square feet. It featured an altar and two rows of pews made of sturdy dark wood and adorned with carvings. A silver chalice stood on the altar and next to it lay a leatherbound Bible.

'Oh my, we've uncovered something very special, Samuel. Cherie will be green with envy.' Maggie blew the dust off the cover of the precious tome, opened it carefully and shone her torch on the page. She attempted to read it. 'It's in Latin.'

'It would be.' Sam peered at the book over Maggie's head. The pages were made of yellowed parchment and the text was beautifully calligraphed. He cast his eyes over the altar, seeking other relics. His attention was caught by a long smudge across the tabletop where dust appeared to have been swept away. He pointed Maggie to his discovery, 'Notice how the dust was disturbed – quite recently, I would say.'

Maggie gazed at it and then at Sam, her

forehead wrinkled with befuddlement. 'That's so curious, Samuel. Someone's been here not so long ago, certainly less than a century. Let's see where this tunnel leads to.'

Indeed, there was a narrow passageway leading away from the chamber. It could accommodate the width of one person but Sam had to walk doubled-up as the ceiling was low. They hadn't covered more than ten yards when they came upon a junction.

'Let's go left,' Sam suggested. 'It looks like this is the main tunnel.'

'We'll have to explore every path,' Maggie said, 'but we can start with this one.'

She took the lead, shining her torch erratically at the walls, the ceiling and occasionally at the ground. She clearly fancied herself as tour guide as she went on with her commentary, 'Priest's Hole dates back to 1645 and that is evident from the plaque over my front door.'

'Yes, you told me about it when I bought the house.'

'But did I tell you about the old rectory?' She didn't wait for an answer, which would have been yes. 'The house stands on its original foundations. The main building was burned down by Roundheads during the Civil War. Funnily enough, by the time they were finished with it only the central chimney breast remained standing. And that explains why the underground chapel and this network of tunnels remained hidden after the estate was rebuilt in 1849.'

'And it would've stayed secret had it not been for an adventurous little lady with a sledgehammer,' Sam jested.

'You see?' Maggie chimed. 'I have my uses.'

Joking and laughing, they reached the end of the tunnel. They came to another stairwell, but this one was obscured by rubble. Towards the top it was blocked. They started clearing away the debris, Sam was carefully loosening and removing stones, and passing them to Maggie who stood at the bottom of the stairwell. She threw them on a pile at her feet. Soon however, they could see that there was no way out. Sam hit a concrete slab that had been laid across the exit. It wasn't budging.

'It's sealed,' he told Maggie.

'I wonder where we are in relation to the house.'

'We've travelled at least three hundred yards north-west. We could be under the road—'

'Church Lane?'

'Yes,' he scratched his chin, calculating the distance in his head, 'or maybe even beneath the foundations of Howard Jacobsen's house.'

'We haven't got the tools to burrow our way out of here,' Maggie pondered, 'though the sledgehammers could come in handy...'

'Are you proposing we smash through Mr

Jacobsen's kitchen floor?' Sam half-believed she was serious.

'Maybe not. Let's go back and see where the other tunnel takes us.'

Upon reaching the junction they took a sharp turn to the left. This passageway was tighter but neater. The walls were made of brick and the ceiling was arched. This had to be the original tunnel, whilst the other must have been added hurriedly and untidily later on.

The unpleasant stench intensified as they navigated deeper along this passage. Sam felt disoriented. His first thought had been that this tunnel led to the church, but now he wasn't sure. The darkness and oppressive narrowness of the walls disoriented him. The odour compounded the sense of being lost and the shortness of breath.

Maggie didn't seem to suffer so much. She continued ahead towards a feeble shaft of light. 'Look Samuel, another tunnel! It's very small. I could crawl through it to see where it goes.'

'Wait!' Sam picked up pace to firstly assess the risks, but Maggie was already gone.

She fell onto her knees and wriggled her body as she slipped into the hole. Sam shone his torch after her to see her slither like a snake. 'It'd better not cave in on you,' he shouted an empty warning.

'It links to the well in the cemetery!' Maggie's voice was distant and muffled. 'It's only a small opening. I found a bucket on a rope. Pretty much disintegrated, but I think it was used to draw water from the well. One could spend days and weeks in here with access to fresh water!'

'Great! Now, come back here, please!'

Maggie scrambled backwards. She was puffing by the time she stood before Sam in her full, soil-dusted glory, but there was a grin of excitement on her face – a sight Sam had been missing badly in recent days.

'Shall we continue?' she asked.

'After you.' Sam executed a polite bow and gestured for her to lead the way.

The tunnel went at a slight gradient and their shoes squelched in oily-black mud, but soon it became elevated again. They encountered a step and above it a heavy oak door.

'The dreadful stink comes from behind there,' Maggie guessed, and Sam had to agree. It had intensified as they drew closer to it.

'Should we go in or wait for an expert to fumigate whatever lies behind that door? It could be Black Death for all we know,' Sam suggested. He wasn't entirely joking.

'Don't be such a wuss, Samuel! Pull up your mask and breathe through your mouth. You won't smell it.'

They pushed the door open. In fact, it was already slightly ajar so it took only a small nudge from Sam's shoulder for it to move. It screeched with the vengeance of unoiled hinges.

'That's the noise I heard in the night,' Maggie commented. 'It was muted but that was the same sound. My first thought was that someone, or rather an animal, wailed in the night. When you said it could've been a bird in the chimney, it made sense, but now I'm sure it was this door. Someone was here four weeks ago, and I can't imagine it would've been an animal. If it was, it would have to be a big one, and then, how would it have got here? Through the well shaft?'

'Well, let's go in and find out. Maybe there is an entrance on the other side of the door.'

They stepped in and shone their phone torches. Stone sarcophagi stood on the floor in still silence, and aged wood coffins sat on arched shelves carved into the walls. Unlike in the tunnel, the floor in this vault was made of limestone tiles.

'We're in St John's crypt,' Maggie declared. 'It's been ages since I was here last – I was a small girl – but I remember it like it was only yesterday. Me and Andrea were helping Grandpa Bernie in the church. We were putting out psalters in the pews before the service. He must've popped out for a minute. We finished the job and sat there bored. Then we climbed up to the organ to play a few notes, but didn't know how to operate it, so we came down and started sniffing around behind the altar. That's when we found the door to the crypt. We knew it led to where the dead were kept in coffins, especially the nobility and the benefactors of the church – Grandpa Bernie had told us all about it. And we also knew not to go there. So we did. And we got trapped. We were absolutely mortified. We screamed for help, kicked and scratched the bloody door but it wouldn't shift. God, I had nightmares for months after that.

'It's a funny door, you see,' Maggie was just getting into the swing of her story. 'It has a handle on one side but not on the other. I suppose nobody expects the dead to walk out of here so they don't need a handle.' She paused and pointed, 'That's the pesky door— Oh my God!' Maggie screamed, held her chest and took a few steps backwards. Her torchlight was quavering over the step at the foot of the handle-less door. There, huddled in a foetal position, lay a human corpse.

It was instantly obvious that this was someone who had died recently. The figure was dressed in contemporary clothes: black corduroy trousers and a light-cream puffer jacket. Next to it lay a colourful scarf with exotic orange, brown and yellow patterns. Sam had an idea who it belonged to.

He crouched next to the body and examined the face. It was indeed Daisy Rotich.

CHAPTER 26

Daisy was clutching a mobile phone in her hand, pressing it to her ear. She must have been desperate to call for help. Alas, there was no telephone reception in the crypt. From the moment Daisy Rotich had become trapped in the vault, she was as good as dead.

Maggie and Sam were also unable to make a call from where they stood and had to return to Priest's Hole to find a signal. Neither of them stayed with the body. Daisy Rotich wasn't going anywhere.

They hurried through the tunnel and climbed out of the chimney rubble on Sam's side.

'I'll call Alec Scarfe,' Sam decided. It had become quite customary now to treat Alec as their first point of contact whenever they found a dead body.

He answered instantly, 'Sam, my man! Good to hear from you. How are things?'

'Not very good, I'm afraid.'

'Oh don't tell me – let me guess: you found a body.' Scarfe gave a dry chuckle followed by a cough.

'You all right, Alec?'

'Yes. I just choked. It's not Covid if that's what you were thinking. So, what can I do for you?'

'Well, we did find a corpse, actually – in St John's crypt.'

A long, baffled silence answered him.

'Alec?'

'I can't believe it! You aren't joking?'

'No. I wish we were.'

'Hang on, do you mean to say you found a corpse in a crypt where corpses are supposed to be kept?'

'Not that kind of a corpse.'

'What kind then, for pity's sake!'

'The kind that wasn't put in a coffin with all the trimmings of a proper burial. The kind that got there by accident, or by evil design. That kind,' Sam elaborated.

'How do you know?'

'It's Daisy Rotich, our guest who went missing from Badger's Hall.'

'Your B&B?'

'That's the one.'

'How come it's always you?' Scarfe sighed after a moment of reflection.

'We were just doing some home improvements when one side of the chimney caved in, and we discovered a tunnel. It led us to the body.'

'I can't get my head around the fact that it's always the two of you... Oh, never mind. I'm sure you're telling the truth – you have a blinking corpse under your chimney. Daisy Rotich, you say?'

'It's definitely her.'

'I will send DCI Marsh. She'll organise a CSI team. I won't be there. Only the critical officers these days – Covid restriction, and all.'

'Thanks Alec. Apologies for calling you rather than the station. I hope I didn't mess up your day.'

'It's not the first time, is it? I'm used to it. And anyway, you found our missing person.'

Deirdre heard the telephone conversation – at least, Sam's side of it – from upstairs. She had listened to it on the landing and, as soon as Sam rang off, came down to find out more. Maggie was only too happy to oblige.

'Why don't we put the kettle on while you tell me all about it,' Deirdre suggested, 'and we could have sandwiches too. It's lunchtime, as it happens. But, if you don't mind my saying, you two stink to high heaven. Go and wash, change your clothes, and I'll make the sandwiches. We'll have them out in the garden. This whole house reeks of dead people.'

They reconvened on Sam's patio. The day

was hot and the air still, but the whiff of death somehow managed to travel outdoors. The aroma of freshly brewed tea was fighting a losing battle against it. Nobody seemed to have much appetite.

Maggie and Sam, between them, described to Deirdre how they had come upon Daisy's body.

'My theory is,' Maggie speculated, 'that she came here sightseeing – after all St John's is a grade-one listed building well worth a visit – and she followed the signposts, explored the cemetery and the church, and strayed into the vault. There was no one around, what with the lockdown coming on the following Monday... Everyone was doing last minute shopping, including the vicar and his wife. Daisy was the only soul inside the church. The door shut behind her. No way she could open it from within, couldn't use her phone to call for help, and ultimately couldn't get out of there any other way.'

'She must have gone up and down the tunnels,' Sam added. 'We discovered that the dust on the altar beneath Priest's Hole had been disturbed. She must've been there, looking for escape routes.'

'That explains the scratching and shrieking noises I was hearing,' Maggie said. 'Poor thing was trying to get out.'

The arrival of the police and forensic vehicles interrupted their conversation. They heard scrunching of the gravel on the driveway, followed by an energetic knock on the door.

DCI Gillian Marsh was standing on the front step flanked by her crime scene investigation team. Despite his head-to-toe protective clothing, Michael Almond, the forensic pathologist, was instantly recognisable because of his slim and square, six-foot frame. His moustache was doing its best to peer from beneath his facemask. There was also the forensic scientist Bobby Hughes, known to Sam from previous *incidents*, and three men – or women – of his team. It was hard to tell people's gender due to their comprehensive body coverage. DC Whittaker was gazing at Sam from behind the small crowd and gave him a curt nod when Sam's eyes halted on him. For once, his impressively large nose was not in evidence as it was covered by his facemask.

'Okay,' said detective Marsh, 'can you lead us to the body.' As usual, there was no *please* and no *thank you* to go with her request. In fact, it wasn't even a request.

'This way,' Maggie called from behind Sam. She clearly wasn't planning to be left out of this investigation.

They all proceeded to the excavation by the side of the chimney, and one by one (as the tunnel was narrow) descended into it, Maggie leading the way, Sam her second in command. Together they recounted how they had come to find the body, and Maggie shared her theory about how Daisy may have become trapped.

'It was probably a tragic accident,' she concluded.

Once at the scene, the CSI team dispersed around the crypt, getting on with their specialised tasks. A small generator and halogen lamps were installed. The whole chamber basked in bright light.

Maggie and Sam were instructed by Marsh to leave. 'We'll take it from here,' she said. 'The less scene contamination the better.'

Maggie pulled Sam's sleeve and when he leant towards her, whispered, 'Let's just stand quietly at the back and listen. It won't do any harm.'

So they stealthily backed into the shadows and virtually blended with the background, eavesdropping, observing and taking mental notes of the forensic findings.

Michael Almond was busying himself examining the body. Every now and again, he would point to an area on the body and ask the photographer to take a picture. Despite the bright lights, his camera would flash. Detective Marsh squatted next to Michael and began interrogating him.

'So, what's the verdict?'

'Do you always have to do that?' Michael asked. 'Can't you wait for the *post mortem*, like everyone else?'

'You know I can't. What did she die of?'

'It could be one of two possibilities, but that's just at first sight. I haven't even turned or moved the body yet. I don't know what I'll find when I open it up and carry out toxicology tests.'

'Yeah, I know all that. So, what's the verdict – at first sight.'

'It could be terminal dehydration. She would have fallen into unconsciousness after a week, maybe ten days, depending on her general health. Or it could be something else,' Michael shifted on his knees and gestured DCI Marsh to slip into the space he vacated. He pointed something out to her, 'Can you see this here?'

'That's quite some nasty gash,' she observed.

'Yes, this close to the temple it could be lethal, or at least, she would've been rendered unconscious, depending on the velocity of the blow. Judging by the swelling, it was powerful. A blunt instrument.'

'Would it have been a deliberate blow to her head?'

'I can't tell you that, Gillian. It could've been a blow, or she could've tripped, fell and hit her head on the step here or the stone floor, or any of those tombs.' He swept his arm over the interior of the vault. 'We'll see what Bobby's team brings to the table. Plus, I need to examine her skull, and the rest of her.'

'So it could've been an accident or an assault?'

'You tell me.'

'How long has she been dead?'

'Three to five weeks.'

'That's a wide range!'

'Like I said, the body has begun to decompose but one has to take into account the unique ecology of this vault. It's been sealed, I understand, until Maggie and Sam got here. The temperature, as well as the saturation and oxygen levels of the air here would've been entirely different from above ground. These small variations will make a difference to the speed of decomposition. Think of the Catacombs of Paris – in some cases human remains have been well preserved thanks to—'

'Yes, whatever you say,' Marsh interrupted Michael's scientific expose which Sam was finding rather interesting. 'I need facts about this particular body. Are we doing the PM today?'

'Tomorrow morning.'

'Today,' she insisted.

Sam's thoughts were still on the matter of the sealed vault. Something had been overlooked. He felt compelled to speak out, 'This vault would've first been opened when Daisy Rotich entered it, don't you think, DCI Marsh? So the balance of oxygen and all those humidity levels and so on that Michael is talking about may have been disturbed then for the first time, not when me and Maggie got here.'

'Good thinking, Samuel,' Maggie chipped in.

'And she would've entered the crypt through that door,' she pointed, 'There was no other way.'

'How do you know that?' Marsh asked.

'We checked. The only other tunnel is sealed and the way we entered... well, let's just say that our floor was in one piece at the time of Daisy's death,' Maggie explained. 'And that door,' she gestured towards it, 'opens behind the altar in the church. The funny thing about it is that you can't open it from inside the vault – there is no handle.'

Gillian Marsh frowned but nodded, reluctantly verifying the absence of a door handle.

'But there is one, of course, on the other side. So, you see,' Maggie cocked her head and wrinkled her brow in a know-all fashion, 'the simple conclusion is that Miss Rotich was admiring the church, ventured into the crypt and the door shut behind her. She got trapped and no one could hear her cries for help. Apart from me, that is.'

'You heard her calling for help? Why didn't you do anything?' the detective's eyes widened in disbelief.

'Because I thought it was a bird stuck in the chimney,' Maggie spoke ruefully.

'Crying for help?'

'It was muffled, and it was more like scratching and creaking,' Sam stepped in to defend his fiancé. 'There were no articulate cries for help, not as such. Maggie mentioned it to me and I suggested a trapped bird. We didn't have reason to suspect anything else.'

'The scratching makes sense,' Michael said. 'Her nails are broken, the fingertips bloodied, and splinters under her skin. It's indicative of her scraping the door with her bare hands.' He lifted his gaze towards it. 'Look here – scratch marks.'

Indeed, four-fingered grooves around the keyhole testified to Daisy's tragic efforts to free herself.

'How come nobody heard her cries in the church? There's a keyhole – she would've shouted through it, her voice would've carried,' Marsh wondered.

'Except that due to lockdown the church was locked – no services were held, no parishioners came to pray, nobody was there to hear her calling out,' Sam explained.

'OK, let's have a look at that door from the other side,' DCI Marsh decided. 'Whittaker, go and get that door opened.'

'You'll need to get the vicar to open the church for you,' Sam said.

Maggie and Sam accompanied DC Whittaker to the vicarage, not because he needed or requested their assistance but because DCI Marsh instructed him to *escort Miss Kaye and Mr Dee from my crime scene while you're at it*. Staying at home once expelled from DCI Marsh's crime scene was naturally not on Maggie's agenda.

CHAPTER 27

Maggie's Journal

I showed DC Whittaker the shortcut to the vicarage through my garden gate. He, Samuel and I speculated about the tunnel running somewhere below our feet. Interestingly, we noticed that there was an overgrown ancient footpath made of cracked slabs which, by our estimates, mirrored the tunnel on the ground. It may have been created on purpose so that no burial slots would have been allocated immediately above the tunnel. It made perfect sense.

As we went past the well, I saw Isaac Wotton in a state of agitation. It isn't natural for the spirits to show emotion – they usually act as if they don't give two hoots about what goes on in the world of the living. Yet, I know they care, otherwise they wouldn't be here. Isaac's agitation was evident in his circling of the well at speed. It looked as if he had mounted an invisible carousel and was swept in its round-and-round trajectory. Was he trying to tell me something? Was this his way of saying that his and Daisy Rotich's deaths were connected? If only he could tell me how!

'There is a passageway between the tunnel and the well,' I informed DC Whittaker. 'I think it may be important.'

'What makes you think that, madam?'

'Please don't call me madam, detective. I really hate it. Call me Maggie, or if that's too familiar, Miss Kaye will be fine.'

'Okay, Miss Kaye, point taken. So, why do you think that well is pertinent to our investigation?'

Of course, I couldn't tell him that Isaac Wotton was zooming above it like a man possessed, so I said, 'I don't know why. I just do know it's important and you ought to look into it.'

DC Whittaker sent a quizzical look to Samuel who raised his brows and rounded his lips in an act of deep concentration. At last he said, 'Well, it's yet another way into the crypt, though admittedly it's unlikely Miss Rotich used it. First, she'd have to negotiate the slippery walls of the well and then squeeze herself into the narrow hole. Why would she do that? And besides how would she know about the existence of that passageway?'

'And if she used it to get in, why didn't she use it to get out?' I added, and only afterwards thought that my comment didn't quite support my request for the police to give the well due consideration. I could kick myself for sabotaging my own theories.

To my surprise, DC Whittaker said, 'Thank you for telling me about it. We take every piece of information seriously. Sometimes we don't know how it will fit in with our inquires, but with time the most unlikely reports start making sense and everything falls into place. I'll pass it onto DCI Marsh. We'll look deep into the well, I'm sure.' He gave me a wink. Based on that pun, I was no longer certain that he'd taken the matter of the well seriously enough.

We reached the vicarage. The detective rang the bell. A short minute later, the mahogany face of Quentin Magnebu and his wide smile appeared in the doorway.

'DC Whittaker, I believe? What brings you to Bishops Well, officer – duty or pleasure?'

'Good evening, sir. I'm afraid, the former.' The policeman said. 'We need your assistance with accessing the church, please.'

'No problem. I'll fetch the key.'

Leanne Magnebu shouted from within, 'Who's that, Quentin?'

'It's the police, dear! Grab the church key! They need to get inside.' The Vicar bellowed over his shoulder. He then turned his attention back to DC Whittaker, and asked, 'May I inquire what you're looking for in my church? Is it something to do with Isaac Wotton?'

'Potentially,' said I.

DC Whittaker contradicted me: 'No, it's unrelated to that case. Unfortunately, a body was found in the crypt. We believe the deceased accessed the crypt via the church and became trapped. We need to check that theory.'

'Dear Lord! A dead person? A real dead person? Not a buried person, you mean?' The vicar bumbled and stared at the detective, trying to process his words.

'Yes, sir. A real dead person who has no business to be there, or to be dead.' It was an interesting way of putting it, I thought, but DC Whittaker hit the nail on its head. Indeed, Daisy Rotich had no business being dead.

Leanne brought the keys and handed them to Quentin.

'They found a body in the crypt...' he whispered as if afraid to wake the dead.

She just gaped at him, then at us, without a word.

'Let's go,' I prompted them.

Quentin Magnebu, being a big man with long limbs, hurried to the church in long strides, forcing the rest of us into a jog. He unlocked the church door and we all poured in. It was already late evening – I didn't know where the hours had gone. We had discovered the body in the morning. It felt like only a few minutes ago. The interior of the church was shrouded in utter darkness.

'I'll turn on the lights,' Leanne offered and felt the wall to the left for the switch.

The Vicar strode on in the dark. He knew the topography of his church by heart and didn't need the light to find his way. Soon the church was fully illuminated and we could all see where we were going. We caught up with the Vicar behind the altar. He waited for us before opening the door to the crypt.

'Is there a separate key to this door?' DC Whittaker inquired.

'No… I mean, I'm not aware of any key,' said Vicar Quentin. 'There's a keyhole but I've never seen a key that'd go in it. Have you, Leanne?'

'A key? No, no key,' she mumbled anxiously. She looked pale and worried. She was probably mortified over what lay beyond that door, as would anyone.

'Yes, that's right. We were never given a key. The door is always unlocked.'

'But you can only open it from this side,' I clarified.

'That's correct, Miss Kaye,' the Vicar confirmed. 'There's no handle on the other side, as you probably know. Shall I do it?' Reaching for the handle, he asked DC Whittaker.

'No, sir. Don't touch it. We must preserve fingerprints if there are any.'

The detective was wearing gloves. He stepped forward, pressed his ear against the panel of the door, and shouted through it, 'Step back! We are coming in!' Then he squeezed the handle. The door swung open into the crypt.

'There is a latch on the wall behind it,' Leanne spoke from the back of our small group. 'You can hook it to the door and it'll stay open.'

'If only Daisy Rotich had known that!' I sighed.

'Who?' Quentin asked.

'We haven't confirmed that's her name yet. The deceased has not been formally identified at this stage,' DC Whittaker shot me a scolding look.

Quentin pushed by him and charged into the vault. DCI Marsh hollered from within, 'Stay away from the crime scene, sir! Whittaker, get him the hell out of here!'

Whittaker didn't need to take any action for the vicar shot back out as quickly as he had entered. He stumbled backwards, the heel of his foot caught on the raised threshold and he fell on his back. Released, the door promptly shut in his face.

Marsh's voice could be heard at the top of its vocal range, 'Open that door! Whittaker!'

While DC Gary Whittaker followed his superior's order, and also put the door on the latch to keep it ajar, Samuel and I helped Vicar Quentin to his feet and escorted him to a pew where his wife was already seated.

'Are you hurt, Vicar?' I asked and peered into his eyes. They were rounded with shock and as black as soot. It seemed as if his pupils had spilled into his irises. His mouth was moving but at first he did not utter any intelligible sounds.

He slumped in the pew and hunched, holding his stomach and retching as if he were about to throw up.

'Oh my God, my God,' he began to chant. 'My dear, dear God!' He raised his eyes to his wife. 'Leanne? My dear, dear God... Oh God!'

Leanne clutched her chest, her fingers digging into the lapels of her crisp linen dress. She was shaking her head mutely, her lips pursed white and her brows knitted in a scowl.

'Poor Vicar,' Samuel said. 'The shock has knocked him for six. Should we help you take him back to the vicarage? He could do with some brandy or sweet tea.'

Leanne only gawked at him.

'God help me,' Quentin was muttering.

It was then that Daisy joined us. As they do, she floated from nowhere and stood still by the altar, seemingly indifferent to all the sudden activity. She was young, at least twenty years younger than when she died. That was normal, too. They do like to travel down memory lane to their happier, younger, more beautiful days.

She was wearing traditional African attire: an elaborately folded head scarf, a bit like a turban. It was teeming with colours: oranges, browns and vivid yellows. It reminded me of the scarf we found lying by her side in the crypt. Her dress too was opulent with rich African themes and hues. She looked radiant and strikingly beautiful: chiselled cheekbones, large eyes and a statuesque figure.

Watching her poised by the altar, it occurred to me that it had indeed been Daisy Rotich's ghost that I had seen cross the church aisle the other day. I had convinced myself that it was a shadow – a trick of light – but it was Daisy moored to the place where she had met her end. She had been here all along, waiting to be found.

CHAPTER 28

The cuckoo clock in Maggie's sitting room declared that it was eight o'clock in the evening. The koo-koo sound echoed through Priest's Hole and was picked up by Deirdre who said, 'Look at the time! You're in luck, the pair of you. I kept your dinner in the oven. Sit down, I'll bring it to the table.'

Sam and Maggie didn't object to being waited upon. They were exhausted after a day of hard labour, contorting their bodies through the underground tunnels and enduring the emotional stress of finding Daisy Rotich. They were also famished, their last meal being the untouched sandwiches at lunchtime. They slumped over the dining table and gawped at each other without the need for words. It had been quite a day.

Deirdre arrived carrying two plates piled with steaming-hot food. 'Steak pie, root veg and gravy,' she announced. They dug in and she knew better than to interrogate them while they were eating. Curious as she was, she sat silently with them, watching as they devoured her homemade pies and peered at her with eyes narrowed with ecstatic pleasure.

Alas, not everyone was as tactful as Deirdre Dee. There was a knock on the door.

'At this hour?' Deirdre observed, nonplussed. 'Keep eating. I'll see who it is, and remind them their manners.'

She hobbled away and in no time returned with DC Whittaker and a uniformed policewoman in tow.

'The police,' she announced unnecessarily.

DC Whittaker smiled apologetically. 'I'm sorry to disturb, but I need to take your fingerprints. It's for elimination purposes only.'

'That's fine,' Sam said. 'Do you want us to come to the station? Is tomorrow okay?'

'No need for travel. PC de Witt here,' he gestured to his female colleague, 'has a portable fingerprinting scanner. She can take your prints here and now, no trouble.'

PC de Witt offered them a reassuring nod and presented a simple device, a little larger than a mobile phone but smaller than a laptop. 'You don't even have to dip your fingers in ink,' she smiled. She was a voluptuous lady with long chestnut hair kept neat and tidy in a pony tail. In her early forties and with her large, kind eyes she somehow didn't fit the image of an active member of the police force – or any force for that matter.

Sam and Maggie took turns to offer their fingertips for scanning. When that operation was completed, DC Whittaker informed them of the progress at the crime scene: 'Unfortunately, further injuries were found on the body which exclude the possibility of an accidental death. We're now treating the death as murder.'

'Oh dear!' Maggie bristled with curiosity. 'What further injuries?'

'We found two gashes on the back of the head. The victim can't have accidentally tripped and fallen twice to hit her head in two different places. There isn't enough blood where we – you – found the body so the assault took place somewhere else, before she entered – or was moved to – the crypt.'

'But she was alive in the crypt – she navigated the tunnels. I mean, she certainly made it to the chapel below our house,' Sam argued.

'She may've been stunned at first, then came to and started wandering about the tunnels, looking for a way out. Anyway, I don't want to get into the ins and outs of this case, and I'm not discussing it with you,' DC Whittaker made a sudden disclaimer, realising that he'd already said too much, 'but I'm telling you this because PC de Witt and I need to seal the access to the tunnel from your house, and I must instruct you not to tamper with it or enter the crime scene under any circumstances—'

'As if we would!' Deirdre expressed her indignation at the very idea of any of them interfering with the police investigation. Alas, she didn't know Maggie as well as Sam did.

'I'm glad to hear that, madam,' DC Whittaker was unruffled by Deirdre's tone. 'Secondly,' he added, 'just a polite notice that our forensic team will be working through the best part of the night around the church, so there may be some disturbance and light pollution. We apologise for that.'

'That's fine. Thank you for letting us know, detective,' Sam nodded.

'Thank you for your understanding. Could we now secure the entrance to the tunnel?'

'Go ahead. You know where it is.'

'We'll just get something from the van to fix over the hole.'

The officers left. Maggie and Sam returned to their pies. Within minutes, the detectives were back carrying a metal floor plate. They placed it over the excavation by the chimney. 'That should do it,' DC Whittaker wiped his hands. 'We'll bid you goodnight and, again, thank you for your cooperation.'

After dinner, Sam mustered the courage to ask Maggie to stay overnight. 'Since we now have a single household bubble,' he started after Deirdre left the room, 'you may as well sleep with… at mine… with me… I mean, it's been a while.'

'A long while,' Maggie agreed.

'And you may not be safe on your own.'

'I definitely may not,' she grinned. 'I'll go and have a quick shower and fetch my PJs.'

When Sam frowned at the idea of pyjamas, she added, 'We have to maintain some decency in front of your mother.'

Having Maggie in his arms after such a long period of celibacy enforced by the lockdown felt like seventh heaven. The warmth of her body and the softness of her curves relaxed his muscles and rendered him utterly and satisfyingly knackered. Sam was ready to pass out, but Maggie wanted to talk.

She scrambled out of bed and stood by the window. The moonlight had been eclipsed by the halogen lamps blazing in the churchyard. The chapel was ablaze with night-dispelling brightness. From time to time, the fluttering figurine of a disoriented Bechstein's bat swooped through the air. The lamps were swarmed by a tiny confetti of moths attracted to the light. The whole night was awake and buzzing with unnatural activity.

'He's there,' Maggie told Sam. 'Isaac is still there.'

'Well, he would be. You always tell me they stick around until they're ready to go on their own terms.'

'True. We don't have his killer, Samuel. It isn't Dr Edmunds, I am sure of that. And I'm sure that Isaac's death is connected to Daisy's.'

Although his head was splitting in half with a tension headache, Sam gave the matter a little thought. He said, 'From what DC Whittaker was saying, it looks like Daisy was attacked outside the crypt – perhaps in the cemetery. Maybe it was Isaac who attacked her?'

Maggie crinkled her forehead in disagreement, 'No, it can't have been. It wouldn't make sense. I think he knew who attacked Daisy – he probably witnessed it. He spent a lot of time in the graveyard – he practically lived at the back of my garden so he may've seen the killer.'

'And he may have threatened to talk. Three days later he was lured to the cemetery and bludgeoned across his head with that vase. There are a few similarities with Daisy Rotich, too,' Sam observed.

'Was it someone from that gang, do you think?' Maggie tilted her head doubtfully. 'Isaac may've been in cahoots with them to start with, and then changed his mind and...' She paused and scratched her head, murmuring something under her breath. She shook her head, 'No, I doubt it. These deaths have nothing to do with the Sexton's gang.'

'Absolutely nothing,' Sam confirmed. 'They would've taken Daisy's mobile phone. That's what they do.'

'Precisely! Great minds think alike,' Maggie beamed.

'Can we leave the rest of the thinking until tomorrow?' Sam pleaded and patted the sheets next to him, 'Come to bed.'

CHAPTER 29

Maggie's Journal

We woke up late the next morning. We had missed our early morning power-walk, but didn't mind that one bit considering the amount of exercise we had done the previous day, and in the night. We lingered in bed, chatting about inconsequential subjects, such as jumping into our hot tub later today and making a shopping list for our next joint trip to Sexton's Canning supermarket. Living in the same household bubble was going to be a blast, as long as the bubble didn't burst.

We emerged into the daylight with a few minutes to spare before noon. Deirdre had already begun lunch preparations, so we settled for buttered crumpets with a nice cup of coffee. We sat on Sam's patio, gazing idly at the busy insects hovering and buzzing noisily over his overgrown garden.

'I'll have to do something about your weeds,' I told him.

'And I'll have to do something about knocking down the fence between our gardens,' he said.

We peered at each other with eyes filled with joyous anticipation of our life together.

Out of nowhere, Gillian Marsh's face appeared over the wall. I nearly fell off my chair with shock. Having Ms Marsh swoop on you in the middle of your brunch could easily result in choking to death. I coughed out a piece of crumpet that I had breathed in when I gasped.

'Detective! What are you doing in our—' I didn't finish. Technically speaking she wasn't in our garden – she was in the graveyard.

'I have Mr Jackson with me – Miss Rotich's fiancé. He came earlier today to identify the body,' she replied without any ceremony. 'He'll be going back to London but he asked if he could meet the two of you. Don't ask me why. I don't know. I told him I'd ask.'

'I don't see why not,' Samuel answered. I was still working on regaining my breath. 'Is he here with you?'

'He's in the cemetery, stretching his legs.'

'Why don't we come out and meet him there?'

'Why don't you,' she concluded drily.

Mr Jackson was a man in his late fifties, some fifteen, maybe twenty years older than Miss Rotich. He had a long, concave torso, stooped shoulders and a tanned, weather-beaten complexion that testified to many years spent living in the tropics. His hair was white with a few straw-blond highlights hinting at its original colour. He wore horn-rimmed bifocals and kept pushing them up to the bridge of his nose with his middle finger which I found slightly perverse.

Gillian Marsh made curt introductions and informed us that she had to go. 'The investigation can't wait,' she explained. 'Have a safe trip back to London when you're finished here.' It was the best she could achieve by way of being polite. I was beginning to warm to her.

'Thank you, DCI Marsh. Please keep me posted,' Mr Jackson called after her.

'When I have something, you'll be the first to know,' she spoke over her shoulder.

The bereaved man turned his attention to us. When I took a closer look into his eyes, I could see the raw grief. Red veins had formed a net over the whites of his eyeballs. His skin was crumpled as if it too had suffered in its own right from many sleepless nights.

'I'm very sorry about your fiancé,' Samuel offered his condolences.

'We knew her for a very short time, but she came across as such a lovely lady – easy to talk to,' I added.

It felt awkward standing there, exchanging these words and not being able to at least shake his hand, but we had to maintain the prescribed two-metre distance.

'Thank you. Thank you, both,' he replied. He had a posh, clipped accent, the sort of accent the upper classes brandished in the fifties. He had been brought up in Kenya, I gathered.

'May I ask, if you can remember, what Daisy said to you? She was a chatterbox,' a faint smile quivered on his lips, 'but did she say why she... Did she say anything of note? What I'm trying to say – I just want to understand why in God's name... I—' his voice wobbled and came to a standstill.

'Yes, I see,' I helped him. 'She did say something that made me think. That morning – it was the Saturday before lockdown began – she said she had something to attend to. It didn't strike me as a place to visit or a monument to see, but rather,' I paused to think of a best way of expressing it, 'well, I think she had something planned – pre-arranged, like seeing someone. Someone she had specifically come here for.'

He nodded slowly, pensively. 'That was my impression, too. She was bored, I thought. I was extremely busy in my new school, meeting the governors and the staff, and she was on her own.

I suggested keeping herself occupied, something like sightseeing, but it never occurred to me that she'd travel hundreds of miles to the West Country. I meant shopping or popping over to the Tower of London. But Daisy... She must've been thinking of coming here, to this county – this particular town... She bought a ticket to Sexton's Canning. Not Salisbury, or Bath, but Sexton's Canning of all places. There's nothing there.'

'Sexton's Canning is our closest train station,' Samuel observed.

'Yes, I checked. Ever since she went missing, I've been wondering why here.'

'Unfortunately, she didn't tell us. In fact, she gave the impression that she was quite interested in sightseeing. She wanted to know about local attractions, I seem to recall.' I remembered blabbering to her about our Early Celt museum, our pride and joy, and the Stone Circle, and every other bit of Bishops' history, but now, on reflection, I wasn't sure that she had asked for it.

'She was just polite, Maggie,' Samuel was at pains to put my words into perspective. 'She listened to you, but perhaps it was good manners, not interest in local folklore. I had the feeling that she had come to Bishops with a specific objective in mind.'

'Yes, Samuel is right. She wasn't a tourist.'

'I wish I knew what brought her here,' Mr

Jackson sighed. 'Never mind, I'll probably never find out. So, you found Daisy—' his voice faltered a fraction, but he pulled himself together, 'you found Daisy's body?'

'By sheer coincidence. We knocked down a wall in our house,' Samuel gestured towards Priest's Hole, 'and the floor caved in. We found her in the crypt under the church.'

We all gazed at St John's. The entrance was draped with police tape, but then so was the courtyard and sections of the graveyard.

'Do you think it'd be appropriate if I had a look inside the church?' Mr Jackson asked.

I didn't see why not. It wasn't our place to guard the church. If DCI Marsh wanted to keep visitors away, she would have posted a uniformed officer at the door. The forensic sweep of the whole area had been going on through the night and concluded in the morning. The men in boiler suits had left with all the evidence that was to be found.

My eyes flitted towards the well – it hadn't been cordoned off. I would bet that DC Whittaker had not taken me seriously when I raised its significance with him. Oh well, his loss … I was disappointed, to tell the truth. And so was Isaac. I could sense his agitation. He was meandering restlessly around the cursed well.

'We can try. It may be locked,' Samuel answered Mr Jackson's question while I was miles away.

We headed for the church and ducked under the police tape. Surprisingly, the door wasn't locked. We entered. There was still a faint whiff of decomposition in the nave, but it could well be mistaken for the musky, damp air typical of old churches. The interior was illuminated by the late morning sunlight pouring through the arched windows. It filtered through the stained-glass panels of the south elevation, splitting into primary colours that splashed in dappled patches on the floor.

'So this is where Daisy met her end?' Mr Jackson spoke softly.

Neither Samuel or I had an answer to that. We walked silently towards the front of the church.

'Was she a religious woman?' I asked, remembering her amulet.

'Not in the conventional – Christian – sense of the word,' Mr Jackson replied. 'What I mean to say is that she wouldn't have come here for spiritual reasons.'

'She was a pagan?'

'Well, she was a follower of ancient, native-African traditions.'

'We found her amulet. Did the police give it to you with her belongings?'

'No, they've kept it. They're not sure if it's of any significance. Apparently you have some occult sect operating here, with links to the church.'

'Nah,' I rolled my eyes. 'Someone should've told them, really – there're no Satanists here, just a well-meaning lady keeping Death at bay.'

Mr Jackson peered at me quizzically.

'So the amulet wasn't the reason she came here,' Sam observed.

'I can't imagine it would've been. You see, Daisy and I aren't – weren't – in the first spring of youth, but Daisy was keen to have children. She loves – loved – children. She was given that necklace by her tribe's witch doctor. It's was to boost her fertility.'

A figure was slumped in the west nave. It was Vicar Quentin. He was on his knees, deep in prayer. He had lit a candle. It was the only candle. Its flame flickered feebly.

'That's the vicar,' Samuel whispered to Mr Jackson.

Quentin heard that. His bowed head jolted out of his reverie and his eyes darted towards us. He didn't look his usual upbeat self. He wore the same clothes as yesterday. I had the distinct impression that he did not sleep last night. Discovering a murder had been committed in his church must have shaken him to the core. He didn't appear happy to see us. He gave us an unblinking stare.

'This is Mr Jackson,' I quickly filled the uncomfortable silence. 'He's Miss Rotich's fiancé.'

There was little comprehension in the vicar's face.

'The body in the crypt,' I elucidated, 'is that of Daisy Rotich. Mr Jackson identified her this morning. He drove from London... wanted to see the church.'

'I hope you don't mind, Vicar,' Mr Jackson stepped forward.

'No. How could I?' Quentin spoke at last. 'You're from London?'

'From Mombasa, Kenya, actually.'

'Ah.'

'We moved to London a couple of months ago – Daisy and I. If we hadn't—' Jackson's voice broke off. He wiped a stray tear. 'Daisy wasn't that keen at first, but then she saw London and, yes... Of course, she'd miss home. We both would.'

'It's the most beautiful place on earth,' Vicar Quentin declared earnestly. His eyes lit up as he did.

'You've been to Kenya?'

'I am from Kenya. It's my home, too.' The vicar rose from his knees. 'Please accept my deepest,' he swallowed and pressed his hand to his chest, 'my condolences. I'll leave you in peace.' He bowed his head and left. He traipsed the length of the church hurriedly, as if he was running away from us.

'Where is the crypt?' Mr Jackson asked.

'It's behind the altar, but I don't think we should go there,' Samuel said. 'We've been explicitly told not to enter the scene.'

Jackson accepted that without protest. We sat quietly in a pew and each of us drifted into our own thoughts. Our guest was the only one to make the sign of the cross – he was praying. When he finished, he said, 'What was she doing here? She wasn't religious – not a churchgoer.'

CHAPTER 30

Maggie's Journal

W e both thought of it at the same time. As soon as we saw Mr Jackson off to his car, we stood on the road, reluctant to go home. We knew we had to confront the vicar. Well, I knew it. Samuel was mooting the possibility of calling the police and letting them do their job.

'And what are we going to tell them, Samuel?' I challenged him. 'That it has come to our knowledge that Quentin Magnebu and Daisy Rotich both come from Kenya? I can already hear Ms Marsh snapping, "So what? Kenya is a big country." We need to dig deeper, until we have a tangible connection.'

'We have enough,' Samuel argued. 'Daisy came to Quentin's church. She told us she had something to attend to that morning – it's blindingly obvious she was meeting him. And that means they knew each other. That's all we need to tell the police and they'll follow it up.'

I pulled a face that I hoped would melt Samuel's resolve. 'But why don't we first have a little chat with him, give him a chance to explain? Come now, Samuel, he doesn't strike me as an axe-wielding murderer. Maybe something went terribly wrong – maybe it was an accident? Let's ask him.'

Samuel relented, but not without expelling a very heavy sigh and commenting about my stubbornness and possibly even a death wish. I told him not to get carried away and assured him that we were doing the right thing. We proceeded to the vicarage.

Leanne opened the door. She looked defeated and tired. A flicker of dismay – maybe even hostility – lit in her face, but quickly faded away.

'We need to speak to the vicar. It's private,' Samuel made our intentions clear in case she harboured the notion that she could act as a buffer.

She transparently did not. She stepped away from the door. 'Come in. I'll let him know you're here.' She glided away.

Quentin appeared from the depths of the vicarage with Leanne in tow. He wasn't smiling. He looked tense. I think, he knew already why we had come.

'It's about Daisy Rotich,' Samuel said without any preamble. 'About you and Daisy Rotich. If we could find somewhere to talk in private.'

'I don't think I should have any secrets from Leanne,' Quentin's voice was low. It rumbled from his ribcage like a distant murmur of thunder. 'Come to the back. We can sit outdoors, in the arbour, without breaking the Covid rules.'

I briefly mused about the triviality of social-distancing rules compared to the sixth commandment that, as we suspected, he may well have broken. Leanne came with us.

We sat down, and it was again Samuel who spoke: 'Daisy Rotich came to see you, didn't she? You knew her from before.'

Quentin bowed his head. 'Yes, I knew Daisy. Twenty years ago it was when she and I were betrothed.'

Leanne whimpered.

Quentin jerked his head up and reached for her hand. She let him hold it. 'But it wasn't legal, my love. Daisy and I were youngsters. We'd been promised to each other by our parents. It was an arranged thing. Her father gave mine a dowry of ten cows – we measure wealth in head count of cattle in Kenya. Cows are currency over there. My father was able to send me off to be properly educated thanks to those cows.'

'She was your wife…' Leanne's breath rattled

in her throat.

'The rites we took were in accordance with our old tribal tradition, but they aren't formally recognised as marriage vows. Not even in Kenya. Speaking plainly, we didn't enter into a legally binding contract of marriage. I am not a bigamist.'

'She was your wife,' Leanne repeated stubbornly.

'No, she wasn't. Not in the eyes of the law. You are my wife – my only wife.'

They peered into each other's eyes tenderly. Leanne's chest rippled with emotion. 'Oh, Quentin... Why didn't you tell me?'

'It was nothing. A long forgotten tribal ritual. By the time I was in Mombasa, training to be a priest, I was in a different world – the real world. I'd left Daisy and all that superstition behind me. And so did Daisy!' He sat by his wife's side, grabbed her hands and squeezed them. 'She was getting married. I met her fiancé this morning – Mr Jackson. Tell her, Miss Kaye!'

'Yes, that's true. Miss Rotich was about to be married.'

'You see!' Vicar Quentin enthused. 'Daisy and I are ancient history. You're my wife.'

'Maybe to you Daisy was in your past, but not to her. She came here for you, didn't she?' I pressed him.

'It's not my fault that she decided to come here. I knew nothing about it. I didn't invite her.

I don't know how she tracked me down. Maybe it was a coincidence – her coming to Bishops, to this church?'

'I don't think so, Vicar. She acted like she'd planned this trip in advance and was here for a reason,' I had to make it plain to him that we knew.

'In that case, she didn't tell me. I didn't know about her plans,' There was a note of irritation in his voice, but he reined his temper in quickly, and tried to reason: 'Maybe, she was hoping to catch up with me on an off chance – I don't know... Maybe she came to the church, hoping to see me, and a tragedy struck: she got trapped in the crypt. I really ought to have that door fixed.' He shook his head, frowning, then addressed Leanne, 'But let me assure you, I had nothing to do with her death. It was a tragic accident!'

'It wasn't an accident,' Samuel countered. 'We have it on good authority – DC Whittaker, in fact – that Daisy was murdered. She was struck on the head twice. That can't have been an accident.'

For a few baffled seconds Vicar Quentin and his wife sat gaping at Samuel and me, their eyes darting from him to me as if urging me to refute what Samuel had just told them. I couldn't of course. 'It's what DC Whittaker told us,' I confirmed. 'They're treating Daisy's death as murder.'

'Well, it wasn't me!' the vicar threw his

arms in the air, palms up, and rolled his eyes heavenward, 'Let God strike me dead on the spot if I'm lying! You don't believe that nonsense, Leanne, do you?'

She slowly shook her head. Her voice was chilling when she said, 'Of course, I don't.'

Quentin's brow was beading with sweat. He was shouting without realising it, 'It was those hooligans! They did it! They'd been stealing, setting fires to our hymn books – they killed Daisy! My God! I should've called the police when it all started! I should've had them arrested. Daisy would still be alive and we could sit down together with her and have a nice chat about the good old days – I'd have explained it to you calmly, and... You'd have liked her, Leanne. Good God, they bludgeoned to death an innocent woman!'

Samuel raised his hand to stop him. 'I really doubt that it was the Sexton's gang, Quentin,' he said firmly, forcing the vicar to shut up and only blink his incomprehension. Samuel explained, 'You see, Daisy was killed and left to die in the church four weeks ago, but you told us that you'd been locking up the church for at least a couple of months, since the thefts had started. How would those boys gain access to the church? They didn't have the key. I'm sorry to have to say this, but you killed Daisy Rotich.'

Quentin's eyes bulged out of their sockets, the red veins I'd noticed earlier reaching bursting point, 'I did not kill Daisy!'

'Someone did – someone with access to the church,' I pointed out.

Quentin Magnebu fixed me with a sharp, penetrating look and expelled a heavy sigh. 'Okay, here is the truth. That Saturday – it was just before lockdown – she did come to see me.'

Leanne grabbed his hand. 'Quentin, stop. You don't have to tell them anything!'

'No, it's all right, love. It'll come out sooner or later, and I truly don't have anything to hide – I didn't kill Daisy. I saw her that morning, that's all. It was early in the morning when she caught me in the driveway. I was on my way to Bristol for the diocese lockdown planning meeting. I was shocked to see her after all those years. I never knew she was coming. We greeted each other amicably – it was a friendly reunion, you could say.

'Of course, I didn't want to bring her home – I didn't want you to jump to the wrong conclusions. I invited her to the church where we could chat in peace. I did tell her I had to rush, but I couldn't send her packing, could I? She said she was leaving the next day.

'We went to the church and sat in a pew, and talked.'

'What about?' I asked.

'About the old days, the spectacle of our betrothal, the fact that I was now a married man and she was about to get married.'

'And then you shook hands, she left and you locked the church, correct, Vicar?' Samuel's question was tainted with sarcasm. He didn't believe Magnebu, and neither did I.

The vicar nodded vaguely.

'So how did she get back into the church, got herself clobbered on the head from behind – twice?' I spoke sharply.

'No, it wasn't as you said, Mr Dee. She didn't leave the church. I did. She stayed there,' he wiped his sweaty forehead. 'Okay, we didn't part on the best of terms. You see, she wanted her dowry back. A stupid idea, really. The ten damned cows her father had given to mine twenty years ago! She didn't ask for the cows back, of course, but she did ask for money: the relative value of the cows in today's money. She said she wanted to bring something into her new marriage, and I owed the dowry back.

'It was a daft idea, I told her as much, and I didn't have the sum she was asking for.'

'How much did she want?' Leanne asked.

'Ten thousand pounds,' Quentin exhaled the words like a curse.

'She insisted, and finally I said I'd see how much I could put together without alerting you,' he gave Leanne a guilty glance, 'but it wouldn't be ten thousand, or anywhere near that amount. I told her I was in a hurry, but I'd be in touch once I organised something. Then I walked away. I left her there in church, alive and well, if frustrated.

She was sat in a pew when I left, you've got to believe me! Anyone could've walked in and killed her. The church wasn't locked that morning. I left it open.

'I didn't kill Daisy! You've got to believe me! Leanne? Please say something...'

His wife was breathing in shallow puffs as if pumping herself up for a massive eruption of bad temper. She glared at Samuel, her eyes narrowed with fury. She managed to overcome it somehow, because when she finally spoke she was calm: 'I was out that morning, shopping. I had lunch at the Old Stables. The church stood open for a few hours until I returned at about two o'clock and locked it. I didn't make much of the door being open. I thought I must've forgotten to lock it the night before. I didn't see anyone. The killer must've come in during that morning and attacked Miss – Miss—'

'Rotich,' I gave her the name she was clearly unfamiliar with.

'Yes, Miss Rotich. It was all very unfortunate and my heart goes out to her fiancé, but my husband had nothing to do with her death and I resent your accusations. False—'

Her dignified avowal of her husband's innocence was disrupted by the ringing of the doorbell. Leanne nearly jumped out of her skin and clutched her chest in distress. 'Who the hell is it now!'

'Let them ring. I don't care. I can't face

anyone else right now,' the vicar mumbled. At this point he seemed bewildered and downcast, but no longer defensive.

'They'll go away. Just breathe. You'll be fine,' Leanne wrapped her arms around his neck and kissed his cheek. She had already forgiven him for the trespasses of his youth, maybe even for the murder of Miss Rotich if one were to assume that Leanne knew something incriminating that she wasn't telling us.

The doorbell resonated again, and for longer. Whoever it was, they weren't leaving.

I decided to answer and tell them to come back later. Then I would go home, and take Samuel with me. I wasn't sure about the vicar's guilt. Somehow I couldn't envisage this annoyingly righteous but harmless windbag of a man committing an act of violence, and moreover, acting with coldblooded premeditation. His motive was also weak. He wasn't a bigamist. Daisy had nothing on him but some unenforceable claim to her forfeited dowry. Why would he go as far as killing the woman? I was battling with those doubts as I opened the door and found DCI Marsh and DC Whittaker on the doorstep.

CHAPTER 31

Maggie's Journal

'Is Quentin Magnebu in?' Marsh inquired brusquely.

She brushed past me before I could reply, and headed for the back door at the end of the hallway. I had left it open and through the gap one could see the people gathered outside. DC Whittaker and I followed her. She confronted the vicar as soon as she clapped her eyes on him.

'Mr Magnebu, why didn't you tell us that you knew Daisy Rotich? I just spoke to her father in Kenya. He knows you and he tells me you and she were very close once – married, he said. You – were – married – to – her,' she put an emphasis on every word. 'Can you explain why you didn't deem it necessary to inform us of it? It isn't a small nuance.'

'I didn't get a chance. I... I was in shock.' He started mumbling disjointedly, composing his thoughts with painful slowness. At last he confronted Marsh with a direct gaze and said: 'I met with Daisy that day, I've already admitted it to Miss Maggie and Mr Dee, but like I said to them: I did not kill her! I wouldn't. Why would I? The church was left open for several hours, with Daisy sat inside. Ask my wife. Please, just ask my wife. It was those youths – the thieves and arsonists!'

'Thieves? Arsonists? The small time, teenage thugs from Sexton's?' Marsh snorted. 'They killed her and didn't even bother stealing her mobile? Some thieves, I say! And they wiped the door handle clean, and meticulously washed the floors with a powerful bleach to remove blood? Are you suggesting they brought the bleach with them on the off chance?'

'I don't know! I didn't kill anyone! I had no reason to kill her!' Vicar Quentin squeezed his temples and shut his eyes.

'Even though she blackmailed you about the death of Alya Imani?'

Now, that was news! As I was still indoors, I pressed my back against the wall to make myself invisible just in case DCI Marsh realised my continued presence and sent me home. I noticed that Samuel was doing the same. He was sitting a couple of metres away from the garden table (social distancing does have its benefits, after all!), obscured in the foliage of a large rhododendron. I noticed him shrink in his chair. The detectives' backs were to him – he stood a chance of remaining invisible to them.

DCI Marsh cautioned the vicar. The dialogue that ensued between them was chaotic, full of exclamations, denials, admissions and retractions. Despite that I was able to piece together a tale of a violent pagan exorcism that had gone terribly wrong – an eighteen-year-old girl, Alya Imani, had died.

At first, Quentin Magnebu attempted to deny his part in the ritual, then he tried to reduce it to the role of a mere spectator, until he finally broke down and cried, 'I thought I was doing the right thing! I was only eighteen. Mziba, our witch doctor, was a powerful man. I believed with all my heart we could heal Alya. I only followed his instructions – did as I was told. I had seen Mziba do it many times, and nothing bad had happened. Nobody had died before Alya!'

'But Alya was pregnant, wasn't she?' DCI Marsh interjected. 'The violence and the shock of the treatment sent her into early labour. She bled to death. Her baby stood no chance at only twenty or so weeks. Did you intend for that to happen? Was it your baby she was carrying?'

'No!' Quentin clasped his hands over his ears. 'No, it wasn't. I hardly knew that girl. I was already betrothed to Daisy. And,' he shot Leanne a furtive glance, 'Leanne doesn't know this, but I can't have children. I'm sorry, my dearest, I never told you and let you think...'

Leanne didn't respond. She didn't seem to have heard him. She was staring into space, her shoulders raised stiffly and her hands laced together as if in prayer. Maybe she *was* praying.

Quentin lowered his gaze and spoke in his sonorous voice that resonated as if it was rising from beneath the ground, 'I believed Alya was possessed by an evil spirit. I know now it was nonsense, a stupid backwater superstition, but then I didn't know any better. Her behaviour was—' He shook his head at the memory. 'She was a danger to herself and to the village. My guess is she suffered from schizophrenia, but you must understand – we had no real doctors, no psychiatrists. I was a young man who'd never been further than the nearest town. It'd taken me years of schooling and travel to realise the absurdity of the superstitions I was brought up on. But it was too late for Alya.'

'Did Daisy Rotich try to blackmail you?' DCI Marsh ploughed deeper.

'She...When I left her, she was alive!' His chest rattled and he broke down in tears.

'Quentin Magnebu, you're under arrest on suspicion of murder. Whittaker, read him his rights.' DCI Marsh concluded the interview.

The two detectives led Quentin Magnebu out of the house and into their unmarked car parked in the vicarage driveway. Samuel and I waited until they were gone before we offered our support to Leanne. She didn't acknowledge us in any way. She continued to sit motionlessly in her chair and didn't as much as blink. I suppose it was the shock. We let her be.

CHAPTER 32

Sam and Maggie spent the rest of the day on the menial task of clearing the rubble of the internal wall they had demolished two days earlier. Sam dismantled the wooden frames as best he could and without bringing the whole house down. Maggie busied herself wheeling the debris and rolls of insulation foam out into the driveway. After lockdown, they would hire a skip and the wall would become a distant memory. Deirdre kept them fed and watered. Her one attempt at sweeping the floors and especially the metal slab over the entrance to the tunnel met with condemnation. She was instantly dispatched from the room.

Very little was being said between Sam and Maggie about the affair of Quentin Magnebu and Daisy Rotich. They were too emotionally shattered to contemplate it. Physical exertion was exactly what they needed to put it out of their minds.

Deirdre was redeployed to cook dinner. By the time they sat down to a shepherd's pie with mushy peas, Priest's Hole looked almost presentable. If it wasn't for the heavy platform by the chimney and the ribbons of police tape crossing over it, one could be forgiven for thinking that life carried on uneventfully in the Kaye-Dee bubble.

Indeed, the dinner was enjoyed in near silence, with Deirdre throwing in random comments about the latest news and the weather forecast for the coming week (which incidentally looked promising). Sam allowed himself to believe that the whole Daisy Rotich saga was behind them.

It wasn't meant to last.

At bedtime, Maggie summoned the ghosts. She sat on the edge of the bed, peering at Sam in a way that demanded his undivided attention, and said, 'I'm not sure we have the right man.'

'Maggie, please, let the police find that out for themselves. It's their job to investigate.'

'But will they? Now that they have the backstory, and Quentin's admission that he saw Daisy that day, they'll be only too happy to pin everything on him.'

'I think you should have more confidence in Gillian.'

'I do, but you know how it is – the police have limited resource. They'll want to close the case quickly and kill two birds with one stone.'

'What do you mean?'

'They'll let the vicar go down for the murder of Miss Rotich and for Isaac. It makes sense that whoever killed Daisy also killed Isaac, but you see,' Maggie inhaled deeply before carrying on, 'Daisy and Isaac are still here. They shouldn't be here if the police had the right man.

'To be honest with you, I expected Isaac to move on after the charges were laid against Dr Edmunds, but that didn't happen. Now, with Quentin arrested and Isaac still hanging out by the well, the only conclusion is that the killer is still at large.'

'The weight of evidence against the vicar is overwhelming – he had lied about knowing Daisy, then confessed to seeing her that day and even volunteered that she had demanded money. It wasn't her dowry, it was blood money, plain and simple,' Sam argued.

'But he was genuinely shocked when he saw her body in the crypt,' Maggie argued. 'Unless he's a damn good actor, that was real raw emotion!'

'Regret? Guilt? Shock at what he'd done? I don't know, Maggie, I'm not a psychologist. And I'm knackered.' Sam wanted nothing better than to switch off the lights and rest his weary bones after a day of hard labour. He gave one last throwaway remark and lay down on the bed: 'He's guilty as hell but, I grant you, maybe he didn't act alone. Maybe Leanne was in on it. The cops will get to the bottom of it. Let's get some sleep.'

Maggie didn't seem to hear his last sentence. 'You know,' she said, 'you may be onto something. Leanne!'

'Who knows?' he mumbled sleepily.

'It's the bleach, you see?'

Sam didn't quite see what Maggie was getting at. He clenched his teeth, forcibly keeping his eyes open to be polite.

'Gillian Marsh said that the attacker used bleach to remove the blood from the floor. Leanne takes care of the church, cleans it, does the flower arrangements and so on. She'd be the one with all the right cleaning materials to hand. Think about it, Samuel!' Maggie was brimming with excitement. Sam couldn't fathom where she got her energy from.

'Well, yes – it wouldn't have been Sexton's teenagers, that's for sure,' he conceded the point.

'Or the vicar!' Maggie shuffled on the bed, sidling up to Sam. 'Just try to imagine him with a bottle of bleach giving the nave a good clean, then driving to Bristol for the ecumenical conference. He'd need two-three hours to clean the church floors, go back home, shower, change clothes. Not likely.'

'Not likely,' Sam repeated mindlessly.

'And then again, what about Isaac—'

'What about him?'

'The morning we found Isaac, think about

it! Quentin wasn't around that morning, but Leanne was. She said she'd only heard us when the ambulance arrived and that she was at the vicarage at the time, remember?'

'Vaguely, yes,' Sam said sleepily.

'But she was lying. I remember vividly that she'd come running from the church. That's where she had been all along – when we found Isaac and called 999, and tried to resuscitate him. All that time, she had been in the church. Not the vicarage! She would've heard us shouting, Harry Wotton arriving and his cries. But she didn't come out, not until the ambulance... Do you think what I am thinking?'

Not again, Sam despaired. 'What is it that you're thinking, Maggie?' he indulged his lovely, but right now very tiresome, fiancé.

'I think she lured Isaac to the cemetery because he had witnessed Daisy's death and knew her killer – whoever that killer was, Quentin or Leanne. Isaac had an expectation of a windfall. Remember? He told Thomas. I'm positive he was blackmailing her. She promised to pay him off. Told him to meet her at the cemetery. There she bashed him on the head and thinking that he was dead tried to drag him to the church. He would probably have joined Daisy in the crypt if she'd succeeded, but we turned up. She had to flee. After that, she just waited, hoping that Isaac would die. When he finally did, he took her secret to his grave. How am I doing?'

Maggie beamed, very pleased with her theory.

'Brilliantly. Only we have no evidence to prove any of that.' Sam yawned. 'Can we go to sleep now?'

'You go,' Maggie sighed and walked to the window. She peered through the net curtain, looking out onto the cemetery. 'He's still there,' she said in a half-whisper, 'hanging out by that well. Day and night, circling... He's trying to tell me something. What is it, Isaac? I know!' She squealed, making Sam jump. He had been dosing off.

'What now?'

'That well, Samuel! We have to check that well!'

'Not now, I hope,' he puffed out his cheeks and exhaled his dismay.

'No, not now. We need daylight. Tomorrow morning.' At last, she returned to bed. Within seconds she was asleep.

Sam turned to face her and embraced her curled up body. It was luxuriously warm and soft. He buried his face in the small of her neck and inhaled her scent. She smelled of lavender soap. Her hair was still wet from her shower and gave its own aroma of wild nettles. Sam closed his eyes, relishing the moment. He prayed to the Lord Almighty that by tomorrow Maggie would forget all about the blinking well.

CHAPTER 33

'Rise and shine, Samuel! We have a well to scale,' Maggie's voice tickled his ears. Sam opened one eye to behold his fiancé. She was dressed in her full-body wetsuit. Sam's eyes popped out in alarm.

'You can't be serious!' he cried and sat upright on the bed.

'I am dead serious, but we can have breakfast first – fortify ourselves before we abseil into the well.'

'You can't do that!'

'Of course, I can. I'm a capable abseiler. I learned how to do it on the many residential trips I went on with my pupils. It was years ago but abseiling is like riding a bike – it'll come back to me. I have fond memories of those trips. We used to go to Pembrokeshire. It has a ragged, rocky coast – perfect for abseiling. We should do it together one day.' Maggie's eyes shone with excitement.

'But this is a slimy, derelict well, Maggie, a far cry from the Pembrokeshire coast. I am not letting you do it. No way!' If he wasn't sitting in bed cross-legged, Sam would be stomping his foot in anger.

Maggie smiled sweetly and perched by his side, her wetsuit squeaking in protest. 'Come now, Samuel, we'll just peep in and see what we can find, if anything. There may be no need for me to descend to the bottom.'

'There'll be no chance of that!'

'We'll see. But first thing's first: a hearty breakfast. Are you ready for a fry-up?'

He was. Sam was ravenous.

Although it was a sunny day, the sun could not reach the depths of the well. Maggie and Sam had to shine their phone torches, and even they proved insufficient. All they could illuminate were the moss- and lichen-covered stone walls. The bottom of the well remained impenetrable.

'I'll have to get a decent torch. Wait here, and don't do anything stupid,' Sam instructed Maggie. He hurried to the garage as fast as his legs could carry him. He didn't trust Maggie alone with that wretched well. He had reasonable suspicions that she would attempt to sit in the rusty bucket and plunge into the abyss, hoping for a soft landing at the bottom.

Armed with a powerful LED torch, he returned to the site. To his relief, Maggie was engaged in a conversation with, presumably, the ghost of Isaac Wotton.

'I know, I know! Something is there... Just be patient, young man. I gave your father my word that I'd get to the bottom of it—'

'I hope you won't take it literally,' Sam joked and handed her the torch.

Maggie switched it on and pointed it into the well. They leant over the ledge, their heads close together as their eyes followed the beam of light. The walls were lined with stone and brick. The deeper the layer, the darker and slimier it looked. The light from the lamp penetrated the depths right to the bottom. The well was almost dry with only a murky puddle at the base.

'You see? Nothing there: no dead bodies, no dangerous weapons,' Sam rejoiced.

'There!' Maggie shouted. 'Can you see it?'

Sam narrowed his eyes and focussed on the circle of light shaking erratically over a small flat object that was partially submerged in the puddle.

'It's a mobile phone,' Maggie identified it.

Sam had to agree: it was an iPhone. The small silver etching that reflected the light of the torch was the Apple icon.

'I bet it's Isaac's. It'd be interesting to find out if anyone knows that it's missing. I can't imagine Harry Wotton would bother looking for it, even if he realised it wasn't returned to him amongst Isaac's possessions.'

'You may be right, Maggie. I'll call DCI Marsh. The cops will fish it out from there.'

'We're not waiting for the cops!' Maggie objected most vehemently. 'I told DC Whittaker to check the well, and he couldn't be bothered. Trust me, Samuel, they'll ignore our report and all we'll get for our trouble will be Ms Marsh chastising us for wasting police time. She may even charge us with something if it turns out it isn't Isaac's phone. You know how she is! No, no, no,' Maggie wagged her finger. 'We're not leaving it with her. I'm going to climb down and fetch the damn thing. Do you think this bucket is strong enough?' She picked up the wonky vessel to examine it.

This was precisely what Samuel feared would happen. There was no dissuading Maggie, he knew that too. The objective was to mitigate the risks. Looking at the rusty winch mechanism of the well, the crumbling body of the barrel and the frayed rope, it was obvious that a different method of descent had to be found.

'No, it isn't,' he declared emphatically. 'This whole mechanism will crumble as soon as you as much as touch it. So don't you dare!'

'I have to get in there somehow. I can't jump,' she protested.

'Wait here,' Sam snarled.

He headed back to his garage. He had left it open, suspecting that he'd need to fetch climbing gear at some point today. Sam used to be a keen mountaineer in his twenties and despite the elapse of three decades he had clung on to his gear. He just had to find it. It was somewhere in one of the five still unopened boxes. Cursing under his breath, Sam rummaged through the junk, discovering and tossing aside objects he didn't even know he possessed. The third box he attacked contained the climbing gear. Sam recovered the harness, a good length of rope and a helmet.

'Wow!' Maggie was impressed when he arrived with the equipment. 'You come well prepared!'

'Yes, and I am going down there!'

'Do you really expect me to hold your weight? Me?' Maggie pulled a frightened face.

Of course, he should've thought of it: someone would need to remain at the top to secure the descent, and it would have to be the stronger of the two of them.

'Okay,' he conceded, 'get the harness on. And the helmet.'

Maggie scowled. 'Ooh, it's covered with cobwebs!'

'Blow them away. You're wearing the helmet or we're calling DCI Marsh.'

Maggie surrendered and braved the spider's nest inside the helmet. Sam clipped the rope to her harness and wound the other end around his waist, tying a solid climber's knot to secure it. He stood with his feet wide apart, one foot propped against the side of the well, the other against the concrete edge of the nearest grave.

'Right, show us your abseiling skills and may God have mercy on your soul, because I won't!'

Maggie climbed onto the ledge and wobbled precariously. To Sam's relief, she seemed to be holding the rope correctly for abseiling: one hand clutching the pulley above her stomach, the other gripping the rope under her bum.

'Hold on tight, Samuel!' she shouted, kicked the edge of the well and disappeared. Sam felt the tension on the rope as he held on to it for dear life. Although he couldn't see Maggie, he could hear her jolly squeaks. At least, she was still alive.

'I've got it, Samuel!' Her voice echoed from the well a minute or so later. 'You can pull me up now.'

That was easier said than done. Maggie wasn't the lightest of feathers. Her feet, even though she was wearing sturdy boots with grippy soles, were sliding over the slimy stones of the well. Sam was pulling with all his might, the friction with the rope leaving bloodied marks on his soft palms. A few times, Maggie slipped and dropped a fraction, giving Sam a near heart attack. Finally, one small step after another, she managed to find footing in the wall cavities, and with a final pull from Sam, Maggie emerged into the sunshine.

'I've got it!' She was holding the iPhone over her head like a trophy.

CHAPTER 34

Maggie's Journal

My hands were shaking with excitement (and also because the rope cut into the groove under my fingers and I saw blood). I rinsed it off under the tap and wrapped a hankie over my hand. I couldn't find a bandage. Truth is, I probably didn't own such a luxurious and rarely needed commodity. I didn't waste time trying to extricate myself from my wetsuit. That would take too long.

I had unearthed Isaac's phone! I was sure it was his. The moment I came to the surface, I noticed the triumph in Isaac's eyes. He was hovering over Samuel's shoulder, rooting for me. It had to be his phone. The battery was spent but Samuel said that he had a lead to connect it to his laptop. We'd be able to see the phone's contents while it was charging.

'Let's hope there are no passwords to get in,' I crossed my fingers.

'In which case, just as I've been suggesting all along, we'll call the cops and they'll know how to circumvent the password. We should do it anyway. This phone may contain vital evidence and what we're doing is tampering with it.' Samuel sounded unnecessarily gloomy.

'We're only checking if this is the right phone,' I argued feebly. I was dying to see what was lurking in its memory.

Although Samuel tried to rise above basic human curiosity by acting with put-on indifference, he wasn't fooling me. He was as eager as I to delve into the dead boy's life because that's what that device was: Isaac's life imprint. It is common knowledge that young people live through their phones. Everything there is to know about them is recorded somewhere between their calls, web search history, text messages and photo galleries. We checked all of those elements, in that order. The incoming and outgoing numbers told us nothing. The police would be able to track down and identify his contacts, but we were helpless against the wall of digits and initials. The same went for the SMS texts. There was nothing we could learn from them. They were composed in an alien language consisting of words we didn't recognise, a wild array of emoticons and amazingly inventive spelling. One could say, the real-life equivalent of Isaac's text messaging would be grunting. His search history included the inevitable soft porn and gaming sites. We swiftly moved on to his photo gallery and that was where we came upon a goldmine.

To being with, we trawled through a patch of selfies displaying Isaac in various stages of nakedness. We squinted with discomfort but kept scrolling. We hit a selection of blurry and dark images which, I guessed with distaste, were most likely snapped under the skirts of unsuspecting schoolgirls. Finally, we arrived at the aforesaid goldmine. The images made my hair stand on end.

'Silly lout! Why didn't he do anything!' I despaired as we viewed the photos, and even one video recording, that told the story of Daisy's death frame by shocking frame.

'He might have been able to save her if he'd stepped in! It wasn't too late. She was still alive at that point,' Samuel said, his face crestfallen.

'Instead of helping her, he was taking snapshots to use for blackmail.' I was sick to my stomach. I couldn't imagine how Harry Wotton would react when I told him. If I told him.

'I'm calling Alec Scarfe now. The police have got the wrong man.' Samuel shook me out of my reverie. He scrolled for Alec's number on his phone.

I gripped his arm and implored him, 'Wait.

Let's confront her with these photos first – give her a chance to confess.'

We found Leanne Magnebu in the church, scrubbing the floors as if she was having a Lady Macbeth moment. She had already covered half of the main aisle with nothing but a bucket of soapy water and a heavy-duty hand brush with bassine bristles. Her knuckles were bleeding and inadvertently she was leaving smudges of her own blood on the floor.

'You can't wash away your sins by cleaning the floors,' I said to her with intended cruelty. 'You'd be better off confessing and sparing your husband the pain of finding out from the police that it was you.'

She started and jumped to her feet knocking over the bucket. Grey, chalky water spilled out and diluted the tracks of her blood.

'What are you talking about?' she demanded. 'You shouldn't be here! The church is off limits.'

'We know you killed Daisy Rotich and then, you tried to kill Isaac Wotton,' Samuel spoke calmly. 'We found Isaac's phone.'

Whatever blood was left coursing through her veins was syphoned away from her face. She went ghostly white.

'Isaac took photographs of you and Daisy in the church. It must've been a pure coincidence.

He was probably after the communion wine. He found the church open – thought he'd grab the opportunity and steal into the vestry behind your back and then creep out with his loot. But before he crossed the aisle he saw you go for her, or maybe he heard raised voices – a heated argument. Did you two argue? Did you confront her about blackmailing your husband?'

Leanne didn't answer. She was just gaping.

Samuel waved Isaac's phone in her face, 'Isaac recorded it. It's all here: as you push her and she falls and smashes her temple on the edge of the lectern, as you seize the crucifix and strike her with it on the back of her head, as you kneel over her to check her pulse with a panicked expression in your eyes, as you take hold of her arms by the wrists and drag her behind the altar, as you push her unconscious body down into the vault… It's all here. Have a look.'

'I have already seen them,' she whispered. Her lips were compressed tightly. She staggered, gripped the side of the nearest pew and slumped into it. 'He showed them to me – he wanted money. They're always after money. Five grand, he said, or he'd call the police. He gave me three days to organise the cash.

'We met on the Thursday morning. That was when he showed me the pictures. He said I could delete them myself as soon as I handed him the money. But I didn't have five thousand pounds. I don't have any income of my own.

'I was desperate. I had to do something to stop him from talking to the police. And I didn't trust him – he was bound to come back for more. I panicked and threw his phone into the well. He swore, pushed me away and leant over— That's when picked up the vase from the grave behind the well and...

'I thought he was dead. I couldn't leave him lying there with his head cracked open. I thought of heaving the body over the ledge and letting him drop into the well – it would look like an accident... But then I thought, it'd be even better if his body was never found. Like Daisy's. I decided to drag him to the crypt. He was heavy but I was making gradual progress—'

'And that's when we turned up,' I said.

'I heard your voices. I fled to the church. There was a chance that you wouldn't see him, but—'

'But we did, and what's worse, Isaac was still alive.' Samuel spoke, grim judgment in his tone. 'You must've been petrified that he'd talk. It was your lucky day when he died in hospital.'

'Believe me, I didn't rejoice. I was mortified by what happened, how quickly it happened – him dying.' Leanne was weeping. She wiped her tears with the back of her hand. The blood from her knuckles mixed with them, leaving her face looking ghastly. 'I didn't set out to kill that wretched boy.'

'And Daisy Rotich? Did you set out to kill her,

or was that opportunistic?' I gave her a hard look.

'She called the vicarage a couple of weeks before coming over. Quentin was out and about as he always is. I answered the call. She probably took me for his housekeeper.' Anger flashed in Leanne's eyes. She stopped to compose herself. 'She didn't give me her full name – said she was Quentin's old flame. The way she said it... I was polite and friendly, but she spoke to me like I was domestic help. She said, "Tell him Daisy called. Tell him I'm in the UK." That was it. I didn't know what to make of her.

'I didn't tell Quentin about the phone call. I don't know why. Probably, deep down I was hoping that'd be the end of it – she'd go back wherever she'd come from and we'd never hear from her again.'

'But she did come,' I said.

'I saw them through the window. I saw Quentin react to her as she approached him. He pulled her into his arms. Then he took her by the elbow and they went inside the church. I had to follow.

'I didn't hear every word, but I heard enough to piece it all together: their marriage and something about the dead girl. Rotich demanded money. No, she wasn't blunt – she knew how to play him. She said all she wanted was her dowry back, but I don't think Quentin was in any doubt that it was blackmail.' Leanne's breath rattled in her chest as he inhaled. 'I had no idea their marriage was invalid. I thought if Quentin had never divorced her then he was—' she couldn't say that word.

'A bigamist,' Samuel helped her.

'Yes, a bigamist and a killer. Rotich implied that she was prepared to make it public. She said, "How would your Church superiors react if they knew?" I couldn't allow this to happen. I couldn't have that woman destroy his life, his career – and our marriage!'

'So you waited for your husband to leave, and then confronted her? Did you threaten her? Did she laugh at you?'

'No,' Leanne gazed at me coldly. 'There was nothing I could say that would make her go away. I had no illusions. We didn't speak. She didn't know I was there. I approached her from behind and hit her with a curtain pole. It didn't do her any harm. She got to her feet – that's when I pushed her and she fell, hitting her temple. You saw the rest in the video.' Leanne shook her head. 'I thought she was dead when I dumped her in the vault. But I didn't mean to kill her. What else was I supposed to do?'

'Anything but murder an innocent woman, and then a young man with his whole life ahead of him,' I said sternly.

Multiple steps resonated on the church's tile floor. Why wasn't I surprised? It was Ms Marsh accompanied by DC Whittaker and a uniformed officer.

'Leanne Magnebu?' she sounded officious, asking her name as if she didn't know her.

Of course, Marsh had somehow worked out Leanne's guilt and was here to arrest her. Samuel and I would leave her to it. I had something more important to do – I had to speak to Harry Wotton.

'Let's go, Samuel,' I said and took Isaac's iPhone out of his lap. I wanted to have the satisfaction of presenting it to Ms Marsh.

As our paths crossed, Samuel and I on our way out – DCI Marsh on her way in, I pressed the phone into her hand. 'It's all there,' I said.

We didn't even stop at home to change from our ridiculous outfits – we headed directly for Mr Wotton's farm. I had promised Harry Wotton that I would find his son's killer. I had the duty to tell him who it was and I didn't give a monkey's if DCI Marsh expected me to keep it to myself, or wait for the outcome of the trial. I knew what I knew, and Harry Wotton would be appraised of the facts today.

We found him in his barn, sprinkling lime in the chicken coops. Mrs Wotton was outside, herding the chickens out of harm's way.

'Mr Wotton!' I shouted from the yard.

He stopped and gazed at me and Samuel. He took off his gloves and put them under his arm. 'You've got news for us, Miss Kaye?'

'I do.'

Mrs Wotton saw us too and hurried into the barn to stand by her husband. She also guessed why we'd turned up suddenly and without warning.

'So you know who did it, then – who killed our Isaac?' Harry Wotton spoke softly as we levelled up with him.

'It was Leanne Magnebu, the vicar's wife,' I said. 'The police have just arrested her.'

'Why? Why would she do that to our boy?'

'She committed a serious crime – murder. Isaac witnessed it. She couldn't afford to let him live. Just remember this: your son hasn't done anything wrong. He was just in the wrong place at the wrong time. That's all.' I couldn't bring myself to tell those two grieving parents about the blackmail. Isaac Wotton was hardly twenty years of age when he died. He was a naïve young man who didn't stop to think about the consequences of his actions. But he didn't have a black heart, like his killer. He was just a boy who had played with fire and got burned.

CHAPTER 35

It was a beautiful summer day. The sun lounged high in the cloudless sky, diluting it to a faint cornflower blue. Harry Wotton had allowed the meadow to flourish in its natural wilderness, just as Maggie had asked. Grass rippled in a soft breeze. Bees and butterflies flitted from flower to flower, buzzing contentedly.

Guests arrived in large numbers to witness the ceremony. Maggie's sister Andrea flew in from New Zealand and, on this occasion, brought her family with her, husband Eliot and their son, Jack. They had arrived a week in advance of the wedding and were staying at Badger's Hall. Maggie's brother Will and his family too had taken a week away from the hustle and bustle of London to enjoy the countryside. Maggie noted, tears welling up in her eyes, that Badger's Hall felt like home again. If only Mum and Dad were around to witness this reunion…

Sam too felt a bout of nostalgia rising in his chest when his children arrived with their partners to celebrate their dad's wedding. Abigail and Campbell chipped in together with their grandmother (Deirdre being probably the main contributor) to fund a honeymoon for the newlyweds in the Lake District.

'You have to give this village a bit of breathing space,' Deirdre explained. 'With you around there's always a risk of someone dying.'

'Thanks, Mum. Good to know what you think of us,' Sam raised a cynical eyebrow, but couldn't help a grin.

Maggie took the comment more literally. 'The dead are gone,' she said mystically. 'It's all nice and quiet in the church and the cemetery.'

'As it should be, dear,' Deirdre nodded. 'That's what cemeteries are for – resting in peace.'

Maggie tried to argue that some souls could be pretty restless, but Sam quickly reminded her that this day wasn't about the dead. It'd be wise to keep them out of today's celebrations.

As well as Maggie and Sam's respective families, nearly the entire population of Bishops Well gathered around the Stone Circle to witness them exchange their vows. The Parish Council was represented by Agnes Digby and Howard Jacobsen. An enormous hamper teeming with jam jars, a cheese board, shortbread biscuits, Rum & Raisin Fudge Extravaganza and a bottle of vintage Bordeaux was presented to Maggie and her husband-to-be with best wishes from the Council. The whole of Bishops AA attended, including their dogs and cats. Cherie and Lisa held hands and wept tears of joy. Wagging his tail and pricking his ears excitedly, Rumpole sat between a tearful Vera and the unusually speechless Henry Hopps-Wood. Vanessa and Alec Scarfe stood rapt and radiant, hankies at the ready. Edgar rolled up with his mother, and she brought her knitting. It looked like she was making tiny booties. God alone knew who they were for! Michael Almond flocked in with his irascible girlfriend Gillian, her dog Corky and cat Fritz. Fritz didn't stay for long, but still – it was the thought that counted. James Weston-Jones represented the Bishops' gentry with his wife and two boys. They had returned home from France especially for this occasion. Mary and Dan Nolan were there as well, Dan chatting with Will, reminiscing about the wild days of Bishop and the Beast, their heavy metal band. Hannah and Matthew were full of smiles. Even the elusive horror writer and Hannah's employer, Daryl Luntz made a guest appearance. Bishops' Morris dancers came dressed in their traditional attire, armed with wands, ribbons, bells and whistles. They were to entertain the gathering with a stick dance choreographed especially for the occasion. The proprietor of the Rook's Nest, Terrence Truelove, Robert Kane of Robert Kane

& Sons Butchers, Kev Wilcox, the chocolatier, Vernon Leitch, the cheesemaker, Ron Worsley, the omnipresent traffic warden and John Erwin, the Jack of all trades constituted the dancing troupe. The town of Bishops Well bubbled with excitement. At long last, Maggie Kaye was to marry!

Maggie looked a picture in a long dress embroidered with the flowers of the meadow. She was wearing a daisy chain in her hair and colourful bangles on her wrists and ankles. Sam peered at her tenderly, blinking away tears of emotion.

Sabine, who happened to be the High Priestess ordained in the pagan faith of ancient Celts, conducted the ceremony. Since the sudden departure of Vicar Quentin, the church wedding had to be cancelled. The pagan rites however proceeded unfettered.

The wedding began with the ritual of handfasting. Maggie and Sam bound each other's hands with colourful leather cords, each colour representing different gifts they brought to their union: strength, kindness, patience, understanding, health and wisdom. At least, some wisdom.

The guests looked on, rather bemused, as the newlyweds jumped over the besom broom symbolising the threshold into their new life together. Sam nearly fell as his foot caught on the stick, but Maggie held his hand firmly and helped him recover his balance on the other side of the broom.

After the ceremony, Sam invited everyone for a feast at Badger's Hall. A procession of over fifty revellers skipped along Badger's Crossing merrily.

Amongst them, Maggie spotted Thomas Moore. He was in the company of an athletic young lady with black and blue cornrow braids. Maggie waved to them and dashed to thank Thomas for accepting the invitation.

'I'm so glad you came, Thomas,' she said. 'Is this young lady your girlfriend?'

'Yeah, you can say that. Tiffany – Tiffs,' Thomas introduced his companion.

She smiled at Maggie lopsidedly, her eyes narrowed with a mixture of curiosity and suspicion. 'Hi,' she offered a tentative greeting.

'Lovely to meet you, Tiffany,' Maggie said.

Tiffany continued to squint and didn't return the compliment. That made Maggie feel slightly uncomfortable. She looked to Thomas for the clarification of his girlfriend's standoffish attitude.

'I had to prove to her that I wasn't carrying on with you, Miss,' Thomas explained, the pained expression of a misunderstood martyr twisting his face.

'Carrying on with me?' Maggie's eyes widened as she echoed Thomas's words.

'You know, when my Mum gave you a

dressing down in the shop at Sexton's, word got out that you and I...' Thomas blushed and chuckled nervously. 'Tiffs heard about it and gave me a bloody nose the next day.'

Maggie gaped at the pair of youngsters in disbelief. 'Are you saying it was Tiffany who...'

'Yeah, she bloody well broke me nose! 'Cos of you, Miss.'

'And I've been blaming myself for putting you in danger with the Sexton's mob,' Maggie started, but then waved her arm dismissively, 'Never mind! All's well that ends well.'

ABOUT THE AUTHOR

Anna Legat

Anna Legat is best known for her cosy crime fiction, The Shires Mysteries, and her legal crime thrillers, Goode's Law and the DI Gillian Marsh series. Murder isn't the only thing on her mind. She dabbles in a wide variety of genres, ranging from historical fiction, through magic realism to dystopia.

A globe-trotter and Jack-of-all-trades, Anna has been an attorney, legal adviser, a silver-service waitress, a school teacher and a librarian. She has lived in far-flung places where she delighted in people-watching and collecting precious life experiences for her stories.

She lives near Bath.

annalegatblog.wordpress.com
@LegatWriter on Twitter
@AnnaLegatAuthor on FB

@LegatAuthor on Instagram

BOOKS IN THIS SERIES

The Shires Mysteries

Death Comes To Bishops Well

At Death's Door

Cause Of Death

Death On The High Seas

Death By Misadventure

BOOKS BY THIS AUTHOR

The Inheritance

Bloodlines

Complicity

Buried In The Past

Life Without Me

Broken

The End Of The Road

Swimming With Sharks

Nothing To Lose

Thicker Than Blood

Sandman

Conspiracy Of Silence

Out Of Sight

Paula Goes To Heaven